Beyond Boundary

By
Don Bozeman

Other Books by Don Bozeman

Cassiopeia, Flight from Savannah

Growing up as a house slave on Rose Lawn Plantation, Cassie Omoru dreams of being free and helping her people. When her well being is threatened by the depraved son of the plantation owner she is whisked away to St. Benedict's monastery. During the Battle of Savannah she falls in love with Andre Dupre, a Haitian soldier in the French army, and becomes swept up in the battle and its aftermath.

The Spelling Bee

When Derek Barton enters his school's spelling bee, little does he know that one of his mentors is interested in more than his spelling prowess. As events unfold, danger lurks for Derek and threatens those closest to him.

Blackberries in the Summer

This is the story of suffragist and business woman Eulalie Salley and her crucial role in the development of the Aiken Winter Colony. Her interactions with the rich and famous people who came to Aiken in the early 20th century provide a fascinating insight into that era and its rich history.

Dedication

*To my wife Sydney for her support
and encouragement during the writing
of "Beyond Boundary,"
and to the City of Aiken and
its people for their unique
blend of history and inspiration.*

Author's Notes

"Beyond Boundary" is a work of fiction. Dialog and activities attributed to any historical figures are products of the author's imagination and are not based on historical fact. Other people or events in the book were created by the author and any resemblance to actual people or events is coincidental.

1

The Return

Alexander Hamilton Devereux didn't see the green expanse of South Carolina pines flashing past his window. He had closed his eyes as the persistent, hypnotic rhythm of the train's wheels transported him back to another place and time. He could see his parents standing on the station platform, his mother dabbing at her eyes while his father struggled to hold back his own tears. That was nearly eight years ago, when this same train had taken him north, away from Aiken, away from his family, and away from the only world he had ever known.

"Ten minutes to Aiken, ten minutes," the conductor announced as he walked through the car. Alex flinched. The conductor's booming announcement startled him from his reverie. He glanced at his watch. It was almost seven. The blistering sun of August was beginning its descent beyond the wall of pines. His stomach growled. He realized that he was very tired and very hungry after twenty hours on the train. The sandwich he ate at the small stand in the Charleston depot was now a distant memory. He sat up straighter in his seat as he pulled a crumpled, yellow sheet from his inside coat pocket. He slowly unfolded the telegram that Western Union had delivered early yesterday morning.

The deafening jangle of the doorbell had jarred him awake. The uniformed bicycle messenger stood nervously on the stoop of the Columbia Heights apartment that Alex shared with three other Howard University students. Alex staggered downstairs and blindly signed for the delivery. He slowly closed the door behind him, leaning against it while staring dully at the yellow envelope. He hesitated to break the seal. He had a dark foreboding. News delivered this early in the morning was never good. He read the telegram again—for the umpteenth time.

"Alex you had better come home. Samson is dying. He wants to see you before he goes.
Mama"

* * * * *

Samson Demosthenes Devereux had lived in Aiken, South Carolina since 1873. He came there with Miss Celestine Eustis from New Orleans when Miss Eustis brought her orphaned niece Louise to Aiken for treatment of her tuberculosis—the same disease that had killed both her parents in France, following the War Between the States. Sam continued to work for Miss Eustis until her death in 1921. Now the cancer ravaging Samson Devereux's lungs would no longer be denied.

* * * * *

"Is that you Alex?"

The voice came from amid the impatient crowd jostling for position at the foot of the train steps. The sun angling across the platform was blinding. He raised his hand to shade his eyes, but the glare prevented him from seeing who was speaking. It didn't really matter. Even after all the intervening years, he immediately recognized the voice of his brother Ben.

Benjamin Franklin Devereux was five years younger than

Alex. He idolized his brother and was devastated when Alex left for Washington. Ben was fifteen at the time, quiet and introspective. As the youngest member of the Devereux clan Ben was heir to all the family hand-me-downs and cast-offs—including his withdrawn and sensitive nature. Ben was always reclusive, the quietest member of the family.

* * * * *

"Ben, is that really you?" Alex shouted, throwing his arms around his younger brother.

"It sho is, Alex! My Lord! It's been so long! Why, you're even bigger than when you left. What you now, six-two, six-three?" Ben asked as he stepped back to appraise the strapping figure standing before him.

"Actually, I'm six-four and I weigh 225 pounds, in case you were going to ask. And, look at you! All grown up! You were just a skinny little kid when I left. Now you're almost as big as I am. I guess we come from some pretty strong stock."

Suddenly, the joy drained from Alex's face. The broad smile disappeared into the wilting corners of his mouth. Ben, so much the image of his father Sam, reminded Alex of the reason for his return to Aiken.

"How's Papa?"

"Not good Alex. Doctor Johnson say the cancer done spread to his lungs and it's jest a matter of time now. He in a lot of pain. The doctor, he comes by twice a day to give him a shot. Papa, he sleeps most the day. Mr. Palmer told the doc to do whatever he needed to keep him comfortable and that he would pay for it. The Palmers have been mighty good to us through all of this.

* * * * *

Samson and Minnie Devereux went to work for Alfred Endicott Palmer following Miss Eustis' death in 1921.

3

The Palmers had been her neighbors in the elite equestrian community of Westbury, New York, on the north shore of Long Island. Mr. Palmer was president of the Nassau Bank and Trust Company. Celestine Eustis seduced Mr. Palmer into becoming a member of Aiken's Winter Colony. He bought a parcel of land from her and had Julian Peabody design and build *The Cove* for him. The thirty-room cottage, from its lofty perch on Coker Springs Road, held a commanding view of the sprawling urban forest that was Hitchcock Woods.

* * * * *

"When did Papa find out about the cancer?" Alex asked as they collected his luggage.

"The doctor found it 'bout nine months ago, but Papa kept on working. He didn't tell nobody for six months. He didn't even tell Mama until he had to stop working. She knowed something bad was wrong; he kept losing so much weight. Papa held on for as long as he could. He jest didn't want to let Mr. Alfred down and he hated to think about jest lying around the house. You know how he had to always keep busy. He was the butler at *The Cove* for years. Mama ran the kitchen. They went to work there right after Miss Eustis died and you left."

"Yeah, I recall Mama writing to tell me that they had gone over to Mr. Palmer's. I remember Miss Celestine saying how much she thought of the Palmer family. I never got much of a chance to meet them. Do you still work there?"

"Naw, I'm working at the Gaston Livery Stable out on Park Avenue. Old man Gaston, he been real sick lately and his son done took over the stable. He splits his time 'tween the bank and his farms, so he hired Mr. Harold Sims to run the stable. You remember him. He used to run his own stable in the Alley downtown. Mr. Sims needed someone to help out and he recollected me from Miss Celestine. The money's pretty good and I gits tips when I pick up folks comin' into the depot. I like being around the horses. Mr. Sims, he let me use this rig to fetch you home. I didn't want you to hafta walk."

"Thanks, Ben. I sure do appreciate that. I wasn't looking forward to walking home after twenty hours on that train; especially not in this heat with two suitcases."

Ben unhitched the horse from the railing and headed him east along Park Avenue. The more direct route would have been down Union to Colleton then east to Charleston. However, that route meant driving down Colleton where all the rich folks lived. Unless you were going to work, or delivering something to one of those homes, any self-respecting member of Aiken's servant class observed the unwritten—and unbending—rule. Stay off the streets of the horse district. A short distance from the station Ben tugged on the right rein, steering the buggy onto Charleston.

"Gee, Adam, gee," Ben commanded, and the sleek, sorrel horse obeyed the instruction to turn right. "When I picks up folks at the station I takes the bigger buggy. That's when I harness up Eve. Her and Adam, they been totin' folks to and from the station for years."

Ben lapsed into silence. He appeared ill-at-ease. It was as if an invisible curtain lowered between the two as they rode side-by-side on the carriage seat. Their old relationship, back when they were equals running around Aiken and playing with the other children, had changed. Something troubling had transpired during the seven years Alex was away studying the law. Ben couldn't put his finger on precisely what it was. He loved Alex and was proud of him, however at twenty-two Ben could sense the arc of his life following that of his father Samson's. He wanted more. He resented that he didn't have the same opportunity as Alex; to go to school, to try to make something more of himself. He didn't blame Alex for taking advantage of the opportunity Miss Celestine had given him, however that awareness couldn't quell the festering envy rising in the pit of his stomach—nor his sense of the unfairness of it all. What about me? Ben thought. Why don't I deserve the same chance at something better in life?

The steel rims of the carriage wheels grated across the railroad tracks before resuming their familiar crunching sound; a sound unique to the sandy, unpaved streets of Aiken. The abrupt, abrasive noise of steel on steel stirred Ben from his bitter musings. It was this same loamy soil, together with the benign winters, that attracted the wealthy horse lovers to Aiken and in turn provided livelihoods for the entire Devereux clan.

"I reckon it's not the worst place in life to be," Ben concluded under his breath.

"What was that Ben? I didn't hear you."

"Oh, it was nothing. I was just reckoning old Adam might need re-shoeing. Something sounds outa kilter when his right front hoof hits the ground. When you's around horses like I is you hear things other people won't pay no mind to."

Alex heard more in Ben's muted response than his words expressed.

"What is it Ben? You seem to be a little down. Is it just Papa, or is something else bothering you?"

"I don't know Alex." Ben hesitated. "It just seems like they oughta be more in life than jest lookin' at the rear end of a horse. I look at you and I sees a chance. I look at me and all I see is more of the same. I don't want to grow old and die still starin' at the ass-end of some old horse, still doin' the same old things then that I'm a doin' at twenty-two.

"I can understand that Ben. For the past seven years, I've seen another world, a world full of opportunity and promise. I've met other colored folks who have done some real important things: professors, doctors, lawyers, writers. I look at my future and I want to do those things. I believe I'm capable of doing something important. I recognize that Miss Celestine paid my way through school so that I could come back to Aiken and try to make life better for the black community here, but I just don't know if I can do that. I don't know if Aiken is ready for an "uppity nigger" practicing law in the white man's courtroom. I don't know if I'm ready to give up the life I could have in Washington."

"You gotta do what make you happy, Alex. I hope its stayin' here in Aiken, but if it ain't, I understand."

2

The Promise

Celestine Eustis built the modest bungalow on Charleston Street for Sam and Minnie Devereux. They had lived there rent-free since their marriage. She left it to them in her will, free and clear. All five of the Devereux children grew up there; in that simple, six-room, shotgun cabin on Charleston Street, in the block wedged between Colleton Avenue and South Boundary. It was the only home Alex had ever known. The small frame house was handy to the exclusive horse district and within walking distance of *The Cove* and *Mon Repos,* the Eustis/Hitchcock cottage. However, like all the homes of those who served the Winter Colony, it was located **Beyond Boundary,** the imaginary line dividing the haves from the have-nots in Aiken society.

* * * * *

The sun had disappeared completely at the west end of Colleton when Ben pulled the carriage onto the gravel driveway of the modest clapboard house. A lone figure waited at the top of the front porch steps. In the gloom, Alex could barely make out the portly form standing there, but as surely as he had known Ben's voice, he knew the rounded silhouette of his mother. She was patiently waiting for her prodigal son to return home.

Looking at her, it was apparent that Minnie Devereux enjoyed her own cooking as much as she loved serving it to others.

"Come here, boy! Let me see what you looks like now that them Yankees has had aholt of you."

She drew Alex to her bountiful bosom. He recognized the fragrance she was wearing, the fancy bottle, still half-full, and still occupying its special spot atop her chest-of-drawers. Miss Eustis had given the perfume to Minnie at a time when the family was packing for a return to New York. "*Shalimar,*" that intriguing name, evoking in Alex images of the Arabian nights. Minnie treasured the gift, using it only sparingly and only for very special occasions, like Alex's homecoming.

She squeezed him as if trying to crush all the long years of separation out of him. The same tears he remembered from the station platform over seven years ago once again rolled down his mother's plump cheeks.

"My, my, how you done growed. I reckoned Ben was a big'un but you done outgrowed him."

"Hey, Mama," Alex said huskily, his long arms encircling her, a lump forming in his throat. "It's sure good to be home. I didn't know how much I'd missed y'all until I saw Ben at the station."

Alex swung easily back into the southern vernacular of his youth, the polish and breeding of seven years quickly melting away.

"How you doin' Mama?" he said, "I know Papa's condition must've been really hard on you and the family."

"It has been Alex, but thank goodness for Cleo and Phoebe. I don't know what I'da done without them two girls. They's been a real blessing to me, and when they won't here, the women folk at Friendship Baptist come by to sit with Sam. The last few weeks has been the hardest. Movin' him, and bathin' him, and gittin' him to the toilet. It 'bout takes all I can do."

"I'm sorry Mama. I shoulda been here."

"Hesh up, Alex," she said sternly. "Yo daddy won't 'low it. He told me not to tell you. He too proud of what you done. Him and me, we never had much schoolin' and he was bound and determined that you git that diploma 'fo you come home. He promised Miss Celestine befo' she passed that he gone make sure you finish yo schoolin'. He seed her the day befo she died. She say 'Sam, don't you let anything stand in the way of that boy finishing school. I want him to come back here to Aiken. Your people need him.' "

* * * * *

Celestine Eustis held a deep and abiding affection for the entire Devereux family. Sam had been loyal to her through all the difficult times; first in France, then in New Orleans, and finally here in Aiken. All the Devereux children, except George, were bright. However, at a very early age she saw flashes of extraordinary brilliance in young Alex Devereux. She lifted the phone and asked the operator to call Martha Schofield.

"Martha, this is Celestine Eustis."

* * * * *

Martha Schofield founded the Aiken Normal and Industrial School for Negroes after the Civil War for the education of the children of freed slaves. Martha came to Aiken from St. Helena Island and the Penn School on the South Carolina coast. She went there as a Quaker missionary from Pennsylvania to teach the orphaned and homeless black children. Martha contracted tuberculosis and moved to Aiken at the suggestion of her fellow teachers. Aiken was noted for its healthy climate and curative powers. She intended to return to St. Helena, but never did. She saw the same desperate need in Aiken that she had found on the coast, and so she stayed. Celestine Eustis was a strong supporter and major benefactor of the Aiken Normal and Industrial School.

* * * * *

"Yes, Miss Eustis, what can I do for you?"

"Martha I believe you know Sam and Minnie Devereux. They work for us here at *Mon Repos.*"

"Yes, I met them when you invited me for dinner."

"Well, they have a young son, Alex, who works here in the stables. He's the same age as Tommy, Jr. and he's smart as a whip. I was wondering if you would take him at your school — as a favor to me. I'll be glad to cover his expenses. I know that many of your students have gone on to college up north and become doctors and lawyers and teachers. I also know that most of them have not returned to Aiken. We both know why. The old prejudices and attitudes die hard. Life here can be very difficult for Negroes. Like you, I want to help change that. The future for the colored race in the South depends on the leadership of bright, educated, young men and women who have the courage and the credentials, and the conviction to challenge the old ways. I believe Alex Devereux can be one of those leaders, and I want you to help me to help him."

"Miss Eustis I will consider it a great honor to have your young Alex at our school. You can count on my full support."

Alex blossomed at Miss Schofield's school. He absorbed all that the staff threw at him with remarkable ease. He excelled in mathematics, physics, English and the other courses the school offered.

The shrill ring of the black, candlestick phone echoed across the sitting room in Celestine Eustis' apartment upstairs at *Mon Repos.* It was early April. The family had remained in Aiken longer than usual to permit Tommy, Jr. to participate in late spring polo matches.

"Hello, this is Celestine Eustis."

"Miss Eustis, this is Martha Schofield. How are you today?"

"I am fine Martha. I just came in from the woods. I was riding with Louise and Thomas. It's a glorious day outside. What can I do for you Martha?"

"I just wanted you to know that Alex Devereux has completed every course required for a diploma from our school, and he's done it in record time. I think, at fifteen, he's the youngest ever to accomplish that. I've never encountered such a precocious mind in my life. We're very proud of him. I'm sure you are as well."

"Martha, as you know, I've been following his progress and I can't thank you enough for what you've done for Alex. Is there anything more he requires to be accepted into college?"

"Our weakest subjects here are classical literature and world history. Alex may require more training in those areas. It all depends on which school he attends."

"Thank you, Martha. When will Alex graduate?"

"Commencement this year will be on April 20. Many of the children need to get home to help with the spring planting season."

"That's great. We're not returning to New York until the first of May. I look forward to attending the graduation ceremonies."

"We look forward to having you there. As a matter of fact, Dr. George Washington Carver from Tuskegee Institute was scheduled to speak, however, he is being honored with an award in Sweden that weekend. He asked if we would please release him from his commitment. Of course, I said yes. But, it was such short notice that we haven't found a suitable replacement. I wonder if you would consider addressing our graduates."

"Oh, Martha, that's so kind of you. I am not practiced at public speaking; however, since this is such a special day for Alex, I'll be delighted to speak. I certainly can't compete with Dr. Carver when it comes to the subject of peanuts, but maybe

I'll find something else to interest the students."

"I'm sure you will do a fine job, Miss Eustis. You've always been an inspiration to the school and to the citizens of Aiken. I look forward to your address."

"Tommy," Celestine called to her nephew as he came in from the stables, "you know that Alex Devereux has finished his work at Miss Schofield's school?"

"Yes ma'am, he told me yesterday that he'll be graduating in April."

"I hate to see his education stop at this point. I was thinking that maybe the folks at Aiken Prep wouldn't mind if he went to some of your classes. Miss Schofield says he can use some more courses in classical literature and world history. He could just sit in back and audit the courses. I'll pay for his books and maybe you can give him a hand after school. Would you do that?"

"Why, yes ma'am. I'd be glad to. I spend a lot of time with Alex in the stables anyway. I'd be happy to help him."

"Thank you, Tommy. It'll mean a lot to me."

The staff at Aiken Prep was eager to please the school's founder, and the teachers were more than generous in their support. After school, Alex and Tommy would sit for hours on hay bales, parsing Latin phrases, debating Plato and Aristotle and dissecting Napoleon's successes and failures. Alex's regular job was grooming the horses and mucking the stalls of the *Mon Repos* stables, which were surrounded by the majestic forests of Hitchcock Woods. With both of Alex's parents working in the big house, he and Tommy Jr. practically grew up together — that is, until 1917 when Tommy left for France to join the Lafayette Escadrille, an American Air Group aiding the French in World War One.

"Louise, I need to talk to you," her aunt said after dinner one evening. It was shortly after Tommy, Jr. had left for France. *Tante* Celestine never used her niece's formal name unless what she was about to say was extremely important.

"What is it?" Louise said. "You sound so serious."

"I am serious," she began. "I've never been more serious in my life. Lulie you are aware that my will gives the house on Charleston to Sam Devereux when I die."

"Yes ma'am, you told me that. I think it's a wonderful gesture on your part."

"Well, it's more than just a gesture. I don't think I could have made it through the death of George and Louise and your illness without Sam. There's more that I have included in my will for them. I've set up a small trust with Mr. Dibble down at Farmers and Trust and I have named you as the trustee. It's to see that they have enough to live on when they stop working."

She paused for a moment then continued.

"There's another item in the will that I haven't discussed with you before. It has to do with Alex Devereux."

"Alex? I knew you had taken a personal interest in the boy, but I just thought it had to do with him and Tommy being the same age and playing together all the time."

"There was that, but it goes much deeper. Do you remember that trial several years ago when that Negro man, Raleigh Neighbors, was convicted of molesting a white girl out in Salley."

"Yes, I remember."

"And do you remember the young white lawyer Judge Haley appointed to represent him."

"Yes. He had just graduated from law school the year before. Mr. Cranston I believe."

"Yes, poor, bewildered, in-over-his-head, Bob Cranston. Mr. Croft, the prosecutor, ate him up and spat him out, and

Mr. Neighbors went to jail for a crime he didn't commit. We only found that out when that white trash Buncombe boy was arrested a few months later for molesting another girl in Salley. Well, under the sheriff's questioning, he confessed. Similarities in the two cases led the sheriff to ask Buncombe about Mary Rogers, the first girl. He finally admitted that he had been with Mary Rogers the night she claimed she was assaulted. The sheriff called her in and after a period of questioning, she finally corroborated the Buncombe boy's story. She said she had been so afraid of what her daddy might do that she blamed her bruises on Mr. Neighbors, who lived nearby. Meanwhile poor Mr. Neighbors sat in prison while his family nearly starved to death. It still took three months to get him released."

"What does all that have to do with Alex Devereux, *Tante* Celestine?"

"The black people of Aiken County deserve better. Now that Alex has graduated from Miss Schofield's school and sat in on some of Tommy's courses at Aiken Prep, I believe he is ready for college. I have written to the president of Howard University and assured him that Alex has the education necessary to succeed at the university level. My brother William is a big supporter of the University and he spoke to Dr. Mordecai Johnson for me. Dr. Johnson is willing to test Alex and, if he passes the entrance exams, to enroll him at the school. Howard University has an excellent law school. If Alex does well in his undergraduate work, Dr. Johnson said he can enroll there. I want Alex to get his law degree and come back to Aiken to practice. I want someone who'll be able to stand between the black people and the white justice system. I've already spoken to Mr. Frampton Poole. He has agreed to help Alex pass the South Carolina bar. If he passes, Mr. Poole said he'll take Alex into his firm. He is an honest and fair man — he also owes me a favor. He knows there are those in the community who will shun him for this, but he's agreed to do it anyway. I told him I would make sure his practice doesn't suffer. Members of the colony will stand behind me — and him. So, that's the other item in my will."

"I think that's wonderful," Louise said. "Your story about Mr. Neighbors reminded me of the time several years ago when we came down for the winter and read about another colored man who had been arrested in Wagener for much the same thing. He was dragged off the train in Windsor by a gang of whites, tied to a tree and blown to pieces by a shotgun; no judge, no jury, just vigilante justice. I think everyone knew that no black man would come near a white girl, let alone molest her. I agree with you. The system needs fixing. I hope Alex Devereux can help."

3

The Death Watch

"**H**e looks so thin Mama."

Alex stood in the door and looked across the room at the emaciated form of his father. A single, small, electric bulb hung suspended from the ceiling, its naked bareness starkly revealing the ravages of the cancer that now riddled the once proud and powerful body of Samson Devereux. The harsh light cast dark shadows in the deep crevices where his once prominent cheeks stood. The sharp scent of witch-hazel permeated the room. The once piercing, blue eyes lay dull and sunken in his skull; eyes that were a legacy of his grandfather, one of Jean Lafitte's pirate band in New Orleans. Nothing lying there was the man he remembered; the loving father, the stern disciplinarian, the steady shelter from the harshness of life — only the empty shell of the man he called Papa.

"He's been slipping away mo' and mo' these past few days. I think he held on this long cause he knew you was coming home. He loved all his chilren Alex, but we both know there was a special place in his heart for you. He be able to slip away in peace now that you home. Go on. He just dozin'. He'd want you to wake him up."

"Papa, Papa." he said soothingly, "It's Alex. I've come home."

Slowly, Sam Devereux opened his right eye. He turned his head in the direction of the sweet voice he had so longed to hear once more.

"That really you boy? I 'bout done give up on you makin' it in time."

"Papa, you knew I'd get here. I wish you'da let Mama send for me sooner."

"Now don't you go fussin' her 'bout that. I knowed you was close to gittin' that piece of paper. I tol' Miss Celestine jest befo she died that I gone be sure you got that diploma. I won't gonna let nuthin' git in the way of that. 'Sides he said with a raspy laugh, "I won't lookin' a whole heap better two or three weeks ago, so hit don't matter much."

"I'm so sorry Papa. I was looking forward to coming back to Aiken and looking after you and Mama and the family. It just doesn't seem fair that God would lead you to the banks of Jordan but like Moses he won't let you enter the Promised Land?"

"Reverend say that the Lord works in 'sterious ways, his wonders to perform. We cain't never know why He do what He do. We jest has to go on and live out the days He give us and leave all the rest up to Him."

"I know Papa, but it's so hard to see you like this."

"When I's gone Alex, don't you think 'bout me this way. You 'member me the way it useta be when we'd go over to Platt's Pond and fish for bream and you and the girls be goin' swimmin'. Them was the good days and them's the ones you needs to hang on to. I gone be jest fine. I's at peace wit the world. Miss Celestine done left some money so your ma will be all right. I know Jesus be waitin' for me on t'other side. Now that I's seed you again, I can go in peace. All I asks of you boy is to look out for your ma and the family. I know it oughta be

George I'm talking to. I don't know what done come over that boy. He jest gone bad is all I can say. I hoped for a while that he was gonna straighten hisself out but it seem like it jest gits wuss and wuss."

* * * * *

George Washington Devereux, at thirty-one, was the oldest of the five Devereux children. He had been a trial to Sam and Minnie since the day he was born. The excruciating delivery of the twelve pound George took thirty hours. Minnie nearly died from loss of blood. When the doctor finally came, he found the baby in an undeliverable breech position. The old midwife, Rosa, had done her best, but this was beyond her midwifery skills. Sam went for Doctor Johnson to come help.

"Get me a lot of hot water and old sheets," he commanded Rosa upon seeing the distress Minnie was in. "We're going to have tooperate on her. Even at that, she's lost so much blood I don't know if she'll make it.

"Sam, clear off the kitchen table, scrub it down, and put a sheet on it, then come back in here!"

Sam did as he was told, quickly reappearing at the bedroom door.

"Okay, Rosa, Sam, we've got to get her to the kitchen."

With Sam at her shoulders and the doctor and Rosa at her feet they were able to maneuver the exhausted, half-conscious Minnie into the kitchen.

"Sam, keep that water boiling. Rosa, you'll need to help me."

Doctor Johnson gave Minnie an injection of morphine. When he was satisfied that she was under, he made a long incision across Minnie's swollen abdomen. Rosa used old rags to soak up the blood oozing from the ragged edges of Minnie's distended stomach and uterus. Meanwhile, the doctor struggled to move the fetus into a position where he could remove it. As he grabbed its legs he saw that the umbilical cord was wrapped tightly around the baby's neck and encircling his torso. It was trapped between the fetus' shoulder and the uterine wall. Young George was turning blue. The doctor turned the boy over, lifted him free of his mother's womb, and unfurled the umbilical cord from around his neck. Reflexive spasms accompanied the infant's attempts to breathe. The doctor held the gasping infant up by his legs and whacked him on the rear. Mucous material erupted from the baby's throat. George let out a scream and then gulped in his first breath of fresh air.

"Rosa, you get him cleaned up while I close up Minnie's stomach," Doc Johnson said after severing and tying the umbilical cord. "Sam keep the water coming. We're gonna need some more rags."

An hour later, with Minnie back in her bed resting and with young George pressed against her bosom, Dr. Johnson was finally able to sit down and have the cup of coffee Sam offered him. He stared across the table at the frightened father. He chose his words carefully.

"Sam, I don't know how to tell you this, but that cord around the baby's neck had cut off his blood supply for some period of time. I don't know for how long or whether there was any permanent damage, but it's something you and Minnie are going to have to look out for as he gets older."

Sam would have reason to recall that conversation many times over the next thirty-one years.

* * * * *

"Papa, we all know George has problems. From early on he was prone to have seizures and he's never been very well coordinated. You told me that Dr, Johnson said there might be complications. What did he say, exactly?"

Sam shifted so that Alex was in his field of vision. He

coughed and reached for the rag on his bed. He swiped it across his mouth and dropped it back onto the bedspread. Fresh streaks of crimson materialized on the folds of the makeshift handkerchief.

"George was a breech baby. He tried to come out butt first. Old Rosa, the midwife, she worked with your ma all night trying to birth that boy. Next morning she say, 'Sam, you best go git Doc Johnson. It don't look lak dat youngun's gonna come out on his own.' The doctor, he come right away, and he seed the boy wadn't turned right. He said, 'Sam, Rosa, we're going to have to cut that baby out.' Well, him'n me and Rosa, we dragged your Ma into the kitchen and he operated on her right there on the kitchen table. Trouble be, when he got in there the cord done wrapped round the baby's neck and the blood was cut off. When it was all over he say, 'Sam that baby may have problems.' So, I say, 'What kinda problems Doc?' and he say, 'He may have seizures and some kinda palsy.' It all depended on how much brain damage they was."

Minnie came over and placed a hand on Alex's arm.

"You best let'im rest awhile. He gits tired out real easy."

"All right, Mama." Alex looked back at Sam, "You get some rest now, Papa. I'll come back in to see you later."

He turned quickly to walk toward the kitchen, hoping his father didn't see his tears.

"I bet you didn't git nothin' to eat on that train did you Alex?" Minnie said.

"No, ma'am," he answered huskily, drying his eyes. "The last thing I had was a sandwich in Charleston."

"Me and Ben reckoned you'd be hungry so we waited supper for you. How bout some fried chicken, turnip greens and cornbread?"

"That sounds good to me. I've been thinking about your fried chicken ever since I got on that train in Washington."

Alex sat across the table from Minnie and Ben. He picked

up his fork and reached for a drumstick.

"What you doin' boy?" Minnie harrumphed as she parried his thrust with her own fork. "You done forgot bout thanking the Lord for His blessings?"

"I'm sorry Mama. I guess I've fallen into some heathen ways up north. If you hesitate at the boarding house you're liable to get left out."

"Well, you best 'member yo manners now that you back home."

Minnie took Ben's hand and reached across the table for Alex's.

"Lord, thank You for bringin' my boy back home safe and sound. He been gone a awful long time and he done changed a whole heap, but he still my little Alex. Bless us Lord and give us the strength we needs to handle the troubles You done laid on us with Sam. I reckon You knows whut You's a doin' but it sho hard. Bless Sam and make his goin' easy. He been a good husband and a good pa and I know he be goin'home to Jesus now. Bless this food to our bodies and our bodies to Your service. Amen."

Sam was still sleeping. It was nine when Alex sat down in the swing on the front porch. They had talked for an hour at the table after the supper dishes were put away. Minnie was tending to Sam. Ben had gone to take Adam back to Gaston's and bed him down for the night. The din of crickets and katydids filled his ears. A whip-poor-will shrilled in the distance, mournfully seeking its mate. Alex suddenly realized how much he had missed the sounds of his youth. The frenzied hubbub of Washington's urban scene masked most of the critter noises. The fact that his father lay dying just beyond the door couldn't mute entirely his joy at being home. The screen door opened. Minnie stepped out onto the porch.

"He still sleepin'. Doc Johnson left some laudanum case

Sam gits restless. I give him a dose. He won't wake up no more til mawnin'."

She settled her heavy frame next to Alex. The beam overhead groaned and squealed in protest at the increased burden.

"Where is George, Mama?"

"Last we heard he was over to North Augusta. He took up with some young woman what work at the casino at Carolina Springs. We don't know nuthin' much 'bout her. A few folks at Friendship say they's seen her once or twice at Storm Branch Baptist out near Clearwater. You may 'member the Springs was started up by some Storm Branch members. It's only a few miles away from the church. It was mostly a swimming hole called the Dragon Club until the bands started comin' in. That's where George 'sposed to be now. Some of the folks round here what goes over there say they's seen him a time or two. They say he has some kinda job at the casino. He ain't been home in more'n a year. We sent word that Sam was bad sick but we ain't heard nary a thing from him."

"What about Cleo and Phoebe?"

"They both be at the Highland Park. They been there since me and Sam went over to work for Mr. Palmer at *The Cove*. Cleo, she works in housekeeping and Phoebe, she works in the laundry. They both say they comin' round tomorrow. They gits Saturdays off."

"You wrote me that they're both married now."

"Yeah. Cleo's married to Jonah Page. He works for the Iselins at Hopelands. He one of the grooms for the horses. They lives over near Miss Schofield's school on Marlboro Street. They got two chilren already. Four-year old boy and two-year old girl. Toby and Maggie. Sweetest little'uns you ever seen. I spec they'll be round tomorrow.

"Phoebe married now too. Lester works for Mr. Ambrose Clark up on Grace. He takes care of the yards for 'im. Lester's last name Mitchell. They ain't got no chilren yet.

"How 'bout you Alex? You got any girls in the big city?"

"I've been out with a few of the local girls. Can't say there's one in particular. There was one girl I really liked; she was in the music school at Howard. Voice of an angel. She had an offer to move up to New York when she graduated. She's been singing in several clubs up there. She sang some with Cab Calloway's band at the Cotton Club. She even appeared in a Broadway musical called *No, No, Nanette*. She fills in sometimes in the chorus,"

"You still hearin' from her?"

"Yes'm. We've been corresponding since she left. She's been up there over a year now."

"She gone come down here to see you?"

"I don't think so Mama. It's hard for Aiken to compete with New York. I guess once you get there it sorta gets in your blood. No, I don't expect to see her again."

"You don't never know. With all them bands what come down to play for the rich folks she may jest wind up here one day."

"I don't know Mama," Alex said wistfully. "I hope you're right."

A figure emerged from the shadows. It was Ben returning from the stables.

"Well, all the horses done been fed and bedded down for the night. I'm plum tuckered out. If y'all don't mind, I'm gonna go on to bed. We got a big day tomorrow, some new horses comin' in and a new fancy carriage. Mr. Dibble down at the bank ordered it. He still likes to drive his cariage to town from Montmorenci when the weather's good. I'll be takin' it out there after we gits it set up and greased. You wanta come? They'll be two horses to ride back."

"Sure Ben. What time will you be leaving?"

"It'll be right after dinner. Probably 'bout one or so."

"All right. I'll be ready."

"You go on, son," Minnie said. " Me'n Alex got some catchin' up to do. What time you wants to git up?"

"Bout six. I needs to be at Gaston's by seven. Good night Alex. It sho good you home."

"Good night Ben. It's good to be home."

"Mama, how's Ben really been doing? He seemed a little out of sorts on the drive home."

"Tell the truth Alex, I been a mite worried 'bout Ben. He ain't been in no trouble or nothin' but he jest seems lost sometimes. He always talkin' bout you and how you gonna be all different when you comes home. He talks 'bout wantin' to go to school. Trouble be, we caint afford to pay for 'im to go. We kinda thought Miss Celestine mighta left some money for his schoolin' but they weren't none. I guess she reckoned one boy in the family with schoolin' was enough. Mind you, I ain't faultin' her atall. She done more for this family than we had any right to expect. It jest hurts my heart to see Ben achin' like he do."

"I'm sorry Ma. Maybe when I get established as a lawyer I'll be able to help him."

"That would be mighty nice if you could Alex. I know he'd sho' 'preciate it."

"Mama," Alex asked hesitatingly, "does Ben have any girlfriends?"

"He was seein' one of the Staley twins for a while but she done got engaged to Luke Tyler. You remember him? He one of the boys what worked for Mr. Fitch Gilbert over to Red Top. He goes with the family when they goes North in the springtime. They s'posed to git married when Luke come back in October. Nowadays, Ben mostly runs round wit' some of the boys over to that pool hall on York Street. I tol'im I don't like some of them boys but he a growed man now and he gonna do what he gonna do."

"Was he doing that before Pa got sick?"

"Naw. He started hangin' round with them boys bout the same time Sam got real bad."

"Maybe I'll have a talk with Ben on our way out to Mr. Dibble's place tomorrow."

"I'd sho 'preciate you doin' that Alex. I got more on my plate than I can handle already. I don't need Ben gittin' into no trouble."

"All right, Mama, I'll do it. I know Ben's a good boy so don't you worry about him. You just worry about Papa. He needs all your attention now.

"I think I'll follow Ben's lead and head off to bed. I didn't realize how tired I am until I sat down in this swing. It's been a long two days. Good night Mama. I'll see you in the morning."

"Good night Alex. It mighty good you home. You sleep tight."

4

Death

The shrill blast of the 7:10 out of Augusta, bound for Charleston, jolted Alex awake. The ear-piercing scream grew to a climax as the train emerged from the walls of the railroad cut along Staubes Lane and pulled into the station at Union Street. The hiss of escaping steam from the locomotive was sharp and clear from across the several blocks to the Devereux house. It took Alex a minute to regain his bearings. A quick glance around the old familiar room reassured him that he was safely home in Aiken.

I slept later than I meant to, he thought. I want to get out and see what changes have taken place since I left.

Childhood memories came flooding back as he heard the clanging of pots in the kitchen and knew that Mama was busily preparing breakfast. Alex stretched and rolled out of bed. The bare, linoleum floor felt cold to his feet. He held vivid memories of the day when Samson lugged the eight foot by eight foot square into his room and unrolled it. It was an unexpected luxury for a boy of ten in his neighborhood to have a linoleum floor. During the next week, he brought every one of his friends in to marvel at the luxury. He smiled as he slipped on his clothes and walked down the hall to the kitchen. On the way, he glanced through the parlor door. Samson was still sleeping.

"Morning Mama."

Alex put his arm around Minnie's broad shoulders.

"Mornin' son. You sleep all right?"

"Yes ma'am. Like a log. I was more tired than I thought. I'd probably still be asleep if the train hadn't come in. I forgot how loud its whistle is."

"Won't take you long to get back in the habit of ignorin' it like we do."

"Has Ben gone?"

"Yeah. He left bout a half-hour ago. You want some eggs and fat-back? I got some biscuits and syrup to go with em."

"Thanks, Mama," Alex said. "That sounds good. Have you already eaten?"

"Yeah, I ate with Ben, but I'll sit a spell with you and have a cup of coffee."

Alex stared out the window. The morning parade of workers streamed past on their way to their work throughout the horse district. Most of the cottages were shuttered and mothballed during the heat of summer but year-round housekeepers occupied a few. Others required regular maintenance and their gardens tended. The off-season could be hard on those who only served while the owners were in residence. A few paid off-season stipends to tide their staffs over and to make sure they would be there in the fall. For most, there were only their savings and odd jobs to bridge the seasons. Many worked as day laborers on the farms surrounding the city, where planting and harvesting tidily coincided with the off-season.

"Mama what does Ben do in the summer months when there are fewer horse people in town?"

"Mostly there's work to do at the stables or at Mr. Gaston's farm. He keeps busy most time. He helps round here when I need 'im. Sometimes he goes off with his friends from the pool hall."

"What do his friends do?"

"Mostly they do odd jobs. I hear tell one of them works some at the mills in Graniteville."

"Are any of them married?"

"Ben won't say, but he never talked about any of 'em bein' married. Why you ask?"

"I was just curious." Alex said unconvincingly.

"I know you boy! What you thinking?"

"Nothing Ma, just forget it. I'm going to go wandering a bit after breakfast if you don't mind. I'm curious about what's been going on around town while I've been away. I think I'll drop in to see how some of my old friends are getting along. I'll be back before Ben comes home for dinner."

Alex walked north on Charleston, retracing the route Ben had taken home last night. He crossed over Park past the cluster of businesses east of the depot. He turned down Richland Avenue and headed toward the downtown, passing Friendship Baptist Church where his family had belonged for as long as he could remember. By the time he passed the hotel at Chesterfield and Newberry his shirt was soaked through and plastered to his back. A few guests at the hotel were sitting on the veranda, fanning themselves to relieve the early morning heat and to shoo away the flies that had migrated over from the stables in The Alley. A block later, Alex stepped into the drug store on the southwest corner of Newberry and Richland.

"Good morning Dr. Johnson. Remember me? It's Alex Devereux."

The tall, angular man looked up from the book that lay open on the counter. He removed his glasses and focused on the young man standing before him.

"Of course! Alex! Your mother told me you were coming home. I'm so sorry about Sam. It's good that you're home. I don't think Sam will be with us much longer."

"No sir. I expect that you're right. He was still sleeping

when I left the house. I sure do appreciate you taking such good care of him for Mama."

"Sam's a good man and a good friend. It's the least I could do."

He glanced up at the large Seth Thomas clock hanging on the wall above the medicine cabinets. "It's about time for his next shot. I'll be driving over in a few minutes. Would you like a ride back home?"

"Thank you, sir, but no. I'm just taking a walk around to get reacquainted with Aiken. So much has changed since I left."

"That's for sure. Time never stands still. By the way, I can't tell you how proud we are that you've finished your law degree at Howard. It's a great school. I trust you'll be practicing here in Aiken."

"I was having some second thoughts, but now that I'm home and realize how much I have missed it, I think I will stay. Besides, Mama's gonna need me."

"That's great news Alex. Well, I'd better get over to see Sam. Drop back in later on and we'll get caught up on everything. It's sure good to see you Alex."

"Thank you, sir. It's good to see you, too. I look forward to that talk."

Alex watched as the doctor retrieved a hypodermic from a locked cabinet and put it into his well-worn black bag. He followed Dr. Johnson out of the pharmacy, watched him climb into his black Model-T Ford sedan and then disappear down Richland Avenue.

Further down Richland, past the Alley,several people were gathered on the sidewalk outside the entrance to the Commercial Hotel where a heated conversation was taking place. Alex headed in that direction. As he neared the crowd, he recognized Mr. Herman Hahn, owner of the hotel and the grocery store across Laurens Avenue. He was shouting at a young black man dressed in the livery of a chauffeur.

"Look here Dave, I don't care who your employer is you can't park your car here. You're blocking the hotel entrance for other cars that need to drop off and pick up customers."

"But, Mr. Herman," Dave said. "Mr. Eugene told me not to leave. He said he'd be right out. He just needed to speak to one of the guests at the hotel."

"I'm sorry. I respect Mr. Grace, but he knows the rules. Just pull around the corner into the alley. I'll tell Mr. Grace where you are."

"Yas suh, Mr. Herman. I hope you'll tell Mr. Eugene you made me move."

"Don't worry Dave. I'll take care of it."

Alex hung back but near enough to hear the conversation without getting involved. As the young man turned to enter his car, Alex recognized Dave Smith from his time at Schofield. Dave had been enrolled in the printing program. He had to drop out when his father became ill. Alex waited until the car came to a stop in the alley before approaching.

"Hey, Dave," he said, "Long time, no see."

Dave spun around, knocking his cap off on the doorframe. He stooped to retrieve it while trying to make out the man who just called to him.

"Alex. Alex Devereux. Is that really you?"

"Sure as shootin' Dave. I just got back into town yesterday. You remember my Pa, Samson. Well, he's in a mighty bad way. We don't expect him to be with us much longer."

"I'm sorry to hear that. I ran into Ben a few weeks back and he said your pa was sick.

"Are you through school Alex? Will you be moving back to Aiken?"

"It sure looks that way. If I can pass the bar exam, I'll be setting up practice here. Mr. Poole's gonna help me with the exam. He said he'll take me on if I pass. From the sound of your conversation with Mr. Hahn it doesn't look like too much has changed."

"Oh, he don't mean nothin' by it. He treats everybody the same way — black or white."

Alex followed Dave as he rounded the corner back to the front of the hotel. Eugene Grace was just emerging from the front door.

"I'm sorry I had to move the car Mr. Eugene but Mr. Hahn made me."

"It's okay Dave. Herman told me. He can be a little fussy at times, but being a businessman myself I understand.

"Who's this young man with you Dave?"

"Mr. Eugene Grace, this is Alex Devereux. He just got back from Washington, DC. He gone be a lawyer here in Aiken."

"Alex Devereux. Do your folks work for Endicott Palmer?"

"Yes, sir. That is they did. My father is very ill and my mother is staying home with him now."

"I'm sorry to hear that Alex. I remember both of them. They are very fine people. Did they work for Celestine Eustis before she died?"

"Yes, sir, they did."

"I thought so. My place is just down the street from *Mon Repos.* I used to see her all the time. Give my best to your folks and I hope your father gets better."

"Thank you, Mr. Grace. I'll tell them."

"I'll see you later Alex." Dave said as he followed his employer to the car.

Alex watched Dave disappear around the corner. He turned to head up Laurens Avenue then changed his mind. It was already ten and if he walked up to the Pastime Billiard Parlor he would have to almost run back home to catch Ben. He made a mental note to visit the pool hall soon. He wanted to see where Ben was spending so much of his time.

Ben was early. The new carriage was in the driveway, the

horses tethered to a small crepe myrtle tree. The buggy, painted a deep wine color with spokes of yellow, had a folding canopy of leather, which was tied back with silver buckled straps. It had a double row of seats upholstered in shiny black leather. It was the most beautiful carriage Alex had ever seen — and there were many that came and went at *Mon Repos.* Two English saddles rested behind the back seat. He ran his hand across the metal step-plate of the running board and whistled. Every detail was perfect.

"Hey, Ben," he called as he entered the house. "I think I may need a bath before I can ride in that new carriage, I've never seen anything like it. Old man Dibble must be doing okay at the bank."

"He is, and remember he also runs a dairy and has a big farm out in Montmorenci."

"Alex, I got a big mess of turnip greens cooked-up with ham hocks," Minnie called. "I also fixed some cornbread. You get washed up and we'll have some dinner before you go."

"All right, Mama. How's Papa doing this morning?"

"He was hurtin' sumpin' awful when he woke up, but Dr. Johnson come by and give him a shot. He restin' peaceably now.

"Doc Johnson say he seed you down at his drug store. He say you done turned out to be a fine lookin' young man. I had to agree with him," she said with a giggle.

Alex deflected the compliment and lit into the turnips and ham hock with gusto. He didn't get much cooking like this in Washington. He crumbled the cornbread into the pot liquor on his plate and closed his eyes. He savored the magnificent flavor combination, reminded anew what a great cook Minnie was.

"We'd better get a move on," Ben said as he gnawed the last shred of meat from a ham hock. "I told Mr. Sims I'd get back before three. He's expecting some new horses in and I have to get 'em over to one of Mr. Gaston's pastures. This is the first time Mr. Sims is gonna let me help with the training. The horses belong to Mr. Arthur Young over to Crossways. He wants them broke to a carriage when he comes down in October."

"Okay Ben, I'm about ready," Alex said as he tilted the plate to drink the last of the pot liquor. "Mama, if you want to have some more of this for supper tonight it'll be fine by me," he grinned.

"We's havin' pork roast and sweet taters. You can have some mo' turnips tomorrow."

Alex looked in on Samson as he passed the parlor on the way out. His father looked even worse than the day before. His breathing was shallow and labored. It couldn't be much longer.

Ben asked Alex to help him raise the top on the carriage. The run out to the Dibble farm was six miles and the midday sun was broiling.

Ben pulled onto South Boundary and turned the horses east through the two rows of oaks that Mr. Dibble had convinced Julian Salley to plant when Julian was the mayor of Aiken. The twenty-year old trees were beginning to arch over and shade the sandy, two-lane road. Mr. Dibble had driven his rigs down this route hundreds of times. Occasionally, he still drove his carriage but mostly he took his yellow, 1926 Pierce-Arrow. He especially liked the car's high, fender mounted head lamps since his trips home from the bank were often after dark when free ranging animals were hard to see.

"Ben, I saw Dave Smith down town this morning. He said he ran into you a few days ago."

"Yeah I was down in The Alley with Mr. Sims. Dave was gittin' a horse re-shoed for Mr. Grace."

"Do you see him very often?"

"Naw, he lives over near Eustis Park. I see him at the pool hall every once in a while. Why?"

"I don't know, just curious about the old gang I guess."

The two lapsed into silence. Alex retreated into his own thoughts. He wondered what George was doing and why he had abandoned the family. He wondered about Ben and where he was going with his life. He was curious about his sisters and how marriage and parenthood may have changed them. But, most of all he wondered about himself. He wondered if he was really ready to re-enter this life that now seemed so foreign to him. Was he ready to settle down to become a small town lawyer in Aiken; to represent his people in a white man's justice system? Was he still bound by his promise to Miss Celestine, or did her death release him? His head told him yes, but his heart told him no. If she had enough faith in him to believe he could make a difference, then his duty was to honor that faith. Notwithstanding the siren call of a legal career in a more tolerant society, he knew that he was home to stay.

"Looks like a bumper corn crop this year," Alex observed, breaking the silence.

"Yeah, everybody's plantin' more corn these days. No one will say why exactly, but we all know a bunch of it's goin' to make moonshine. Ever since prohibition started the corn crops has got bigger and bigger. I suspect a lot of it's being shipped up north. I've seen trucks come through town with license plates from New York and Illinois. A feller'd have to be blind to not know what's happenin'. They's also a lot of corn goin' to feed all the horses that's comin' into town with the Yankees."

"What about cotton? There seems to be a lot less than I remember."

"Yeah, every year the boll weevils gits worse and worse. Somebody said we lost over a third of the crop last year."

The twin silos bracketing the Dibble dairy barn emerged above the oaks surrounding "The Vale of Montmorenci," Henry Dibble's estate. His impressive two-story mansion sat several hundred feet back from the main road. Lush gardens ran down to the creek and lake behind. The idyllic Dibble farmstead sat on the periphery of the 720 acres that comprised his farm and dairy.

"Man, I never came out here before." Alex said in awe. "I knew Mr. Dibble was rich, but I never dreamed he was this rich."

"Yeah, he done all right with that bank and his dairy," Ben said. "He gives Mr. Gaston a lot of business even though they's both bankers. I 'magine this rig done set him back over two-hundred dollars. I don't make that much money in a year."

The four-space carriage house was attached to the stables, which were across a lane from the dairy barns. Ben guided the horses there and jumped down to secure their reins to a hitching post. He proceeded to unhitch Eve and Adam from their doubletree and remove their harnesses.

"Mr. Dibble's man Harold say he'll bring the gear back to Gaston's later in the week. Ain't no way we gonna haul it back on the horses. You still 'member how to strap on a saddle Alex?"

"I don't know. It's been a while since I was at the Hitchcock's, but I expect it'll come back to me."

Alex reached into the carriage to retrieve Adam's saddle and blanket. He threw the blanket over the horse's withers and followed up with the saddle, pulling the girth strap under and cinching it tightly through its ring. He pulled the stirrup down.

"Looks like you ain't been gone at all Alex. You may wanta check that cinch when we gits onto the road. Old Adam blows up sometimes to keep the strap from tightening. More'n once he throwed me off."

"Thanks. Ben."

"Now gimme a hand and we'll roll this new rig into that third bay. Don't want it to get dusty or rained on until Mr. Henry gits a chance to drive it."

Ben and Alex each picked up a stave, turned the buggy around, and backed it into the stall.

"Okay, let's head for home. It looks like rain." Ben shouted.

He hoisted himself onto Eve's broad back and gave her a slight nudge with his left heel. The horse leaped forward and tore off at a gallop.

"Wait for me," Alex shouted as he found the stirrup with his left foot and launched himself into the saddle. Adam lost no time taking off after Eve. Alex hung on for dear life. A quarter mile down the lane, as they turned onto the main road, Eve slowed to a trot and Adam quickly caught up the distance.

"I haven't ridden a horse in a while," Alex said. "I'm sure my legs will feel it tomorrow."

"You'll get the hang of it again real quick," Ben said.

They covered the six miles back to the Charleston Street house in less than an hour with Ben leading the way. Alex returned to the thoughts he had been pondering on the trip out to Montmorenci. He was startled when Ben made the turn onto Charleston off South Boundary. There were so many things he had to sort out over the next few days — not the least of which was his pursuit of a South Carolina license to practice law.

5

The Wake

Minnie was sitting in the porch swing, her apron pressed to her face, her elbows on her knees. Alex knew instantly that his father was gone. He hopped down from Adam, wrapped his reins around a yard post, and ran up the steps. Ben trotted up on Eve and followed Alex to the porch.

"I'm so sorry Mama," Alex said. "We should have been here."

"Don't go beatin' yoself up Alex. Sam went peaceably. He opened his eyes one last time and squeezed my hand. He tried to say sumpin' but the words won't come out. He jest smiled and closed his eyes and he was gone."

"I know it's hard Ma," Ben said, sitting down by his mother, "but it be for the best. Pa was sufferin' mightily these past few weeks. He knowed the end was close and he'd done made all his goodbyes. He was a good man and he had a good life. He gone rest in peace now and be with the Lord."

"Ben, you go on and take the horses back to the stable," Minnie said as she lifted her head. "See if Mr. Sims'll let you call the hotel and tell the girls. They gonna want to come and see their pa before he goes to the funeral home. I spec you better call Mr. Will Miller over to the funeral home too. See if he can come over with his hearse 'bout six o'clock. Alex, you come and help me with gittin' Sam's clothes together for Mr. Miller. Sam say he wants to wear his "Sunday-go-to-meetin" suit with the tie what Miss Celestine give him."

Minnie rose from the swing with great effort. Alex took her hand and led her into the parlor. Ben was sobbing as he jumped down from the porch. He drew his sleeve across his face, untied Adam's reins, and climbed into Eve's saddle for the lonely ride back to Gaston. His slumped shoulders mirrored the ache in his heart.

Alex led Minnie into the parlor. Sam looked at peace, as if he'd just gone back to sleep. Minnie kneeled by his bed and moved his arms across his chest and straightened his legs. She knew that rigor mortis would begin soon and she wanted Sam to look right for her family. She kissed Sam, brushed his hair back, and smoothed it out.

"Come with me Alex." she said, leading him into her bedroom off the parlor.

"Sam's clothes is in the right side of that chifforobe. You git his suit and shoes out while I gits a shirt and tie and some underwear from his dresser drawer."

Sam's dress suit was wedged in between two of his butler uniforms. Alex ran his hand down the front of a morning coat and thought of the hundreds of times he'd seen his father dress for a day of work at *Mon Repos*. The finality of the moment struck him. He cried. He picked up one of Sam' handkerchiefs, dabbed at his eyes, and turned to see if Minnie had seen him. Her back was turned. He quickly stuffed the handkerchief into his pocket and composed himself..

"Here you go Ma. Pa always looked good in his suit when we went to church."

"Yeah, your pa sure cut a fine figger. I had to keep a close watch on him," she giggled. "The ladies was always givin' him the eye. Truth be told, Sam never fooled around none. Me and him loved each other and we was all we needed. They gone be a big ol'hole in my heart with him gone." She began to cry again.

Alex left the room to avoid breaking down in front of Minnie. He knew that as the head of the family now he had to be strong for everyone else. Minnie took all the clothes and put them into a large box she had picked up at Hahn's. She had known this day was coming and she wanted to be prepared.

Alex walked back out to the front porch and sat down in the swing. The softly flowing motion of the swing had a soothing effect and soon his spirits revived. He sat there for several minutes listening to his mother bustle around inside. The hypnotic 'squeak-squawk' of the chain lulled him to sleep. He was unaware how much time had elapsed when he was awakened by the raucous sound of a dilapidated Model-A pulling into the driveway. A large, raw-boned, black man got out and walked up the steps.

"You must be Alex," he said. "I'm Lester. Lester Mitchell. I'm married to your sister Phoebe. Ben called me over to Mr. Clark's and I come right on over. Ben said he called Jonah over to Hopeland's and he gone pick the girls up from the hotel. I sho am sorry about Mr. Sam's passing. I sho was proud to know him. He a good man."

"Thank you, Lester. It's good to meet you. I'm sorry it had to be under these circumstances."

"Yeah, we don't got no control over these things. When the good Lord calls, we just gotta go. I figger Mr. Sam in a better place now. He was in a lot of pain for a long time. And, Miss Minnie done bout wore herself out lookin' after him. I know she don't want to let him go but it gone be a blessin' in the long run."

"I suppose you're right Lester, but right now it's really hard to understand. Papa wasn't all that old. I guess cancer is no respecter of age."

"If you don't mind Alex I'm goin' on in to see Mr. Sam and pay my respects to Miss Minnie."

"Not at all, Lester. You go on in. I think I'll wait out here until Jonah and the girls show up. It's been a long time since I last saw my sisters."

"That's fine Alex. When this all be over ya'll have to come over to see me and Phoebe at our place. Miss Minnie taught her all 'bout cookin'."

"I look forward to that Lester."

Lester nearly filled the doorframe of the parlor as he entered the house. Alex returned to his swinging and his thoughts. The next sound he heard was the crunching of gravel as Ben returned from the stables.

"I see ol' Lester done got here. What you think of him Alex."

"I don't know. We just exchanged a few words. He seems nice enough. He sure is a big man."

"Yeah, he stands six-foot-five and weighs 'bout two-fifty. Don't many people mess with him."

"Ma says they've been married about three years but don't have any children yet."

"Yeah, Phoebe say she don't know why. She wants some kids. Who knows? It'll jest happen one o'these days I reckon."

"I hope so."

A rusty, dilapidated, formerly four-door, Model-T turned the corner from Colleton. The sedan had been modified so that the back seat area was now a truck bed. Two small heads peered over the sideboards. Phoebe and Cleo sat up front with the children's father, Jonah Page. Cleo took after Minnie. She was already exhibiting some of her girth. Phoebe on the other hand had maintained her youthful figure. Alex pondered the strange twist of fate that had allocated their parents genes in such a fashion. He rose from the swing and went down the steps. Phoebe was first out of the truck. She rushed up to throw her arms around him.

"Alex it done been way too long since you been home. I'm sure glad you made it before Pa passed. Did you get to talk to him any?"

"Yeah Phoebe, we had a good conversation last night. He said he was waiting for me to get here before he went. I believe that. The human spirit has an amazing capacity to will things. We said our good-byes. He went peacefully — about two o'clock."

"How's Ma doin'?"

"She seems to be holding up pretty well. Of course, she knew it was coming and had steeled herself for it. Nevertheless, it's still an awful shock to the system. You had better go on in to see her and Pa now, before Mr. Miller gets here. I'll be in in a few minutes after I say hi to Cleo and meet Jonah and the kids."

"All right, Alex. I'll talk to you some more later," Phoebe said as she moved to go inside.

"You must be Jonah," Alex said, extending his hand to the wiry, copper-skinned man emerging from the truck.

"Yeah, I'm Jonah," he said with no change of expression.

"It's good to meet you at last. Mama wrote to me about you and Cleo and the children."

Jonah's response was little more than a guttural grunt. He brusquely took Alex's proffered hand then turned immediately to go inside while Cleo helped the children down from the truck bed.

"Don't pay him no mind Alex. He jest gits cantankerous sometimes. Anyway, I want you to meet your niece and nephew. Toby is four and Maggie is two. Say hello to your Uncle Alex children."

Toby grinned and said, "Hey Uncle Alex."

Maggie glanced shyly from behind Cleo and hung onto her skirt for dear life, barely sneaking a peek at this strange man.

"Maggie's the shy one. She'll come around when she gets to know you a little better. You sho looking good Alex. Them folks up north musta took good care of you."

"I can't complain. But I sure do like Mama's cooking a

whole lot better."

"You gotta be careful or she'll fatten you up like me," Cleo said with a trace of sarcasm.

"I think you look wonderful Cleo. I've missed you all these years. It's great to be home again. The kids are sure cute. I see some of Sam and Minnie in them."

"Yeah, Toby can be a handful sometimes. Pa was always egging him on. I think he saw a lot of himself as a boy in New Orleans when he teased Toby.

" I'm gonna go on in and see how Ma's doing."

"Go ahead, Cleo. I'll keep an eye on the children for you."

"Thanks Alex."

"You kids come on and I'll tell you a story."

He led them up the steps and sat in the swing with Toby on one side and Maggie on the other.

The long, black Cadillac hearse pulled up at precisely six. Minnie and the girls were inside the house with Sam. The men sat on the porch with the children.

"Hey Alex," Mr. William Miller called out as he lowered the folding gurney from the back of the hearse. "I heard you was home. It's good to see you. I wish the circumstances were a bit better."

"Thank you, Mr. Miller. I would've been home sooner but Mama didn't want to interrupt my studies. I'm just glad I got here before Papa passed."

"He sure was proud of you boy. Every time I saw him at church, he'd tell me how you was doing. I'm glad you got to say goodbye to him."

Mr. Miller and his assistant wheeled the gurney up the steps and into the parlor. He paid his respects to the women and asked Minnie if there were any special requests she might have for Sam's preparation for burial.

"Jest make him look real, you know, like Sam always

looked. The clothes we wants you to use is in that box over there."

"Do you want visitation to be at the funeral home or here?"

"I think it be better over there, it so hot. Ya'll is better prepared to keep folks cool."

"That'll be fine Miss Minnie. When do you expect you'll have the funeral?"

"I don't know yet Mr. Miller. I ain't talked to the reverend yet, and they's some kinfolks of Sam's that's gotta come up from New Orleans. Lemme see, it's Friday so I spec it gonna be next Saturday. I don't want to mess up Pastor Pope's Sunday service. Why don't you plan on Saturday, and if it gone be different I'll git Ben to call you."

"I reckon he'll be buried in the Aiken Colored Cemetery?"

"Yes suh, Sam done bought a plot for him and me back when Miss Celestine was here. I got a piece o' paper round here someplace. I'll git one of the boys to fetch it over tomorrow."

"That'll be fine, Miss Minnie. Now, if you don't mind, me'n Henry gonna take Mr. Sam to the funeral parlor. It'll be best if ya'll say your goodbyes before we leave."

Mr. Miller picked up a large white shroud and unfolded it to spread over Sam's body. He and Henry lifted Sam's emaciated frame onto the gurney and tucked the shroud around him. Alex sprang up to open the front door as they wheeled it out and gently loaded it into the hearse.

"Alex if you'll bring Miss Minnie over to the funeral home tomorrow we can take care of all the details. Once again, I offer my sincere condolences to the family. The colored community in Aiken is gonna miss Sam. He was a fine man."

William Miller closed the rear door of the hearse and backed out of the driveway. Sam Devereux departed his beloved home on Charleston Street for the last time.

6

Carolina Springs

The girls had gone home with their families. Ben said he had to go back to Gaston and feed the horses. Alex was back in the swing with Minnie. She was furiously fanning herself with one of the fans that Mr. Miller left behind. The illustration on the fan of a kneeling Jesus in the Garden of Gethsemane seemed appropriate for the occasion.

"Mama, what's the problem with Jonah?"

"That be a long story Alex," she said. "It all started when George was still here — maybe two, three years ago. Cleo was over here one Saturday night with Toby. Jonah come in 'bout nine pretty much liquored up and him and Cleo got into a real knock-down-drag-out fight. When it looked like Jonah might hit Cleo, George stepped in between them and grabbed Jonah. He say, 'don't you never lay no hand on my sister.' That kinda surprised Jonah and he backed away. He say, 'George, Cleo my wife and she gotta do what I say.' Well one thang led to another and finally Samson had to come in between 'em. He say, 'George, I know Cleo be your sister but she Jonah's wife. Now I ain't gone tolerate him a beatin' on her but they gotta work out they own troubles.' George looked real mean at Samson and he left. When we got up the next mawnin' George was gone. He

45

blamed Sam for lettin' Jonah treat Cleo bad and he jest wadn't gonna live with that. Him and Cleo was real close. She hoped him to git through a bunch of his troubles.

"I don't think Jonah ever beat Cleo after that but he treated her pretty bad. Him and Samson got into it sometimes when Jonah was drunk. Sam told him he needed to straighten hisself out and start treatin' his family like a real man. Jonah didn't come round too much after that. It was usually jest Cleo and the chilren."

"Did you or Papa ever see George after that?"

"Oh he come round a few times when he knowed Sam won't home. I tried to git him to come back home but he say he happy where he be. That was after he went over to Carolina Springs to work."

"What does he do over there?"

"I think he works mostly in their ice house and around the bar. He helps to clean up after the parties. They gits real big crowds on the weekends when the bands and singers from outta town come in."

"What do you know about the young woman he's living with?"

"Not a whole lot. He won't talk about it the few times I seen 'im. I think she come with one of the bands. That band broke up and she jest stayed on."

"Mama, do you think it would help if I went over there and talked to George?"

"It sho won't hurt none and maybe he'll listen to you since you ain't been around through all his troubles."

"Do you think Lester would let me use his car?"

"I spec he will. Lester is good folk. He been real good to Phoebe. They saved up their money to buy that little house they got. They wants chilren real bad but so far Phoebe ain't got pregnant. It'll happen bye-and-bye; in the good Lord's own time I reckon."

"Since it's Saturday, I expect George will be at the Springs. It must be their busiest night of the week. I think I'll go on over to Phoebe's and see if Lester will let me have the car. Don't you wait up for me. I'll probably be late getting back."

"All right Alex. You be careful on those roads. Specially on Saturday night when so many crazy folks be out."

"I will Mama."

Alex stepped off the porch. It was already dusk. Darkness would come soon. He hurried up the street toward Park Avenue.. The Mitchell house was at Abbeville and Union. As Alex approached the house, a guttural snarl came from beneath the front porch.A mangy, blue tick hound crawled out.

"Easy boy. There's no need to get riled up." Alex extended his hand and the dog edged closer to sniff this stranger in his yard.

"Phoebe, are you in there?" he yelled.

In a few seconds, the battered screen door swung open and his sister emerged, wiping her hands on her apron. She yelled at the dog.

"Brutus, you back away. He ain't gonna hurt you.

"Alex, what you doin' up here?"

"Now come on Phoebe. Is that any way to greet your own brother? I've just come visiting. Is Lester home?"

"Naw. He drove over to his pa's house on York Street. Mr. Page, he cuts meat for Mr. Hahn down at the grocery store. On Saturdays, Mr. Hahn lets the help take some of the older meat home since they's closed on Sundays. Lester, he gone over to git some pork chops for our Sunday dinner. His ma and pa is coming over. He'll be back directly."

"How are you doing Phoebe?" Alex asked. "Is life treating you well?"

"I can't complain none. Me'n Lester is able to save a little since we don't got no chilren."

"Yeah, Mama said you'd been trying but no luck so far."

"Yeah, we're disappointed but Doctor Johnson says to just give it some more time."

The sound of a car rumbling into the back yard interrupted the conversation. Through the kitchen window, Alex saw it come to a wheezing stop under a pecan tree loaded with green-husked fruit, which were just opening to drop their nuts. Alex heard the door slam and Lester's footsteps on the back steps.

Well, hey Alex," Lester said with a surprised look. "We didn't know you was comin' over. We'd a waited supper for you."

"That's okay Lester. I should have mentioned it while you were over at the house. I hadn't planned to come over but me and Mama got to talking about George and she kind of asked me if I'd go over to North Augusta and talk to him, maybe get him to come to Papa's funeral. I figured Saturday night was the best chance to catch him at the club. Since I don't have a car I was wondering if you might let me use yours to go over there."

"I guess that would be all right Alex. Tomorrow's Sunday and I don't need it to get to work. Phoebe and me can walk to church. Just bring it over there and I'll give you and Miss Minnie a ride back. Phoebe'll probably want to go see her ma anyway.

"The spark advance is kinda tricky so you'll need to play with it a little when you start her up. She sounds like she's gonna fall apart sometimes on these washboard roads but she's pretty solid. Might wanta check the oil before you start back. She burns a mite. Needs a ring-and-valve job but we can't afford that yet."

"Thanks Lester, I really appreciate this. I'll take good care of the car for you."

"You want a glass of tea befo you go Alex?" Phoebe asked.

"Thanks, but no, Sis. It's already getting late and I want to get back before all the Saturday night crazies get on the road."

The rickety screen door, slammed back into place by its

heavy spring, closed noisily behind Alex. He strode across the broom-swept back yard, green pecans crushing and snapping under his feet. He eased himself into the driver's seat. The instrument panel consisted of a battery indicator, a key slot and a light switch. The spark advance lever and the accelerator were behind the steering wheel; left and right. The choke was to the right of the battery meter.

Alex advanced the spark about a quarter and pulled the choke out making sure that the gear lever to his left was disengaged. With his foot on the brake, he pressed the starter on the floor with his left foot and the noisy engine sprang to life. The motor was still warm from Lester's' trip, so Alex closed the choke and returned the spark advance to zero. He switched on the lights and pressed the left foot pedal. The car began to move forward. He turned onto the street, advancing the accelerator and picking up speed. He continued down Abbeville to Hampton where it turned into Trolley Line Road to Graniteville and on to North Augusta.

Alex had not driven much in Washington. Slowly the old touch and feel returned and he was comfortable enough to move the accelerator lever forward a few more notches. Traffic was light for an early Saturday evening and he was through Graniteville in a few minutes. He followed the route down and through the Horse Creek Valley, past all the textile mills and the drab, lookalike milltown houses. He passed through Warrenville, Langley, Bath and all the other dreary little clusters of misery that comprised the valley.

Alex knew only a few Negroes who had worked in the Valley. The lint-heads, so called for the white cotton fibers that clung to their hair at work, resisted integration. Aided by the post-Reconstruction Jim Crow laws, they were able to keep the Valley almost lily-white. Truth be told, the lives of these un-reconstructed "rednecks" eking out subsistence livings in the Valley's mills, were less well off than the Negroes who worked in the cottages of the Winter Colony. Nonetheless, they clung to their air of white superiority.

Clearwater was the last village before beginning the ascent into North Augusta. The tall smokestacks and towering walls of the Cherokee Mills dominated the landscape around the small community. Cherokee, along with the Graniteville mills, was responsible for a large percentage of all denim fabric manufactured in the country.

Carolina Springs burbled out of the sandy loam of old Hamburg, the original settlement that later became North Augusta. The spring became a stream as it trickled down to the creek that carried the water two miles to the Savannah River. For many years, members of Storm Branch Baptist church used the springs for swimming and picnicking. Gradually, the popularity of the site led local entrepreneurs to make improvements to the swimming hole and to begin holding dances there, where local entertainers provided the music. The casino gained in popularity and reputation and soon became a regular stop on the "Chitlin Circuit", venues across the south that attracted black entertainers from across the nation. In its heyday, Carolina Springs hosted most of the luminaries of black entertainment, including Cab Calloway, Louis Armstrong and Ella Fitzgerald. The new owners constructed a new and larger casino on the site that could accommodate 1000 patrons. Its status became such that the white population of the area clamored to attend. Southern prejudices and Jim Crow laws severely constrained the public mingling of the races. To circumvent that the owners cleverly constructed a separate entrance and viewing area for white patrons. They flocked to the shows in droves. Buses trolled up and down the boulevards of Augusta, carrying jazz fans to the club.

In the depths of the dog days of summer, most performers at Carolina Springs were from the surrounding area. With 1000 perspiring bodies, the heat inside the casino became overwhelming. The most prestigious performers booked their gigs in the fall and winter months.

This particular Saturday night featured the Jessie Crump Orchestra "Raisin Cain" with his wife Ida Cox as soloist. Ida rose from dire poverty in Toccoa, Georgia where she was a sharecropper's daughter to become a staple of the jazz and blues world of the '20s and '30s. She met Crump in Atlanta while appearing with jazz great Jelly Roll Morton.

Alex entered the casino just as Ida finished singing *The Seven Day Blues*, which she and Crump had recorded that summer in Chicago for Paramount records. Ida bowed, acknowledging the enthusiastic applause.

"Thank you all for such a warm welcome to Carolina Springs. Jessie and me have been trying to work in an appearance here for months and I'm glad we finally made it. As you may know, we're both from just across the river in Georgia and this feels like a homecoming to us. We're gonna take a short break, get something cold to drink, and then we'll be right back. Thank you. Thank you very much."

Alex moved around the edge of the room toward the bar area at the back. He had to dodge the multitude of waiters who were scurrying to deliver drinks to the private tables along the walls and in the back of the room. The crowd streaming toward the restrooms near the entrance jostled him. The immediate area around the bar was dimly lit to limit interference with the performers on stage. Alex made out three people mixing and serving drinks. He slipped silently onto a barstool.

"Hey George," he said.

George wheeled around. He was loading chipped ice into the large bins at either end of the bar. He looked both surprised and bewildered.

"Alex, when did you git home. Last I heard you was still up north."

"George, you know Pa died?"

"Naw, I ain't heard nothin' bout that. I knowed he had that cancer and was mighty sick. Last time I was over to Aiken Ma said it was gittin' worse and he probably was gonna hafta stop working for the Palmers."

"He did, about three months ago. He told Mama not to tell me so that I would finish school before coming home. I got home Friday. He died Saturday afternoon while I went with Ben out to Montmorenci to deliver a buggy to Mr. Dibble.

"We got to spend some time together Friday night. He said he was waiting for me to get home before he died. We talked a lot about you George. He cried. It tore him and Mama up something awful when you left. Mama wanted me to come over to see you and ask you to come home for the funeral. Papa said your leaving home was the worst thing he ever went through. He said he loved you and wanted the best for you. He didn't fully understand why you ran off like that."

"Alex I couldn't stay round and see Jonah treat Cleo the way he did. Me'n her was real close. I begged her to leave him and come home but she said she couldn't because of the chilren. Me'n Papa got into a big fight about it one night when Jonah showed up three-sheets-to-the-wind. He was bout to hit Cleo when I grabbed him. Papa stopped me from hitting him. He took Jonah's side in the fight. I won't goin' to stay round and see no mo of Jonah's abusin' Cleo and Papa 'lowing it, so I jest left.

"One of the fellas that worked shinin' shoes at Mr. Conkle's Tailor Shop where I worked sometimes, told me they was lookin' for help over to Carolina Springs so I jest hightailed it over here. Been here ever since."

"Mama says you've taken up with one of the singers here."

"Yeah, her name is Mary Waters. She come up from Savannah with a small jazz band. They played a few days and then the bandleader said they was breakin' up. He said they was havin' trouble gittin' work and he won't able to pay 'em no more. Mary didn't have no money and didn't wanta go back to Savannah. She'd jest got out of a bad situation and was scared to go back. I'd saved up a bit so I got a little place in town and asked her to move in with me. I was surprised when she said yeah. We been together 'bout nine months now.

"They won't no foolin' round at first but she got over my stutterin' and my other problems and we gits along pretty good. I been a lots better since she come. She make me take my medicine and all.

"She helps round the club and fills in when they ain't no singer available. She got a good voice and the regulars like her a bunch, so she decided to stick around."

"What do you know about her?"

"Her pa played trumpet up to New York. He was white. Her ma ran round with'im when he come to Savannah for a show. She grew up on one of the plantations west of town. When she was eighteen, she moved into town to work at a hotel. That's where she met the horn player. Mary says her grandpa was the plantation owner's son so she more'n three-quarters white. Sometimes the white folks that come here ask her why a white girl is workin' in a black nightclub. She tells em to mind they own business. We gits some evil looks when we walks down the street together. Them peckerwood honkies ain't never got over losin' the war."

"You best be careful George. You go around talking like that and you'll get your head busted open. I wouldn't antagonize the white folks anymore than necessary. You are aware that you still occasionally find black folks hanging from trees around here — or a big cross burning in the yard."

"I hear you brother. I'm careful when I'm around them white folks."

"Is Mary here tonight?"

"Yeah, she jest went out back for a smoke. She'll be back directly."

"Will you introduce me to her?"

"I reckon so, but I don't want you startin' up nothin'."

"I assure you George, I have nothing but the best of intentions."

At that moment, a sensuous young woman with her long black hair tied back in a ponytail with a bright yellow bow rounded the far end of the bar. She walked toward George but her eyes were fixed on Alex. She placed her hand on Georges's shoulder.

"George, who is this handsome young man?"

"Mary Waters, I'd like you to meet my younger brother Alexander Hamilton Devereux."

"My, my. That's about as big a mouthful as George Washington Devereux. Yo daddy sho had a thing for big sounding names."

"How do you do, Miss Waters. I guess George hasn't told you about his father Samson Demosthenes Devereux or his other brother Benjamin Franklin Devereux."

Mary stared at George in wide-eyed amusement.

"George, why have you been keeping all this from me. It sounds like you have a very interesting family."

"I didn't think it was necessary since I done pretty much left my family behind."

"You told me you had a big fight with your father but nothing more. Maybe Alex here will fill me in with the details." Mary said.

"Mary I don't want to drag Alex into this. He was away in Washington goin' to law school when this all happened."

"Law school! My, my. You done got an educated black man in your family. This gets more interesting all the time. Why don't you sit down on this barstool and tell me all about it Alex?'

"I would love to Miss Waters …"

"Call me Mary, please."

"As I was saying, I would love to but I came here tonight

to plead with George to come home for his father's funeral. He died yesterday and the funeral will be held next Saturday."

"Oh, I'm so sorry Alex. I didn't mean to be so flippant. George, I didn't know your father was sick."

"I didn't want to get you involved with my family's problems. I didn't think you'd ever meet them til Alex showed up here tonight," George said.

"Mama asked me to come over and talk to you George," Alex said. "It would mean the world to her for you to be there. Pa's gone now and Jonah doesn't come around much so there won't be any trouble. How about it? And, Miss Waters—Mary —can come as well. That way she can get the whole family story from the horse's mouth so to speak. I know that everyone would like to meet her. She's charming and gracious — not to mention beautiful."

"Why Alex," Mary said. "Such a flatterer. I don't know how George can refuse such an invitation. I tell you what. I'll work on him this week and see what I can do. I believe I can persuade him to come. Where can we call you with an answer?"

"Ben works at Gaston Livery Stable. They have a phone there and I'm sure they'd be glad to give him your message. George please come. It's time to start mending some fences. You're the eldest child. You should be there."

"We'll let you know by Friday. Mary and me'll need to arrange for time off if we do. The weekends are our busiest time. We'll see what we can work out."

"Thanks, George. It'll mean a lot to the whole family. The people at Friendship keep asking about you. There's a lot of love waiting for you if you'll come.

"I'd better get going. I don't relish driving back through Horse Creek on a Saturday night. It's good to see you George. And, it's good to meet you Miss Waters — Mary. Sorry, old habits are hard to break." Mary stood on her tiptoes and pecked Alex on the cheek.

"It's good to meet you too, little brother," she whispered throatily. George didn't seem too pleased with her display of intimacy. He shuffled off toward the icehouse, a bucket in each hand. His awkward, rambling gait seemed less pronounced than Alex remembered, and he definitely was stuttering less. Leaving home, finding love, or both had had a positive effect on his brother.

Alex turned to leave just as Ida Fox took the stage for her second set. She sat her glass of bourbon-and-branch-water on a stool and gestured for the band to begin playing the next number. After the downbeat, she launched into a sultry number called *The Blues Ain't Nothing Else But.*

7

The Valley

The heavens had opened while Alex was inside the club. Steam was rising from the roadway but the air had lost some of its sultry oppressiveness as it flowed in through the car's open windows. The stars hung like crystal raindrops in the moonless sky. The lights were out in most of the mill houses along the Augusta highway as Alex started the climb back up to Aiken and home. The haunting words of Ida Fox's song echoed in his ears. The Blues had a way of penetrating one's very soul.

Alex approached the intersection with Howlandsville Road when he noticed a pickup truck pulling out from the honky-tonk on the corner. He knew it to be a favorite hangout for mill workers on Saturday night. Charlie Wright, the owner, was all too happy to cash their paychecks. He always got a large percentage back in booze and billiards.

The truck fell in behind him as he turned left at the Warrenville Mill. He felt a tingle rising on the nape of his neck. A truck full of liquored-up rednecks in your rearview mirror, on a Saturday night in August, in Horse Creek, was chilling. He advanced the gas lever two notches. The two lights in the rear view mirror clung to his rear bumper He didn't know if they were bent on trouble or were just hassling him. In either event, he didn't like the situation. If he could make it up the hill, past

Graniteville, he would probably be all right. The speedometer needle was bouncing around 35 miles-per-hour and the old car was vibrating like mad. He pushed the speed up to forty, and the gap between his rear bumper and the pickup didn't change. Now he knew that he was in trouble.

Alex heard the rush of water from the Horse Creek diversion canal spinning the dynamos at Gregg's Mill, generating power for the looms and the lights. Their high-pitched keen screamed through his open windows. He turned right onto Trolley Line Road and felt the car shudder. The truck had rammed into his back bumper. Alex was afraid to push the Model-T any faster. The vibrations were already so severe he thought the wheels might come off.

He saw the truck's lights swing to the left and begin to pass him. There were no other cars on the road. In the dim light, he could make out the bearded face of the drunk that had stumbled down the steps at rhe bar. Suddenly, a high-powered beam of light cut through the night from the truck's passenger window. Alex was nearly blinded. He saw the silver barrel of a pistol emerge, framed by the light from the open window. He jammed on the brakes. The muzzle of the gun flashed. The bullet flew through the car. It didn't hit anything. It passed through both windows. He was not hurt. The truck continued on as Alex slowed. It turned onto a side street, up toward the Graniteville cemetery. Alex passed and saw the truck's tail lights disappear over a rise. He was shaking violently. He had trouble gripping the wheel. He slowed the car and continued on to Aiken. He turned off at Laurens and drove downtown. He pulled into the Alley and stopped in front of the police station. He looked at his watch. It was just past nine. Still shaking, he stopped the car and went inside.

The desk sergeant looked up from the form he was filling out. He was recording the sordid details from the latest Saturday night stabbing at a club on Cherokee Street, near the railroad.

The victim had been transported to the hospital on Richland Avenue West. Blood from a slash across his face had soaked through a towel. There was a stab wound in his stomach. The sergeant reckoned he would live but he'd carry the mark of that night to his grave.

"Whadda you want?" the policeman demanded of Alex in a loud and belligerent voice. Alex remembered Sam's numerous warnings — always respond quietly and courteously if you are ever questioned by the police.

"Sir, I was driving back from North Augusta through the Valley when a pickup truck pulled out from that club at Howlandville Road. It started following me. When we started up the hill on Trolley Line, they started to pass me and shined a flashlight in my window. The next thing I knew someone stuck the barrel of a pistol out the window and started shooting at me."

"I don't see no blood, boy."

"No sir, the bullet passed through both windows. I could hear the *whoosh* when it went past my face."

"What happened then?"

"They speeded up and turned off toward the cemetery."

"It don't sound like you got no proof that you was shot at," argued the desk sergeant.

"Well, when we turned onto Trolley Line they rammed the back of my car. I can show you the dent and scratches on the bumper."

"That don't make no nevermind. If what you say is true the whole thing took place outside the city limits. If you want to file a formal complaint, you need to do that with the sheriff's office. Now get outta here. I got a lot of work to do."

Alex stared at the arrogant face gaping down from the bench. He knew from past experience that arguing with "the man" was a waste of time. It was also laden with danger. He bit his tongue and slowly exited the police station. He leaned with both hands against the car, smoldering and muttering under his breath. After a few minutes, when his temper had subsided, he got in, started the car, and eased onto Newberry Street. Inwardly he was still seething at the open prejudice still lingering in his hometown. He thought that during the years he was gone things would have changed between the races. It was as Sam used to say, *The more things change, the more they stay the same."*

It was almost ten when he pulled the car into the Charleston Street driveway. He sat for a moment, still shaken by the events of the past hour. It was bad enough to have a bigoted redneck take a shot at him. It was even worse to see that nothing had changed in his absence. The same prejudice and discrimination that existed when he boarded that train north was still alive and well.

There was still a light in the Devereux kitchen. Alex walked in the back door. He found Minnie sitting at the kitchen table reading her bible. She jumped up when he entered.

"I sho glad you home in one piece. I worries a heap when my chilren goes out at night. Too many bad things happens. I has double worries tonight. You goin' to the Carolina Springs and Ben goin' over to that pool hall. I told him he ought not to do that tonight with his pa lyin' at the funeral home, but he jest say, 'Ma I needs to git outta the house for a while.' He left a little while after you.

"Some of the ladies from the church come by to sit a spell. They brung over a heap of food. There's some chicken and potatoes in the warming oven if you's hungry."

"Thanks, Mama. I am a little hungry. I haven't eaten tonight."

"Was you able to talk to George?" Minnie asked while Alex took a plate from the cabinet and loaded it with food.

"Yes'm, he was at the club. He seems to be happy over there. I got to meet his girlfriend too. Her name's Mary Waters. She came up from Savannah with a band that broke up while they were playing here. She didn't want to go back to Savannah; had some bad memories there. George rented a little apartment in North Augusta and asked her to stay with him. She agreed. She makes sure he takes all his medicines regularly and he seems a lot better than I remember.

"Her mother worked at a hotel in Savannah," Alex continued "and she took up with a white horn player from New York named Waters. The upshot of that was Mary. The horn player skedaddled back to New York when he found out her mother was pregnant, leaving Mary's mother to fend for herself and to raise Mary.

"Mary was exposed to the many musicians that played at the hotel's club when she was growing up. She had a good voice and began to sing with some of them. That's how she got hooked up with the band that came to Carolina Springs. She and George seem happy together."

"What George say 'bout comin' to the funeral?" Minnie asked.

"He said he'd think about it. I encouraged Mary to come with him thinking that might convince George to come. She told me she'd work on him. They'll leave a message for Ben at the Gaston stables by Friday. If they come they have to make arrangements to be gone on Saturday which is the club's biggest day."

"What you think Alex? He gone come?"

"I don't know Ma, but if I was a betting man, I'd say yes."

"I hopes you right. It won't be fittin' for a man's oldest child to stay 'way from his funeral."

Minnie looked at Alex oddly. She still knew her boy.

"Alex you seem bothered. You and George didn't git in no fight, did you?"

"No ma'am, nothing like that."

"What it be then. I still knows that look on yo face."

"It was something that happened on the way home."

"I knowed it! That the same look that you got when you come home from school with a bad mark. What done happened?"

Alex was quiet for a moment, hesitant to burden Minnie with more trouble on top of Samson's death.

"It's no big deal, Ma. You've got enough to worry about."

"That don't matter none boy! You tell me what's a troublin' you!"

Alex knew from past experience that when Minnie took on her mama lion role she would not be denied. She wouldn't let anything come between her and her cubs. Alex relented. He knew she would badger him until he told her what was bothering him.

"It happened on the way home from seeing George. A bunch of mill workers came out of a juke joint in Warrenville. They followed me through Graniteville and began to bang into my back bumper. When I couldn't go any faster they passed me. They shined a flashlight into my car. Next thing I knew, a gun muzzle appeared. I hit the brakes so they'd go past, but not before they got a shot off. Thank goodness, it passed through the car without hitting me. They took off up the hill toward the Graniteville cemetery without knowing whether they'd hit me or not."

"Lord have mercy," Minnie said.

"I know, but as bad as that experience was, I'm more upset with the Aiken police. I went to their offices in the Alley to report the attack and the police officer in charge basically told me to get lost. He wouldn't believe anything I said and told me to take it up with the sheriff since it all took place outside the city limits. I had hoped the attitude toward blacks would have changed since I left, but obviously it hasn't.

"I had some doubts about whether or not I wanted to come back to Aiken and practice law. I can assure you that the reaction of the desk sergeant at police headquarters removed all those doubts. I'm home to stay and I'm going to do everything in my power to change the way black justice is meted out in this town."

Minnie sat transfixed by Alex's tale. She was all too familiar with police treatment of blacks in Aiken, but it had never hit so close to home. She knew there were many honest, law-abiding men on the police force, but she also knew there were some who were bigoted rogues and who were abusive to blacks. She had heard stories of young men arrested on trumped up charges and held for days at the city jail without legal representation or bond hearings.

"Lawsy me, Alex. You coulda done been kilt. What you gonna do now? You gonna go to the sheriff?"

"No ma'am. I'd probably get the same old runaround I got from that Aiken cop. What I'm going to do is get my license to practice law before the South Carolina bar, and I'm going to try to change the system from within, through legal means. While some powers-that-be may flout the law, I believe the legal system, through the courts, through the judicial process, still recognizes the law as the foundation of our civilized society and will work to see that it's not corrupted. If that's so, then I believe I can have a positive impact on the system; especially for black defendants."

"I'm glad to hear you say you gonna stay Alex. I needs you. The family needs you. The black folks in Aiken, they need you. But, you gotta know when you goes up against the man you is askin' for trouble. Them courts may be lookin' out for the law but the law mean different things 'cording to the color of your skin. What you seen happen tonight show that."

"I know Mama, but if we don't have the law to turn to then we don't have anything. I believe in the law and I believe it can bring equal justice to everyone — black, white, yellow, red or green.

"What time did Ben leave for the pool hall?"

"Why you ask?"

"Since I have Lester's car, I think I'll wander over there and have a look around. If Ben's mixed up with the wrong crowd we need to know. I just want to see for myself."

"You be careful Alex. They some rough boys what hang around on Saturday nights. They won't know who you is, you been gone so long. Jest watch your back is all I'm a sayin'."

Don't worry Ma, I'll be careful. Maybe I can give Ben a ride back home. Lester said I could bring the car back to church tomorrow."

Alex rose and took his dishes to the sink before heading back out the kitchen door.

8

The Black Cat

The Pastime Billiard Parlor at the corner of York and Kershaw was a dilapidated, unpainted, clapboard shack with windows only in front. The only illumination outside was the two weak gooseneck lights on the sign hanging over the door courtesy of *The Coca-Cola Bottling Company of Aiken.* Alex parked alongside the building, off Kershaw, and went in. To the right of the door was an L-shaped bar with half-a-dozen stools down each side. Beer taps and a small kitchen filled the back wall. To the left were six ramshackle wooden tables covered with linoleum. Several men sat around the tables nursing their beers and staring through the smoky haze at the pool tables in the rear.

There were six pool tables in two rows of three each. Two hooded, incandescent lamps hung low over each table. They only accentuated the vast swirls of blue cigarette smoke being blown about by the large oscillating floor fans on either side of the room. The bright green felt of the tables reflected the harsh light back into the faces of the players, creating garish, shadowy masks of teeth and hair.

There were four players at three of the tables, three at two others and two at the final table. Most of the bystanders had gathered around that table. A heavy-set bald man sat on a stool just off to the side. He had a beer in one hand and a wad of bills in the other. After each game, he moved wooden rings along an overhead wire, tallying the winnings.

"That's it for me," one of the players said. "How much do I owe?"

"Lemme see," the bald man said as he looked up at the rings. "You owe Albert five dollars — less the house cut. That'll be fifty cents."

The loser reached into his pocket and pulled out several bills. He handed five dollars to Albert who in turn handed a fifty-cent piece to the bald man.

"Thank you boys, see you next week."

The bald man pocketed the money then reached up with the shortened cue stick and reset all the tally rings to zero. It was then he noticed Alex.

"Howdy, son. You new round here. I don't recollect seeing you before. My name's Cecil Hawkins. I own this establishment."

""How do you do Mr. Hawkins. I'm Alex Devereux."

"Oh, you must be Ben's brother what just got back from up north. I was sorry to hear about your pa passing. I didn't know him much. Heard he was a mighty fine man. Ben's always bragging 'bout you and how you gone be a lawyer. You done finished school?"

"Yes sir. I finished just last week."

"You coming back to Aiken?"

"Yes sir. I plan to practice law here as soon as I pass the bar exam."

"That'll be good. We need more educated black folk around here. They's a lot of folks moving in and settin' up they businesses here what with all the rich Yankees coming to town."

"I plan to practice both civil and criminal law. I'm sure I'll do a little of everything until I get established.

"Have you seen Ben tonight, Mr. Hawkins? Ma said he

was coming over here. I wanted to give him a ride back home. There's a lot to be done before the funeral and he needs to be at home to help out."

"He was here earlier, but he left with two other boys about an hour ago."

"Do you know where he was going?"

"He didn't say. They's several of them boys what hang around together. Sometimes they goes to *The Black Cat* when they leaves here."

"What's that?"

"It's a juke joint on up York. 'Bout three blocks."

"Thank you, Mr. Hawkins. I'll be going."

"If you plan on going up there to *The Black Cat* you gone wanna be careful. The police done raided that place several times."

"What for?" Alex asked.

"I can't say for sure," he said with arched eyebrows, "but I hear tell they ain't no girls at that place."

"What are you saying?"

"I don't know for sure, but you can figger it out for yoself."

Alex pulled alongside *The Black Cat* and entered through a side door. The inside of the club was even dimmer and more dismal than the pool hall. When his eyes finally adjusted to the light, he spotted Ben sitting at a corner table with two other young black men. One of the men had his arm draped over Ben's shoulder. Alex walked up to the table from behind Ben. The man sitting across from him looked up anxiously.

"Can we help you mister?" he said. Ben turned to see who was behind him. His eyes flared in momentary terror.

"What are you doing here Alex?"

"The better question is, What are you doing here Ben? You'd better come on home with me. Your dead father is lying in a casket over at Miller's funeral home and your mother needs you at home."

"Who dis Ben?" the man with his arm on Ben's chair back asked. "What right he got telling you what to do?"

"This my older brother Alex. He jest got back from school up north. He the one I been telling you 'bout. He gone be a lawyer."

The questioner didn't respond. He looked at Alex with hooded eyes and a drunken leer. He dropped his arm and picked up his beer. He turned the bottle up and took a long, slow draft, emptying it.

"Well Ben I guess you better mind yo big brother," he slurred, with the accent on big.

"Ben looked down at his hands, his fingers reasting on the edge of the table. He appeared torn between obeying Alex and saving face with his friends.

"I reckon I best go on home," he said without lifting his eyes. "tomorrow Sunday and Ma got a lot to do. She plan on going on to church. She'll be plum wore out. Folks'll be comin' round to bring dinner and visit with the family. 'Sides I gotta go feed the horses in the mawnin, fo church."

"Yeah, why don't you do that," hooded eyes said. "You don't want to keep yo Mama waitin'. We gonna stay on a while longer." He flashed a knowing grin at the other man while dismissing Ben with a flip of his wrist.

Ben slowly disengaged from his chair and stood, obviously torn by competing emotions; fear, embarrassment, anger, resentment — all in full view on his contorted face. Finally, he turned away and followed Alex from the *Black Cat*. Alex started the car, backed out of the lot, and turned down York. Ben stared out his window, silently, until Alex turned east on Richland.

"Why'd you hafta do that Alex? I won't hurtin' nobody."

Alex ignored Ben's protest.

"Ben, tell me about those men you were with."

"That ain't none of yo business Alex. You goes off to school and thinks you can jest come back atter all these years and tell me what to do. I's a grown man. I can do what I please."

"Not if what you please is going to kill your mother and ruin your's and the family's reputation as well."

"I ain't doing nothin' wrong. We was jest having a few beers on Saturday night."

"Don't lie to me Ben. Have you slept with that man?'

"Naw, Alex!" Ben bristled. "Him and that other boy been doin' that but I ain't done it. They been tryin' to git me to go with 'em to a house they has, but I ain't done that yet."

"Do you want to do that Ben?"

"I don't know Alex. I ain't had no luck with women and I keeps wonderin' if they's something wrong with me."

"You mean in a sexual way?"

"I don't know. They keeps makin' it sound like a natural-born thing to do, but I don't know. The bible say lying down with a man be a sin. I don't wanta be doin' no sinnin'."

"Ben, you must know that homosexuality is a crime. I want you to promise me you'll stay away from that place and those men until we can straighten this thing out. All right?"

"I reckon so Alex. You ain't gonna tell Ma 'bout this are you?" he asked, his voice cracking.

"No Ben, as long as you stay away from them and promise me you'll talk to me about it."

"Okay Alex," Ben said hesitantly before changing the subject.

"What you doin' with Lester's car?"

"Ma asked me to go over to Carolina Springs and talk to George. See if I could convince him to come to Pa's funeral."

"And?"

"I'll tell you all about it when we get home."

9

The Requiem

True to his word, Alex said nothing about the incident at *The Black Cat* the night before. Ben was gone when he awoke. Minnie was getting ready to go to church. "You comin' with me, Alex?" she asked as he passed her bedroom.

He was not in a frame of mind to face the barrage of questions and attention he would get at Friendship. On the other hand, he owed it to Minnie to be supportive of her in her darkest hour. And, he had to get the car back to Lester.

"Yes ma'am. Just give me a few minutes to get ready."

He went into the kitchen and made a sandwich of fig preserves, butter and a biscuit, eating it on the way back to his room. His lone black suit was getting shiny in the seat and at the elbows, but he really couldn't afford a new one. He slipped it on and knotted a red and black tie around the fraying collar of his white shirt. He swiped at his black shoes with an old rag and stepped into them. He was ready.

Friendship Missionary Baptist Church began as a clandestine "brush-arbor church" for Negroes during the Civil War. After the war, the members were invited to attend the white First Baptist Church. Then a sudden influx of displaced blacks from Ellenton and Hamburg, following race riots in those two towns, overwhelmed the white congregation. Members of First Baptist assisted the Friendship congregation in building a small wood-frame structure on Richland Avenue at Kershaw. In 1893 that building burned under mysterious circumstances, With the continued assistance of First Baptist and a white architect missionary from the north named Otts, the church was replaced with a splendid, yellow-brick edifice.

Alex pulled into the parking lot behind Friendship Baptist and hopped out to help Minnie down. Parishioners on foot, in buggies, and in automobiles were converging on Friendship for the 11 o'clock services. Lester and Phoebe were crossing Richland as Alex and Minnie started up the front steps.

"Mornin' Miss Minnie. Hey Alex," Lester called.

The couple fell in behind and followed them down to pew number six, left; recognized as the Devereux seats for forty years. The choir emerged from their robing rooms and climbed the steep stairs to the choir loft at the rear. The Devereux and Mitchell families sat as the minister, Reverend Jonathan Pope, crossed to the pulpit and gestured for everyone to rise. Miss Marcy Lewis, following the end of the processional music, began one of Sam's favorite spirituals, *Climbing Up the Mountain.* The choir came in on cue.

> Climbin' up d' mountain children
> Didn't come here to stay
> And if I nevermore see you again
> Gonna meet you at de judgement day

At the sound of the old, familiar refrain Minnie collapsed on the bench, sobbing. Alex sat and held her hand as two white robed attendants converged to console her. After a few minutes, Minnie composed herself, rose to her feet, and joined in the singing. Her saintly smile said she was now communing with

Sam through the words he so loved. There were three more songs, two prayers and a collection before Reverend Pope rose to deliver the morning's sermon.

"Jesus said, 'Come unto me all ye who labor and are heavy laden, and I will give you rest. Take my yoke upon you and learn of me; for I am meek and lowly in heart; and you shall find rest unto your souls,' Matthew 11, verses 27 and 28.

"There are those among us today whose hearts are heavy laden, whose labors in the vineyards of the Lord have worn them out. However, Jesus said come to me and I will give you rest. As children of God and believers in Jesus Christ, we can take him at his word. No matter how sorrowful and grief stricken we are over the loss of a loved one, Jesus has an answer for us. 'Come unto me and I will give you rest.'"

For the next forty minutes, Reverend Pope poured out both blessing and beneficence on his congregation, liberally sprinkled with *amens* and *praise the Lords* from the congregation. His words were both balm and catharsis for the broken hearts of the Samson Devereux family. With the last organ notes fading and the benediction concluded, Minnie Devereux's faith was renewed and she was prepared to face the trials of the week ahead. She was determined that her Sam would get the farewell celebration and sendoff he deserved. Surrounded and supported by family and friends she would make him proud of her.

Alex escorted Minnie and Phoebe to the back of the church where well-wishers besieged them. Ben had arrived from his stable chores and waited out front under one of the oak trees planted when the church was built in 1894.

'Mama, excuse me for a second," Alex said. "I want to speak to the Reverend."

Alex swam upstream through the surging crowd still exiting the sanctuary and congratulating Reverend Pope on his splendid sermon. Alex caught Dr. Pope's eye and signaled that he would like to speak to him. When the pastor finished the last handshake, he walked over to where Alex waited in the shadows of the narthex.

"So you are the Alex your mother and father have been telling me about! You had already left for Howard before I was called to Friendship. It's certainly good to meet you at last. Congratulations on your new law degree."

"Thank you sir. I just wanted to thank you for the kind words you had for my father and for the comfort they gave to my mother."

"You're entirely welcome Alex. I assure you they came from the heart. There are not any two people who have meant more to me, and to Friendship Baptist, than your parents. I trust I'll be seeing you back in pew number six often in the future."

"Yes sir, you will."

Alex nervously shifted from one foot to the other.

"You seem disturbed son. Is there something else you want to share with me?'

"Actually, Reverend there are two things. I went over to North Augusta last night to try to convince my brother George to come to the funeral next Saturday. I assume you are aware of his estrangement from my Father. I would appreciate any help you can offer to get him to come. Maybe you could call over there this week and talk to him. I would certainly appreciate it."

"Yes Alex, I've spent many hours with your parents trying to make sense of George's behavior. I'll be glad to call him. I agree that George should be here for many reasons. Now, what's the second thing on your mind?"

"It's a subject that is very sensitive. I know that conversations between a pastor and a member of his congregation are held in strict confidence, but I need your assurance that what I'm going to say to you will not go beyond us."

Reverend Pope looked puzzled—and surprised.

"You have my word Alex. Nothing is more sacred to me

than the trust of my flock."

"Reverend, I suspect that my brother Ben is mixed up with a bad crowd. I found him last night with some other young men at *The Black Cat* club out on York Street."

"That den of iniquity!" Dr. Pope muttered. " I'm reasonably sure," Alex continued, "that the men he was with are engaged in homosexual activity. Ben swears that he has not participated in any such activity, but it doesn't look good to me. Mama says he's been going out almost every Saturday night since Papa became bedridden. He was very angry and evasive about the whole thing. I was wondering if you could have a talk with him — tell him about the legal and moral implications of such actions. Ben has always been a sensitive boy and he hasn't had a lot of luck with girls. I don't want to believe that he is a homosexual, but I don't think he will ever level with me. I think he will with you, in confidence, and that you may be able to straighten him out."

"My God, Alex! I had no idea. Ben has been a faithful member of the church and has helped me out on numerous occasions. Like you, I can't believe this. I certainly will talk to him, but I think it best to wait until after Mr. Sam's funeral. Do you think anything bad will happen before then?"

"No sir, I don't think so. He promised he wouldn't go back there until we had a chance to talk this out. Ben's a man of his word. He won't go back on a promise. Do you think I should be here when you talk to him?"

"No! He'll be more open and forthright if he knows I'm the only one to hear his story. It'll be best if you're not here. You realize of course that I won't divulge anything to you that he tells me."

"Yes sir. That's why I came to you. Ben will feel free to speak his heart without fear. Thank you Reverend Pope. Now, I'd better get my mother home. She's going to have a lot of company this afternoon."

"I'm sure she will. Tell her that Ada and I will drop by around four, before the evening service."

"I will. Thank you. Goodbye Pastor."

"Goodbye Alex."

Crowding five people into the old Model-T was difficult but they managed. Lester parked in the driveway while Alex and Ben got out. Phoebe embraced her mother.

"Mama, Lester's folks is comin' over for Sunday dinner. When we gets through I'll ask Lester to bring me back over here. I know you's gonna have a heap a folks comin' by today. Cleo say she'll be comin' over too. She gone leave the chilren with Jonah. They'd be causin' too much commotion with company around. Sides, Jonah ain't so excited 'bout big crowds. I spec we'll be back by three."

"You go on now baby. We'll be all right. We already got a table full of food in the kitchen so they won't be a lot to do. I got up in the middle of the night and cleaned the house. I jest couldn't sleep"

"I thought I heard you rambling around," Alex said, "I had trouble sleeping myself."

By the time Phoebe and Cleo arrived, a steady stream of visitors had already passed through the Charleston Street house. All the women in Minnie's prayer groups and sewing circles had made their appearances, offering heartfelt condolences to their grieving sister. Most of the accompanying men gathered on the porch with Alex and Ben. They were not as well practiced in the art of consoling a widow as the women were. Their conversations turned to the weather, crops, horses and other manly subjects. Cleo and Phoebe came out to make sure their iced tea glasses remained full and that food was available.

Alex glimpsed Ben going out the back door. Ben sat down on a bench under the spreading branches of a red maple that Sam planted when he and Minnie first moved to Charleston Street.

He excused himself from the men and walked over to Ben. Most of the men reckoned it as just two brothers comforting each other. Alex knew that Ben was hurting over more than the loss of a father.

"Hey Ben," Alex said softly. "You want to talk about it?"

"Naw. Not right now. I jest wanted to git off by myself and try to sort things out."

"You still mad at me for last night?"

"Naw, I knowed you was jest tryin' to look out for me. I know it look bad Alex, but I won't lying to you. I ain't done what you thinkin'."

"I believe you Ben, but if you keep hanging around with those boys something bad is bound to happen. Look, I know you don't want to talk about this with me. Maybe you ought to talk to Reverend Pope. He seems like a good listener and as a pastor, he will keep anything you say in confidence. I'm sure he can give you better guidance than I can. Preachers get a lot of training in such things. One of my roommates at Howard was studying theology. We used to have some real lively discussions about religion and stuff. Think about it."

"I don't know Alex. Since I ain't done no sinnin' with them boys what I got to say."

"Maybe Dr. Pope can advise you on the legal and moral issues. He can also probably advise you on the best ways to avoid these sorts of temptations. Can't hurt anything."

"Maybe when the funeral done over I'll go by and see him."

"That's great Ben. And remember, I'm here any time you want to talk."

"Thanks Alex."

Alex rejoined the group on the porch where Lester was telling a bawdy joke about Mr. Ambrose Clark. Reverend Pope and his wife Ada drove up as the laughter was dying down.

"Afternoon Gentlemen," Dr. Pope said as he helped Ada up the steps. "You go on in dear. I'll spend a few minutes out here with the men. I need to find out what was so funny when we drove up."

Lester gave an "aw shucks" grin, kicked at the ground and said, "It was just a little joke I was telling bout Mr. Clark. I don't reckon it's fitten for yo ears."

"All right, Lester, I'll pretend I didn't hear anything. How about the rest of you? Ya'll doing all right?"

"Yes sir, Reverend, things 'bout as good as you can 'spect, what with Mr. Sam's passing," Otis Brooks said. "They gone be a big hole where he was. Mighty good man. It good that Alex back. He gone be able to take up some of the slack for Mr. Sam. He gone be a big help for Miss Minnie."

"I'm sure you are right Mr. Brooks," Dr. Pope said as he noticed Alex standing at the back of the crowd. "I believe Alex Devereux will be a big help for all of us. Well, I better go inside and see Miss Minnie. See y'all in church."

The sun had faded in the west when the last well-wisher left for home. Lester took Cleo and Phoebe home about five. Ben rode back as far as Gaston's to look after the livestock. Alex was alone with his mother.

"Mama I knew you and Pa had a lot of friends but never this many. I'll bet there were more than a hundred people here today."

"We been blessed Alex. Between the church folk and all the people what been working in the white folk's homes we knowed more'n half the black folks in Aiken. It be a good place to live and raise a family. I sho glad you gone stay round to be a part of it."

"Me too, Mama. I've seen a lot of things in the last two days — both good and bad — that tell me this is where I belong."

Late Monday afternoon Minnie and Alex walked the few blocks to the Miller funeral home on Kershaw. It was conveniently located just a half-block from Friendship Baptist.

"Morning Miss Minnie, Alex," William Miller said as he opened the front door of his funeral parlor. "I reckon you come to see Mr. Sam and make all the final arrangements."

"Yas suh, Mr. Miller. We needs to pick out a casket and see 'bout the cemetery lot for Sam. He done picked one out in Pinecrest several years ago, and we already done put up the tombstones for both us. Sam reckoned if we didn't do it when we had a little money that it'd be a burden on the family later. Does we need to do sumpin' to 'low you to dig the grave?"

"No ma'am, we have all the records and we'll let them know when we go over there."

"That sho a relief," Minnie said. "I'd hate to be picking out a grave site in my state. Bad enough we gotta pick out a casket."

"Yes ma'am, Miss Minnie. Burying a loved one is hard under the best of circumstances. We aim to make the process as easy as possible for you."

"Thank you Mr. Miller, I 'preciate that. Now if yall'll show me some caskets we'll git on with it."

"Yes ma'am, just step this way into the showroom."

Alex followed his mother into an anteroom that contained a half-dozen caskets arranged in descending order of price; from the plushly quilted mahogany model to the unadorned pine box at the far end.

"How much this one be?" Minnie asked, running her hand over the highly polished mahogany.

"That's our premier model. The Haney family selected that one just a few weeks ago. It normally goes for $125, but because of Mr. Sam's standing in the community I can let it go for $100."

"I'd sho like to have that one for Sam but we ain't got that kinda money."

She wandered past the four shiny, metal caskets until she came to the lacquered, pine box at the end.

"How much this one be?"

"That's our most economical unit. It retails for $25."

"I'd sho like to do better by Sam, but we just cain't. 'Sides, once he in the ground it ain't gone make no never mind. Ashes to ashes and all dat stuff. I reckon we'll take the pine one."

"Whatever you say Miss Minnie. It won't affect our level of service in the least. Now, what about flowers?"

"Sam was kinda partial to gladiolus. They's in bloom now. You thinks maybe you can make up a big spray of 'em?"

"I think we can do that, and I'm sure the folks at Friendship will be sending lots of flowers as well. Now, what about the visitation?"

"I was thinkin' we'd do an open casket on Friday and Saturday mornin'," Minnie said, "with the funeral 'bout two o'clock."

"That'll be just fine Miss Minnie. Will you or some members of the family be here during the visitation hours?"

"Yassuh, we gone divide it up 'mongst me and the chilren." Minnie hesitated, fearful of posing the next question.

"Now I needs to ask ya 'bout t'other expenses. Sam took out a burial policy. It won't much but I's hoping it'll cover most everything."

"With the casket, transportation, flowers, preparation and burial the total cost will be $250?" Mr. Miller paused to observe Minnie's reaction.

"That be a mite more'n I'd reckoned on. If the chilren heps me out a little bit maybe we can come up with that much. You think maybe ya'll could throw in a couple of metal flower urns for the graves?"

"I think we can arrange that Miss Minnie," Miller smiled. "Is there anything else I can do for you today?"

"You think we might be able to see Sam now?" she said with a catch in her voice.

"Yes, ma'am, we've got him all prepared. Just follow me."

Mr. Miller led Minnie and Alex to the back of the building

and down a narrow hallway, stopping at a door with a large push handle in the center. He pressed on the handle and the thick, heavily insulated door swung open revealing a row of cooling platforms. Containers beneath each platform held large blocks of ice. Additional ice was located in deep chests along the sawdust-insulated walls. Sam was the only client present on this occasion. He was lying on one of the platforms. A white satin sheet draping the body covered all but Sam's face.

"We don't do all the final make-up and preparation until the day before the viewing, so he don't look quite as good as he will," Mr. Miller said.

Minnie let out a tiny cry. Her beloved Sam, already very light-skinned, revealed a pallor that shocked her. The thought that he could somehow feel the cold brought her pain even though she knew there was no logic in the feeling. Dealing with death brought out many conflicted feelings — feelings that normal human logic could not assuage.

"He looks so peaceful Ma," Alex said. "He looks like he just lay down to sleep and didn't wake up. He told me that night when I came home that he was at peace and ready to go. I believe he's found that peace now."

Tears welled in Alex's eyes.

"You be right Alex. Me'n Sam talked a heap 'bout dying and what happen after we's gone. Sam knowed what was a comin'. He said he was jest trustin' in Jesus to take him over Jordan to the other side. He say he gone be waitin' for me over there and I believes that."

She caressed Sam's face and kissed him on the lips. She burst into tears. "I reckon we best go now. Sam don't never like to see me a cryin' none."

Alex held his mother's arm as she stepped onto the porch. Perspiration dripped from her face.

"I think I'll sit here on the porch for a spell Alex. Catch my breath," Minnie said.

"Okay Mama. I'll go on in to see if Ben is home yet. I want to talk to him about the funeral."

The oppressive heat abated as the sun began its slow descent beyond the Colleton oaks. The languid drone of bumblebees gathering the nectars from the yard flowers added solemn counterpoint to the somber scene.

Alex walked through the house. There was no sign of Ben. Normally he arrived home before six, in time for supper. The hairs on Alex's neck rose. Was Ben going back on his word? Had he gone back to *The Black Cat?* Alex had to know.

"Mama, Ben's not home," Alex said as he crossed the porch. "I think I'll walk over to Gaston's and see if he needs some help. Can you hold up on supper until we get back?"

"Sho Alex. I's jest gone warm up what we had for dinner. Why you think Ben ain't home yet?"

"He said they were getting a bunch of new horses in and he had to get them stabled and fed. I reckon he just got tied up."

Alex didn't like lying to Minnie, but if he told her what he was really thinking it would devastate her.

11

Quincy

A lone electric bulb, suspended from the pulley beam over the carriage loft door, swung gently in the breeze. An occasional whinny arose from the bowels of the large brick barn. One of the horses, plainly upset at his new quarters, took his frustration out by battering the wall of his stall with steel-shod hooves. Alex detected no human presence about the place. His worst fears now seemed all too real.

He tried to prepare himself for the coming confrontation with Ben. The 15-block walk to York and Kershaw gave Alex plenty of time to think. He didn't want a confrontation with Ben, but he needed to convince his brother to abandon what Alex saw as a certain pathway to destruction. Ben was sitting at the bar with the same man with the hooded eyes and slurred speech. Alex took the stool next to Ben.

"You lied to me," Alex said.

Ben whipped around in alarm at the sound of Alex's voice.

"Alex! What you doin' here?"

"You promised me you wouldn't come back here until we had a chance to work this thing out."

"I can explain Alex. It's not what you think."

"It looks pretty plain to me. You're sitting here with the same man you said you wouldn't see again."

Hooded eyes spoke.

"Why don't you jest go on home and leave us alone man. Ben be growed up 'nough to take care o hisself."

"Apparently, I disagree with you … whatever your name is."

"It's Simon," Ben said, "Simon Pettigrew."

"Well Ben," Alex said testily, "if it's not what it looks like, why don't you enlighten me?"

"Simon called me over to the stable. He say Quincy bad sick and he need my help."

"Who is Quincy?" Alex asked.

"He the other man what was at the table the time you come in."

"And what does that have to do with you?"

"Simon say Quincy gone need to go to the hospital and he ain't got no money. He say maybe I be able to hep out."

"What's the matter with Quincy?" Alex asked.

"He done stepped on a rusty nail in the back yard and his foot all swole up. His whole leg be big as a tree and it all green. He cain't even open his mouth," Simon interjected.

"Where is he now?" Alex asked.

"He at our place on Ravenel. His fever done gone real high."

"What's the address?"

"It be 701 Ravenel Street," Simon said.

"When did this happen."

""Bout three, four days ago," Simon said.

"Ben, ask the manager if I can use his telephone," Alex said.

Ben stepped over to the man by the cash register and whispered into his ear. The man pointed to the wall phone behind him. Ben motioned Alex over.

"He say you can make a local call for a dime — no long distance."

Alex reached in his pocket and handed a dime to the bartender before walking over to the phone. He lifted the earpiece from its cradle and tilted the transmitter up to his mouth. He turned the crank on the side of the wooden box and waited.

"Operator."

"Ma'am can you connect me to Dr. Johnson's pharmacy?'

"Yes sir."

Alex heard a click as the operator inserted a plug into Dr. Johnson's line and pressed the button to begin ringing his phone. Five rings later, he heard another click as the doctor lifted his earpiece.

"This is Dr. Johnson. How can I help you?"

"Doctor this is Alex Devereux. I spoke to you last Saturday at the pharmacy."

"Yes Alex, what can I do for you?"

"I'm with my brother Ben. A friend of his has been injured. I believe he may have tetanus. Can you see him?'

"What's his name?"

"Quincy Patterson."

After an awkward pause, the doctor continued.

"I know his family. Where is he now?"

"He's at 701 Ravenel Street."

"I'll be right over."

"Come on Ben, Simon, the doctor is on his way to your place."

701 Ravenel was a half-mile west of *The Black Cat*. They were there in ten minutes and had hardly entered when a car pulled into the driveway. Dr. Johnson jumped out with his black satchel in hand.

"Where is he?"

"He in the back bedroom, Doc." Simon said. "Follow me."

Quincy lay on a sweat soaked mattress with no sheet. His body was rigid and he babbled incoherently. Saliva spilled from his gaping mouth.

"You boys hold him still while I get his temperature."

Quincy's thrashing about negated using an oral thermometer. Dr. Johnson reached in his bag and pulled an anal thermometer from a metal tube.

"Hold him still now."

He inserted the thermometer. Quincy jumped and then settled down. The doctor looked at his watch. After two minutes, he removed the thermometer.

"His temperature is 104 degrees. We need to get it down. Do you have any ice?"

"We got a little in the ice box," Simon said.

"Bring it to me, with some towels," Dr. Johnson said.

While Simon fetched the ice, the doctor cut Quincy's pants leg off and examined his foot and leg."

"Gangrene's setting in. See that redness creeping up his leg. It'll kill him if we don't get this leg off. We don't have time to get him to the hospital. Once those red lines reach his groin he'll be beyond help. "

Large open sores had formed on Quincy's leg below the knee. Audible gas escaped from the bursting pustules. Their noxious odors hung in the stifling, fetid air of the small room. Alex glanced at Ben. His brother was pale and looked faint.

"Sit down Ben, before you pass out," Alex said. "Dr. Johnson and I have got this covered."

"Simon, just keep the ice in the kitchen," Dr. Johnson shouted. "Spread some sheets on the table then come in here."

"Alex, you and Simon help me get Quincy to the kitchen. Alex you grab him under the arms. Simon, you get his good leg. I'll hold his other one. Now, on the count of three, lift him. One, two, three."

They struggled down the narrow hallway and put Quincy face-up on the table. Simon placed the iced towels along Quincy's sides.

"Ben, bring my bag in here."

Dr. Johnson removed a pair of rubber gloves, a roll of gauze, a vial of anesthetic, a bag of yellow powder, a scalpel and a saw from the bag.

"Alex, I want you to stand at his head and hold this gauze pad over Quincy's nose. I will wet it with chloroform. Whenever he starts to rouse, I will tell you to drip more onto the gauze. Okay?"

"Yes sir."

"Simon you and Ben hold him so he can't move. Everybody ready?"

All three men nodded nervously. Ben still looked faint. There were tears in his eyes.

Dr. Johnson placed several towels under Quincy's leg above the knee. He took the scalpel in his gloved hand and began an incision around the leg, cutting through to the bone. Blood spurted from the femoral arteries. Quincy cried out in pain.

"Drip some more chloroform onto the pad Alex. There. That's enough."

Once the bone was fully exposed, the doctor took his saw and severed the femur. Ben fainted. Dr. Johnson tore open the bag of sulfur and sprinkled it over the bloody stump. He grabbed the icy towels and wrapped them around Quincy's leg, securing them with suture twine. He wrapped the severed limb in a sheet and placed it on the counter by the sink.

"We have to get him to the hospital where he can get emergency care," Dr. Johnson said. "It remains to be seen if the sepsis and gangrene reached beyond his leg. We'll know after a few hours. Simon, run over to that store on York and call the hospital. Tell them to send an ambulance here immediately and to have the emergency room ready when we get Quincy over there."

The ambulance roared down Hampton toward Richland Avenue, its siren wailing and its red lights flashing, with Quincy, Simon and the severed limb in the back. Dr. Johnson followed. Alex and Ben stayed behind.

"You all right now, Ben?" Alex asked.

Ben was ashen. He was shaking and tears streamed down

his face.

"Yeah, I guess so. I ain't never seen nothin' like that before. I sho hope I don't never see it agin."

"Let's go home Ben," Alex said. "We've had enough excitement for one night. And Ben, I'm sorry I doubted you. I would have done the same thing for a friend."

"Thanks Alex. That mean a lot to me," Ben said as he dropped into step alongside.

It was almost ten when they got home. Minnie was nervously pacing back-and-forth on the porch.

"Where you boys been?' she asked in a highly agitated voice.

"One of the horses they brought in injured himself and Ben had to call the vet. I stayed with Ben to help him."

Lying to his mother was no easier the second time around. Ben gave Alex a look of thankful relief.

"He gone be all right?"

"Yassum," Ben said. "He jest needed a few stitches where he cut hisself on the latch."

"You boys come on in. I left some food in the warming oven and they's iced tea on the counter. Now that I knows both of you is all right, I'm going on to bed. It been a tirin' day fo me."

"Good night Mama," Alex said. "See you in the morning."

"Night Mama," Ben echoed.

12

The Storm

A fierce summer storm came roaring through Aiken on that Tuesday morning. Alex awoke to hear crashing thunder and the rifle shots of snapping limbs. He ran to his window in time to witness a huge, long-leaf pine crash into the wash shed behind the house next door. Sheets of tin sailed across the field behind like giant kites. Large, black, bulbous wash pots rolled down the street.

"Mama, Ben, are you all right?" he yelled.

Alex bolted down the hallway to find Minnie cowering in the kitchen. Ben held the back door against the wind, each gust threatening to propel him across the room. The sound and fury passed as quickly as it had arrived. Except for the rain, there was an eerie quiet.

"Had to be a tornado," Ben said. "They was one come close to the stables last year. Took down several of Mr. Gaston's pecan trees. I was in the barn. It sounded like a freight train come through—jest like this'un."

"Come on," Alex said, "let's see if anyone's hurt.

Trees and limbs were scattered up and down Charleston Street and as far down Colleton as they could see. The tops of several pines were twisted out and the debris hurled along the street. A massive oak had split in two. One-half dropped onto the house across the street. The other fell across Charleston, blocking the street. The neighbors were pouring out to assess the damage.

"Mr. Clark, you all right?" Ben shouted over the roar of the wind. Elijah Clark was 91 and had worked as a butler for a member of the Bostwick clan. He lived across the street.

"We all be okay, Ben. One a them limbs done knocked a hole in my kitchen ceiling. Ya'll got any tarpaulins you might patch it with?"

"I'll check in our shed, Mr. Clark," Ben said.

Five minutes later Ben and Alex clambered onto the Clark roof and began affixing a ten-foot square tarp over the gaping hole.

"That oughta hold you till you can get it re-shingled," Alex said.

"I sho thanks you, Alex. I been meanin' to drop by since I seen you come home. Then Sam up and died, so I kinda felt like I oughta leave you folks be for a spell."

"It would have been okay, sir," Alex responded. "Drop over whenever you feel like it."

The brothers continued their survey of the neighborhood, walking two blocks down Colleton to Beaufort Street. The widespread destruction was replicated on both streets. Several trucks and wagons navigated the piles of debris blanketing Colleton to the west. The red lights of an ambulance flashed in the distance. Alex concluded that the wealthy enclave was in good hands and could do without his and Ben's services.

Minnie was sitting at the table with a cup of coffee when the boys returned. Her cup chattered in the saucer when she tried to set it down, her hands still unsteady from the fright of the tornado.

"What you boys find?" she rasped. "They anybody been hurt?"

"No Mama," Alex said reaching for her hand, "Mr. Clark

has a hole in his roof. Me'n Ben nailed a tarp over it. It'll keep the rain out until he can get it repaired."

"Thank God they ain't nobody been hurt. I ain't seen a storm like that come through here in years."

"I think I'll go over and check on the horses," Ben said. "It look like that twister was headed that way. How 'bout you Alex. You wanta go with me?"

"No. I think I'll walk downtown to see if they need any help. While I'm there I'll stop in to see Mr. Poole. I need to get started on my bar exam as soon as possible. I can't live on the meager savings I have left from the money Miss Celestine gave me. I have to get to work."

"All right then," Minnie said. "You boys gone be back home for supper?"

"Yes ma'am," Ben said. "How 'bout you Alex?"

"Probably so," Alex said. "It depends on how much time Mr. Poole can spend with me."

The trip downtown, normally a fifteen-minute breeze took Alex half-an- hour. He dodged several downed trees and stopped to help a city crew remove a pine that had fallen across Park Avenue, east of the depot. West of York there was no evidence that a storm had passed through. It seemed to have cut a narrow path of six blocks from south to north across the eastern side of the city.

Alex was sweaty and tired when he arrived at the foot of the stairs leading up to Mr. Poole's office over the Farmers and Merchants Bank. He wondered if he should wait to see Mr. Poole when he was clean and more refreshed. He decided to go ahead. A portly, middle-aged, woman with red hair responded to Alex's knock.

"Yes, may I help you?"

"Good morning. I'm sorry that I've come unannounced. We don't have a telephone. My name is Alex Devereux."

"Oh yes. Alex Devereux." She drew out the five syllables as

if they were toxic. Mr. Poole said I should expect you to come around soon. I'm sorry to hear of your father's passing."

Her message of condolence dripped with icicles.

"Is Mr. Poole in?"

"He just arrived a few minutes ago. There was a lot of damage over near the school on Pine Log where he lives. Thankfully, his house was spared, but Mrs. Carter next door had considerable damage. He stayed with her until help came."

"Will he be able to see me this morning?"

"Let me check. You can have a seat while I ask him."

Alex sat on one of the sturdy, straight back, wooden chairs across from the receptionist's desk. Diplomas, certificates and pictures of Mr. Poole with various dignitaries filled the walls. One, prominently displayed behind the receptionist's desk, showed Mr. Poole on the capitol steps with Aiken's congressional representative, James Byrnes. The door to the inner office opened and the red haired lady reappeared.

"Mr. Poole asks that you wait a few minutes. There are a few urgent matters he must attend to and then he will see you."

The awareness that Alex was worthy of an audience with her boss in no way diminished the chill in the room.

Alex picked up a law journal from the lamp stand. He thumbed through it briefly while he waited. One article immediately caught his eye. The criminal activity surrounding prohibition had spurred congress to pass a law banning the mail-order purchase of handguns. He wondered if the "lint-head" that shot at him on Saturday got his gun through the mail. The door opened before he was half-way through the article. Mr. Poole came across to shake Alex's hand.

"Come in Alex. I've been looking forward to your visit. I was sorry to hear about the passing of your father."

The warmth expressed in the comment was in stark contrast to that of his receptionist.

"When is the funeral?"

"Thank you, sir. The funeral is set for Saturday at two o'clock. My father was determined that I should finish school before I came home. He wouldn't even let my mother tell me about his illness until last week."

"Sam came by to see me a couple of times while you were away," Mr. Poole said as he ushered Alex into his office. "He had a few minor legal things he needed taken care of, but mostly he wanted to be reassured that I was in complete agreement with Miss Eustis' wishes in regard to you. Especially after she passed away. Sam was extremely proud of you and he wanted more than anything to see you come home and become a lawyer here. I assured him that I intended to carry out her wishes, both in letter and in spirit."

"I had no idea. Pa never let on to me. He was a strict disciplinarian. He didn't show warmth and affection easily. It's good to know he was proud of me, and that he told you so."

"Alex I will do everything I can to see that you pass the South Carolina bar exam," Mr. Poole said as he fiddled nervously with a letter opener on his desk. "Nevertheless, I must be honest with you. It will be an uphill battle. Many of the people who have to pass on your qualifications are men who are only a generation removed from the war and the bitterness engendered by reconstruction. Their views, mostly formed while sitting at the knee of a wounded father or a widowed aunt, reflect a far different vision than some more enlightened individuals may have. Many of them still view the world through their own distorted lenses of history. They see the institution of slavery as the natural state of God's plan. To them the white race is superior and therefore was given dominion over the black race. Now, their inability to wrest power back from Washington and return the South to its former agrarian, slave-holding glory, has led them to transfer the blame onto the black man himself. Many of these men will smile and shake your hand, all the while holding a dagger behind their back, metaphorically speaking. The good news is that for every Ben Tillman there's a Jimmy Byrnes. I will try to see that those more inclined toward improving race relations are chosen to make the decisions."

Alex sensed the depth of Mr. Poole's despair and elected to leave.

"What should I be doing in the meantime?" Alex asked as he stood.

"I want you to come into this office as often as possible. I have prepared several papers that I want you to study. I also want you to read some specific legal treatises I have that compare South Carolina law to other states. It is these differences that will trip you up if used by those aligned against us."

"Thank you sir. If I may, I'd like to take these papers home to read. When do you think I will be allowed to take the bar exam."

"The next scheduled exam is October 15th. I will try to get you on the list to take it. No guarantee, but I have a friend in the examiner's office who may be able to pull it off. If we can slip your application in without disclosing your race, we'll have a better chance. That means you have a lot of studying to do in the next couple of months. I'd also like you to sit in on a couple of trials that are coming up in the September session of district court. I'm defending a farmer charged with murder. He claims the victim, a farm neighbor, stormed into his home on June 21 brandishing a club of some sort and he shot him to protect his family. The prosecutor says it was premeditated. I'll let you sit in on some of the preparations as well.

"Do you have any other questions for me?"

"No sir, but I am curious about something."

"What is that?'

"Your secretary acted as if she thought I shouldn't be here. Did she know about your agreement with Miss Eustis?"

"Miss Rhodes has been with me for fifteen years. She's a very good legal secretary, but she sometimes let's her personal biases influence her work. I try to cut her as much slack as possible. Her grandfather was conscripted at the end of the war. He was forty-five years old. He died in the great explosion at the siege of Petersburg. Her father never let the family forget it. I'll speak to her."

"Thank you Mr. Poole. I'll be getting on back home now. There's still some more cleanup to do after the tornado. I'll try to spend as much time as possible studying these papers during the next few weeks and I'll come in as often as possible. Do you have a date for the trial yet?"

"No, it hasn't been docketed, but it'll be sometime the week of September, 12. I'll know before the end of August. Take care Alex."

13

The Lynchings

Much of the debris had been cleared to the side of the road along Park Avenue as Alex made his way back home. The oppressive heat and humidity of the morning had returned with a vengeance after the soaking rains. In the distance Alex saw Ben turning onto Charleston.

"Hey Ben! Wait up!" he yelled.

Ben turned to see Alex trotting toward him.

"Slow down Alex. It too darn hot to be runnin' like that."

"I didn't know if you heard me."

"How did it go with Mr. Poole?"

"Pretty good I think. He says he's got everything on track for me to take the bar exam in October, barring any major obstacles. He says there are people in the system who won't take kindly to a Negro becoming a lawyer in Aiken. He feels he has enough allies in Columbia to overcome their objections. I sure hope so."

"Things, they done changed some in the seven years you's been away Alex, but not all that much. A black man's still gotta be keerful what he say and how he acts round white folks. I ain't told you 'bout whut happened two years ago. It too raw still."

"What Ben. You sound so serious."

Ben heaved a big sigh and began.

"One day Sheriff Howard and three deputies went out to Monetta to serve a search warrant on a black family, the Leemans. The sheriff done got some letter, wit nobody's name on it, sayin' the family what lived there was moonshiners. They was in the sheriff's car and they won't wearin' no kinda uniforms. They come running up to the house and surroundin' it. Some of the family was outside in the fields and some was workin' 'round the wash pots out back. Fo you knows it, they was shootin' all over the place. Two women was killed along with the sheriff. One son, a daughter and a nephew was arrested for the killin' and took to jail.

"The whole town done got all stirred up. The trial was set for jest a week later. Befo you knowed it, the two boys was sentenced to the 'lectric chair and the daughter to life in prison. Well, they was sent off to a jail in Columbia for safekeepin'.

"Jest a week befo they was set to die, some folks up north raised some money and hired a white lawyer from up to Spartanburg to see if he could stop the executions. Well suh, him and a NAACP lawyer got the state court to hold everything while they looked at it. After the judges looked at the case, they says the three was tried too fast and they ordered a new trial.

"Them three was brought back to Aiken and the new judge say the son won't guilty and the other two was gonna git a new trial. The boy was let go and started walking back to Monetta. He won't even outta town befo he done been arrested again by the new sheriff. He was one of the deputies at the house when the sheriff was killed. He say they was a warrant for Demon Leeman's arrest on 'nother account. So all three was locked up at the Aiken jail. That night a bunch of Ku Klux Klanners done busted them outta jail, drug'em out north o' town, and shot'em to death.

"They was a big racket bout the whole thing. Some big reporter from New York come down and stayed for several days tryin' to find out what happened, but they won't nobody gone point fingers at nobody else. The whole sorry mess was swept under the rug and it done gone away without nobody bein' helt to account for killin' them chilren.

"That why I was so upset 'bout them men shootin' at you. Things is still bad 'tween us colored folks and some of them white folks, 'specially the mill workers out in Horse Creek. Ever one of them is a Klanner."

"I had no idea Ben. That explains why Ma got so upset when I told her."

"That why you gotta be extra keerful, you bein' a black lawyer and all."

"I know Ben. People seem so helpless against the white man. When I get my license I hope I can help to change things and give Negroes recourse to the law — and the ability to prosecute those who violate their rights."

"Me too, Alex, me too."

Minnie was sweeping the front yard with a mulberry brush-broom, trying to remove all the leaves and pine needles accumulated during the storm. Perspiration drenched her housedress.

"Mama you better let us finish that," Ben said, "befo you has a heart attack."

"Sho nuff, Ben," she wheezed, "I'm plum tuckered out. Come on in. I got some fried chicken and fried corn ready."

"Mama, I haven't had chicken that good since I left," Alex said as he placed the third drumstick bone on his plate. "You could make a fortune teaching those folks in Washington how to fry chicken."

"You jest butterin' me up for sumpin' Alex. What you up to?"

"No kidding Ma. I've never seen anyone who cooks as

good as you. It's no wonder Miss Celestine wouldn't let you and Papa go. One day I read some of her recipes from that book she wrote about New Orleans Creole cooking. Sure sounded good."

"I'll let you in on a little secret. I learned as much bout cookin' from her as she did from me. Miss Celestine was a good cook too.

"That be 'nough 'bout my cookin'. What you find out from Mr. Poole?"

"Well, it looks good even though he says there are a lot of hurdles to jump between now and October when the next exam is given."

"Lak what?"

"He says there are some men who must approve licensees for the bar in South Carolina who don't look kindly on Negroes being lawyers, but he thinks he can get around them."

"I sho hopes so! Be a shame you done all that studyin' and cain't be a lawyer here."

"Don't worry Ma. One way or the other we'll get it through," Alex said leaning back from the table and rubbing his stomach.

"Alex, come on and help me with the trash in the yard," Ben said. "I hasta git back to the stables at four."

"Okay Ben, let me change my clothes. I'll be right out."

They finished the cleanup, Ben left for Gaston's, and Alex went in to wash up. He picked up the papers given to him by Mr. Poole and went out to the back porch. He sat down in an old rocking chair whose caning had seen better days. He began to read the several titles.

> Tort reform in South Carolina
> Arguments on Corpus Delecti rulings
> Definition changes in Real Property case law
> Standing requirements in the pursuit of tort relief

Poll taxes and their effect on minority voting in
South Carolina

Among the several topics listed, it was that last one that jumped out at Alex. He had never voted in South Carolina. As far as he knew, neither had either of his parents. The window to the kitchen was open. He could see Minnie bustling about preparing a dish for their supper.

"Mama, did either you or Papa ever vote?" Alex called through the screen.

"Lawsy me no!" she yelled back.

"Why not?" Alex asked.

"Fust of all, they was a tax to vote. Me'n yore Pa didn't have no extra money for that. Second, they won't enough black folks to make no difference. We knowed the white folks was gonna git the people they wanted elected. Third, too many black folks suddenly lost their jobs if they tried to vote. No sirree, we didn't never vote."

Subconsciously, Alex knew all these things to be true. He had just never thought about them in their legal context. This was another thing he hoped to change. He stared at the document in his hand and felt a tinge of the white-hot rage he had witnessed among the black intelligentsia at Howard when they discussed civil rights. If the rights of blacks in Washington inspired such passionate feelings, how much deeper must be the suffused outrage here in Aiken among educated black people. Ah yes, he smiled to himself, the real education of Alex Devereux is just beginning. There were oh so many reefs and shoals he must navigate if he expected to reach the safe harbor of black justice in Aiken, South Carolina.

14

The Visitation

By Thursday, the crowds coming to pay their respects and offer condolences slowed to a trickle. The table and the kitchen counters still groaned under the weight of a myriad of casseroles, cakes and pies. Alex felt he must have gained at least five pounds in the past week, but still he couldn't get enough of all the dishes he had been deprived of for so long.

"Alex, me'n Cleo is gonna sit with Sam tomorow mawnin," Minnie announced at breakfast on Thursday. I want you'n Ben to come over 'bout two o'clock and stay till Mr. Miller closes up at nine. Phoebe and Lester is gonna sit Saturday mawnin' up to funeral time.

Then we all gonna follow Sam to the church in Mr. Miller's big, black Cadillac. The chilren and Lester and Jonah will be in another car. If George show up, he gone ride in the limousine with us. Mr. Miller say it'll hold seven folks."

"Mama we haven't heard a word from George. Don't get your hopes up that he'll come."

"I ain't Alex," she said with a catch in her voice, "I jest sho hope he do."

Ben was late getting home from the stables that night.

Several Pullman cars had arrived with polo ponies for an upcoming international match. It was unusual for one to occur in the heat of summer, but scheduling conflicts in the fall had dictated it. Ben was tired and dirty after stabling and grooming several of the priceless ponies. He just wanted to bathe, get a quick bite to eat, and hit the hay.

One of the few luxuries Sam had allowed himself was the installation of a water-jacketed coal stove in the washhouse to heat water for Minnie's pots and for the oversize tub they used for bathing. Ben emerged from the bath and traipsed across the backyard with a Turkish towel wrapped around his midriff while he dried his hair with a smaller version of the same.

"Mama," he said as he opened the back door, "I forgot to tell you that George called today at Gaston's. He say he comin' to the funeral and he gone bring his friend Mary Waters with him."

Minnie plopped down at the table and buried her head in her arms, heavy sobs racking her stout body.

"Lawsy me," she said after regaining her composure, "the good Lawd, he done answered my prayers. Praise be to Jesus, all my chilren gonna be there for Sam's funeral."

"That's great news Ben," Alex said, rounding the corner from his room. "I hope we can convince George to come back home for good. I don't think Carolina Springs is the best place for him to be."

"Me too, Alex," Minnie said. "I want to git all my family back together lak it used to be. I sho thanks you for gittin' him to come to the funeral. He won't be comin' if you didn't go over there."

"Don't give me too much credit Ma. I expect Mary Waters was more responsible than me. She seems to have George pretty well under control."

"I don't care who gits the credit, I jest glad he gone be here."

There were only a few people in the viewing room with Minnie and Cleo when Alex and Ben got to Miller's on Friday afternoon. A couple that worked with Sam at *The Cove* and some old acquaintances from the *Mon Repos* days.

"I 'member one time when Miss Celestine 'lowed the help to finish off some of the wine after a party. Ol' Sam got a might tipsy. He nigh fell down the back stairs. He was mighty embarrassed. Me'n Ellsworth Givens took him out back to the stables and dunked his head in a horse trough. He come up a sputterin' and thrashing about. We got him cooled off so's he could go back in the house. I don't think Miss Celestine ever done that again. Won't nothing hurt but Sam's pride."

"That sounds like Sam," Minnie said laughing. "He won't never much of a drinker. Ever once in a while he lakked to have a little of that moonshine the Evan's boys brought 'round. He'd only do that if he don't gotta work the next day."

"Minnie we sho sorry bout Sam," Henry Goings said as he took Minnie's hand. "He was a good man. He gone be missed. We'll see ya'll tomorrow at the funeral."

"I sho thanks ya'll fo comin' by. It means a lot to me."

"Hey Cleo, how you doing?" Ben said.

He gave his sister a big hug.

"It been a bit of a rough patch. Jonah ain't made things no easier. He been out drinkin' some. It jest seems lak he ain't able to find hisself no more. I'm worried 'bout him losing his job over to the Iselin's. I cain't take care of Toby and Maggie by myself."

" It been like this ever since him'n George got into it," Ben said. "I sho hope they ain't no fuss when George show up at the funeral."

"George comin' to the funeral!" Cleo exclaimed. "Mama

you didn't say nothin' bout George comin!"

"I was afraid ya'll would get all upset. George comin' with his girlfriend."

"Don't worry Cleo," Alex said. "I don't think either George or Jonah will disrespect Papa's funeral. I'll try to keep them separated."

"Thank you, Alex. I'm gonna walk back home with Mama. Jonah gonna pick me up when he gits off work."

An increasing number of friends and church members flowed through Miller's as the work day wound down. Alex remembered most of the faces. He had a tougher time putting names with them; former Sunday school teachers; classmates from church, students from Schofield's, workers at *Mon Repos*. Alex rose to get a drink of water. He stood by the cooler looking out the front window. A black sports car pulled up around eight o'clock. The tall, blond man behind the wheel looked familiar. It had been eight long years.

"Hello Alex," Thomas Hitchcock Jr., said as he embraced his old friend. "It's been an awful long time."

"Mr. Hitchcock, how nice of you to come by. I thought you would be in New York."

"Call me Tommy. Normally, I would be, but I came home to participate in a polo tournament. I'm so sorry about Sam. I have nothing but fond memories of him and your mother. She still making that fabulous fried chicken of hers?"

"She sure is, Tom. Drop by the house sometimes and she'll offer you some."

"I'd love to Alex, but I'll only be here a few days then I have to get back to New York. How's Miss Minnie holding up?"

"She seems to be doing fine. Papa was sick a long time and she knew what was coming. With the help of family and friends she's holding up pretty well."

"That's good. I understand you've finished your studies at

Howard. I know *Tante* Celestine would be very proud. She put great store by you — as did we all. What are you going to do now?"

"I'm going to honor her wishes and set up shop here in Aiken. Mr. Poole had agreed with Miss Celestine to help me get past the bar exam and to offer me a position at his firm. If it all works out, I'll be practicing law by the end of the year."

"Good for you Alex. Aiken can use men like you. I'll be keeping an eye on you. If there's ever any way I can help you, please give me a call. I can still pull a few strings around here."

"Thank you Tom. Thank you very much."

"I think I'll pay my respects to Sam now. Remember what I said. Call me any time."

Thomas Hitchcock Jr. walked over to the open casket, crossed himself, bowed his head, and said a small prayer for the soul of Samson Demosthenes Devereux. He added a postscript. He asked God to keep watch over his old friend Alexander Hamilton Devereux as well. He pulled a handkerchief from his coat pocket and dabbed at his eyes as he pushed the door open.

The last well-wisher left as the dusk of late summer was fading. When the boys got back home, Jonah had already taken Phoebe home and Minnie was nodding in the porch swing. She awakened to the sound of their feet on the steps.

"Did many folks come by whilst you was there?

"Yes ma'am, quite a few Alex said. "You'll be surprised at one in particular."

"Who that?"

"Mr. Tommy Hitchcock, Jr."

"Well I'll be! What he doin' in town?"

"He's playing in a polo match on Monday. He asked me to give you his best."

"He always was the sweetest boy. He sho helped you a lot. All the Hitchcocks is good folk. Well this be the last day we gone have Sam with us. It sho sad, but we all needs to be at peace along with him. All us better git to bed. Gonna be a long day tomorrow. They's some food I left out for you. I'll see you in the mawnin'."

Minnie wearily lifted herself from the swing and trundled off to bed, lost in her private thoughts of Sam.

15

The Funeral

Minnie was cooking breakfast on the day of Sam's funeral when she heard the back door opening.

"George! Is that you boy? Come on in here and let me see you." She grabbed her eldest son in a bear hug and squeezed him.

"Yeah Ma. It me. It good to see you. It good to be home. I'm sorry I won't here for Papa 'fore he passed."

"I'm sho he done forgive you for that."

George pushed the door open and beckoned to someone on the back porch.

"Mama, this Miss Mary Waters. She work with me over to Carolina Springs."

A beautiful young girl who could have stepped out of a cotillion line on Colleton Avenue emerged from the shadows. Minnie gasped.

"Lawsy mercy, boy, what you gone and done?" she cried.

"What you mean Mama?" George protested.

"You knows what I means boy," Minnie said, fixing George with a doleful stare. "What you doin' with a white woman? You know you gone git yoself strung-up by some of them redneck peckerwoods."

"Miss Minnie," the girl said, "I know I may look white, but

my mama growed up on a plantation as a field worker. She was a mulatto. My papa was a white man from New York. He left us right after I was born. My mother stuck by me, raised me, looked after me; so I chose to be black like her. She still works at that same hotel in Savannah where I was born."

"But chile it ain't the same up here. Them rednecks sees you with a colored man they's gone shoot first and ask questions later. What been happenin' over to Carolina Springs and North Augusta when you been seed together?

"Mama," George spoke up, "we been keerful 'bout goin' out in public and around the Springs folks don't make no never mind, they knows Mary's story. We ain't never together when the crowds is there. I works in the bar area and Mary she out front waitin' tables or singin'. Our place, it in the black part of town and don't nobody bother us. We comes and goes mos'ly after dark anyway."

"It still a trouble to me. I know Mary be a sweet girl and she treat you good, but I seen too many black foks kilt. I knows trouble when I sees it. But, this be ya'll's bizness. I jest gonna pray that nothin' bad gone happen."

"We gonna be careful, Ma," George said. "I won't let nothin' bad happen."

"I sho hopes so. Alex say you doin' a lots better with the talkin' and the fits. He say Miss Mary makin' sure you takes your pills when you s'posed to."

"Yes ma'am, Mary been takin' good care of me. I don't have the spells much no more and I been talkin' a lots better."

"Thank you, Mary," Minnie said, turning to the young woman. "I cain't tell you how much grief I done had a thinkin' 'bout George over there alone. I sho glad he found you."

"We found each other Miss Minnie," Mary corrected her. "I don't know what would've happened to me when the band broke up if George hadn't been there. He saved my life. I couldn't go back to Savannah and I didn't know anyone up here"

"George always had a big heart," Minnie said. "He jest got crossways with his pa and Jonah. I hopes and prays all that be 'hind us now."

"George," Alex said, "I've talked to Cleo and Jonah. I told them you may be here for the funeral. Jonah says he'll let bygones be bygones if you will. We don't want any trouble during the funeral so please be on your best behavior and just stay away from Jonah as much as possible."

"I ain't gonna cause no trouble if he ain't. He been treatin' Cleo any better?"

"They's been doin' better," Minnie interjected. "He still be drinkin' more'n he oughta, but he ain't been 'busin' her lak he did befo' ya'll got into that fight, and Cleo, she seem a mite mo' content now."

"How 'bout Cleo's chilren, they all right?":

"Growin' lak weeds. They's smart as whips, too," Minnie beamed. "I takes 'em some when Cleo workin'. We has a good ol' time.

"George, you and Miss Mary gotta be hungry. Don't 'spect you had no breakfast befo you left. Ya'll sit down an' I'll whip up some mo' eggs and grits."

Ben came in from Gaston's as they all sat down to eat. He gave George a big hug.

"Ben this is Mary Waters," George said. "We works together over at Carolina Springs."

"Alex done tol' me all 'bout ya'll Miss Mary. He say you mighty pretty, but he wrong. You beautiful."

Mary blushed.

The clock edged toward noon. Lester and Phoebe arrived. Lester wore his best church suit with a blue tie. Phoebe had on the black two-piece suit she bought at White's Department Store for her wedding. The white ruffled blouse at her throat softened the strain evident in her face.

"Hey Mama, how you holdin' up?" Phoebe said as she hugged her mother.

"I'm okay, Baby. I done cried all the tears I got. You know George be here?"

"No'm, when he get here?"

"Him and his friend Mary Waters come in 'bout breakfast time. They's in the kitchen gittin' a bite 'fore the funeral. You and Lester go on in to see 'em."

George and Mary were sitting at the kitchen table with Ben and Alex. George hopped up to welcome his sister.

"Hey, Phoebs. How ya doin'? Hey Lester."

"I's fine George. How you?"

"Doin' tolerable well. It sho good to see ya, Sis. You too Lester."

"Phoebe, this my friend, Mary Waters. Me'n her works together over to Carolina Springs."

From Alex's description of Mary, Phoebe knew what to expect, but she was not prepared for the sheer beauty of the girl sitting before her. She stumbled over her words.

"Miss M-m-ary it sho good to meet you. Alex done told me 'bout you after he come back from over there. Why, you even prettier than he say."

Mary blushed again.

"Phoebe, why don't you and Mary get acquainted while I talk to Lester and George? We're going to sit outside. Come on boys."

Alex led the others to the chairs under the pecan tree in the side yard. Jonah and Cleo drove up with the children just as they sat down. Cleo ran to embrace George. Jonah hung back with Toby and Maggie.

"Oh George," she cried, "it been so long since I seen you. How you doin'?"

"I'm doin' all right Cleo. You lookin' good. You done lost some weight."

"Jest a bit. Tryin' to stay way from the sweet stuff."

"Why don't you take the kids in to meet my friend Mary Waters? She work with me in North Augusta. I'll be in to see you directly."

"Jonah, why don't you stay out here with us and let the girls catch up?" Alex said.

"Toby, you and Maggie go on in with your ma," Jonah said. "I'll be in soon."

He sat down in the chair farthest from George without speaking to him. Alex took note.

"I wanted to let the women be alone for a while, but there's something else I want to talk to you about. It's especially important for you to hear this George. I haven't told anybody but Mama about this. When I came home from seeing you George, a car started following me after I went through Warrenville. It followed me through Graniteville and up the hill toward Aiken. Then they started hitting the bumper on Lester's car — I checked it Lester and there was no damage. They passed me going up that long hill on Trolley Line Road. When they got even with me somebody in the car took a shot at me. I had hit the brakes and the bullet just barely whizzed past my head and out the other window. They kept going and turned up the hill toward the cemetery. They didn't know whether I was hit or not. I went straight to the police, but they wouldn't even listen to me. The cop on duty said it was outside their jurisdiction and I should see the sheriff. I didn't even bother. I'm sure I'd get the same runaround.

"George, if they'd shoot at me riding alone you can imagine what they'd do if they saw you with Mary. You've got to be extra careful driving through the Valley. Maybe she should wear a shawl over her head and face."

"You couldn't see who it was shot at ya?" George asked nervously.

"No, it was dark when I passed that juke-joint in Warrenville.

I had to slow down for the left turn across the railroad tracks. That's when I saw them leaving the club. There wasn't much light. One had a bottle in his hand. The other man stumbled down the steps. He got up cursing and shook his fist at me like it was my fault he fell."

"You think they could tell you was black?" Lester asked.

"Yeah, there was enough light for that. I heard the man that fell yell 'let's git that nigger. He oughtn't be out here this time of night. Niggers knows to stay outta the Valley after dark'."

"Wish I'da been there with my shotgun," Jonah chimed in. "They won't be shootin' at no more black men."

"Jonah, you shoot up a car full of whites," Alex said, "and the sheriff would chase you to kingdom come. You know the law has different rules for blacks and whites."

"What you gone do 'bout that when you gits to be a lawyer, Alex?" Jonah asked sarcastically. "You think they gone pay 'tention to a black man?"

"I don't know Jonah, but I aim to try. It has to start somewhere, and it might as well start with me.

"We'd better get back inside. It'll soon be time to leave for the funeral."

"The eleven family members climbed into the three cars and headed up Charleston for Miller's Funeral Parlor. It was one-thirty. Ben rode with Lester and Phoebe. Alex and Minnie climbed into the back seat of George's borrowed car. Jonah trailed behind with his family.

The two limos for the family were lined up under the side portico. The hearse was parked in front. Mr. Miller waited on the front stoop as the family arrived. Two attendants stepped forward with him to open the car doors.

"Hey Miss Minnie. We all ready for you. Mr. Sam is in the front viewing room if the family wants to spend a little private time with him."

"Thank you Mr. Miller," she said as she stepped from the car. "We gots all the family here. George done come over with his girlfriend. I been prayin' we'd all be together for Sam. He gone be lookin' down and smilin' now."

The family trailed Minnie into the parlor. George hung back tentatively. He harbored mixed feelings about seeing his dead father. He wanted to see Sam, but at the same time, he didn't. These past two years had strained their relations almost to the point of no return. He edged into the room behind Alex and slowly crossed to the casket. When he saw Sam lying there, George broke down and fell to his knees, his hands grasping the pallbearer's rail. Fearing he was having a seizure, Minnie reached for George. She knelt by her grieving son.

"It all right George. It all right. Let it all out. It been a long time acomin'. Sam done forgive you a long time ago. Now it time fo' you to put it all in Jesus' hands. He say they ain't no burden he cain't bear."

"Mama I didn't think I'd ever be able to forgive Papa and Jonah for what happened to Cleo and the way they treated me. Now, Cleo seem all right with things and Jonah look like he doin' better. Lak you say it 'bout time."

Alex and Ben rushed over to help George and Minnie to their feet. Minnie stood holding onto George for a long moment while the others shuffled nervously about. Jonah looked on disapprovingly before silently leaving the room. He stepped onto the front stoop, and with a shaking hand fished a Camel from his pocket. He lit up and took a deep, exaggerated draw before expelling a long plume of blue smoke He looked clearly unnerved by the scene he had just witnessed. Cleo joined him.

"What's the matter Jonah? You oughtna left like that."

"Don't you be tellin' me what I oughtna done! Ol' George, he act like he all broke up now that his pa's gone. I ain't buyin' it. He just tryin' to wiggle back in now that Sam's done gone so's he can git some of that money he done left."

"What money? Pa ain't got no money!"

"That what you think. That what they wants you to think. I was up in the hayloft over to Hopeland's a while back right after Mr. Sam got real sick and he left work over to the Palmer's. I hear Miss Hope and 'nother woman down in the tack room a talkin'. She say Miss Celestine done left some more money in her will that was helt in some kinda trust fund. I don't know what that mean but she say it won't to be tetched 'less Alex finish school and come back to practice law in Aiken. If he don't, they don't git it."

"Jonah, why you make up a tale lak that? You jest still mad at George and wanna stir up trouble."

"Don't you tell me what I done heard! I ain't lyin' to you. Jest ask George. Somehow or tother he done found out 'bout it and now he wants some of that money for hisself."

Cleo watched Jonah take the last puff on his cigarette. She eyed him with suspicion, but a tiny seed of doubt crept into her mind. Jonah dropped the butt on the floor and twisted it out with his foot.

"Come on back in and behave yoself. This Pa's day and we don't need you stirrin'up no ruckus."

Jonah dutifully followed Cleo back inside.

Minnie, Phoebe and Mary were seated across from the casket. The men were standing near the window nervously fiddling with their unaccustomed ties. Mr. Miller entered the room.

"Well, it's that time Miss Minnie. We needs to git Sam over to Friendship if the service is to start at two. If all of ya'll will follow me we'll get you into the limousines. Mr. Kendall and Mr. Fields will see to Mr. Sam."

The family crossed through the other viewing room to the side door and loaded into the waiting cars. The two attendants wheeled Sam's casket out the front door and down the ramp. They backed it up to the hearse and rolled it in before clamping it into place. Mr. Kendall walked over to the funeral director and whispered that all was ready. He drove the second car and Mr. Miller the first. Mr. Fields drove the hearse.

Six members of Sam's Sunday school class waited at the bottom of the church steps. As the hearse came to a stop they moved forward to take their positions. Mr. Miller ushered the family up to the narthex while the attendants led the pallbearers up the steps with the casket. The organist began playing *"Going Home"* as the procession made its way down the aisle to the catafalque below the altar. The family followed and took their seats in the two reserved front rows. As she made her way down the aisle, Minnie was pleased to see that every pew was filled and that several people were standing in the rear. The Palmer family was represented as well as the Hitchcocks. Tommy, Jr. sat in the choir loft. All the sanctuary seats were taken when he entered.

Floral offerings filled the area below the altar on either side of the catafalque. Blankets of red gladiolus flowers cascaded over the altar rail. Minnie was overcome with gratitude for the outpouring of love represented by the flowers. She knew that Sam was beloved in the Aiken black community but she never knew it was to this degree. That recognition made it all the more meaningful that his entire family was there.

Alex and George sat on the aisle of the right front pew with Minnie in between. Ben, the girls and the children came next with Lester and Jonah at the far end. Alex made sure that he kept George in tow and away from Jonah. Two of Sam's brothers from New Orleans, along with a gaggle of cousins and other relatives, occupied the other front pew. A few distant relatives overflowed into the second. Three white-clad nurse-attendants occupied the second pew directly behind the family.

Reverend Pope requested everyone to remain standing as he offered a brief prayer for the soul of Samson Devereux and for God's abiding comfort to the loved ones he left behind.

"Thank you all for the testimony you give by being here to honor the life of Samson Demosthenes Devereux, a good and righteous man. It is at times like this that we realize how brief our temporal life is and how it can be snatched from us in the blink of an eye. Sam knew that, and he lived his life accordingly. Through his faith and through his works he was continually prepared to meet his maker. Today we each need to search our hearts to be sure we can make that same statement.

"Miss Minnie, children, loved ones, this is not a sad day. This ceremony is only a recognition that Brother Sam is now embarking on a greater journey. He now sits in heaven on the right hand of God where he will eternally enjoy the rewards he built up while here on earth. It is a day to celebrate the life that earned those rewards and to praise God for allowing this man to dwell among us for all these years. So together, we celebrate Sam Devereux and rejoice in his life.

"Sister Mary Carthell will now favor us with one of Sam's favorite hymns, *"His Eye is on the Sparrow."*

From the choir loft at the rear, the lyric soprano voice of Mary Carthell flowed down over the audience. When she reached the line *'his eye is on the sparrow and I know he watches me'* audible sobs rose from below. Minnie struggled to remain stoic, rivulets of tears betraying her deep sorrow.

"Thank you Mary," Reverend Pope said. "That song embodies all that Sam believed, and trust me, God's eye is still on the sparrow and he still watches over all of us.

"I will now read a passage from the Old Testament, from the Book of Wisdom, The Songs of Solomon, Chapter 121."

I lift mine eyes unto the hills, from whence cometh my help.

My help cometh from the Lord, which made heaven and earth.

He will not suffer thy foot to be moved: he that keepeth thee will not slumber.

Behold, he that keepeth Israel shall neither slumber nor

sleep.

The Lord is thy keeper: the Lord is thy shade upon thy right hand.

The sun shall not smite thee by day, nor the moon by night.

The Lord shall preserve thee from all evil: he shall preserve thy soul.

The Lord shall preserve thy going out and thy coming in from this time forth, and even evermore.

"Blessed be the name of the Lord."

Looking directly at Minnie, Reverend Pope spoke words of comfort.

"In this time of sorrow and of celebration, always know that the Lord is with you. He walks by your side. He lifts you up when you stumble. He leads you through troubled waters. Jesus said, 'Come unto me ye who labor and are heavy laden and I will give ye rest.'"

Cleo stole a glance in Jonah's direction. He sullenly stared straight ahead, not a shred of compassion evident on his stony face. She prayed that they could get through the entire funeral without any confrontations.

The Reverend Pope sat down as Mary Carthell rose to sing a stirring, heartfelt rendition of *Amazing Grace.* Few dry eyes remained in the Friendship sanctuary when she finished. One of the nurse/attendants reached over to console Phoebe who was sobbing uncontrollably. Lester held her hand while brushing tears from his own eyes.

"Thank you Sister. Yes indeed, God does enfold all of us in His amazing grace. We can rest in the assurance that the grace that saved Brother Sam is available to all who will come unto the Lord and accept him as their Lord and Savior.

"I will now read from the New Testament, the gospel according to John, Jesus' closest and most favored disciple. John heard him utter these words in the flesh as they are recorded in Chapter 14, verses 1-4. The disciples were with Jesus in the Upper Room having observed the Passover meal when Jesus began to speak to them, preparing them for his crucifixion on the morrow."

'Let not your heart be troubled: ye believe in God, believe also in me.

In my father's house are many mansions: If it were not so I would have told you. I go to prepare a place for you.

And if I go and prepare a place for you, I will come again, and receive you unto myself, that where I am, there ye may be also.

And whither I go ye know, and the way ye know.

After all the things Jesus had told them that night the disciples were confused and upset. They sensed the deep sadness of his words but they did not understand their context. They could not see the future as Jesus could. They could not know that he was preparing them for his death the next day on Golgotha, on that old rugged cross.

Thank God for John and the other disciples who remembered and recorded His words that night. Imagine a world in which there was no Gospel, no *Good News*, to tell us of Jesus, and his sacrifice for us. To tell us of His willingness to hang on that cruel cross with blood flowing down his face from the mocking crown of thorns placed on his head by His tormentors. For His willingness to suffer the metal spikes through his hands and feet and the spear thrust into His side.

"Without that sacrifice, Miss Minnie would have no hope of rejoining her beloved Sam in that heavenly choir. How bleak, how dismal, life would be if all we had to look forward to was an eternity of darkness. Thank the Lord that he sent his

Son to suffer the indignities of the cross so that we can have everlasting life. As we leave this sanctuary today, I ask you to reflect on what Christ did for you. Go forth from this place renewed in His spirit and dedicated to living your life in His image. Go forth with the renewed promise that rang out in that Upper Room, 'I go to prepare a place for you.' Sam now dwells in the glorious mansion prepared for him. Go forth from here and lift your eyes unto the heavens. Seek ye your own mansion. Let us pray.

"Oh God, giver of life and sustainer of spirit, grant us Your benediction as we leave this place of worship. Remind us of our duty to love one another and to live our lives in such a manner that we will store up treasures in heaven. Bless Sister Minnie and her family. Give them peace. Bless this congregation as we mourn the departure of a faithful and beloved member, Samuel Demosthenes Devereux. All praise be to You and Your Son, Jesus Christ. Amen."

The comforting lyrics of *Just a Closer Walk with Thee* wafted gently down from the choir loft as the family followed Sam up the aisle for one last time. The hope implicit in the final stanza swept over Minnie — in reassurance and consolation.

> *When my feeble life is o'er,*
> *Time will be no more,*
> *Guide me, gently o'er*
> *To Thy kingdom's shore, to Thy shore*

The tears were gone now, in their place the slightest hint of a smile, as she silently visualized Sam standing on that distant shore, waiting for her.

16

The Burial

Alex once again made sure that George and Jonah got into different cars for the journey to the cemetery. As he reached for the door to the lead limousine, there was a touch on his shoulder. He turned to see Tommy Hitchcock.

"Alex, I won't be coming to the cemetery with you. That's a private time for you and your family. Just know that my thoughts and prayers are with you now and as you begin your legal career. I know you will do well, and remember what I said — call me anytime. Give this to Minnie for me when you get home," he said, handing Alex a sealed envelope. "Bye, Alex, take care of yourself."

Young Hitchcock drifted back into the crowd swirling around the funeral cortege and made his way to the little sports car parked down Richland. Alex stuffed the envelope into his inside coat pocket and climbed in next to his mother.

The procession wound slowly through the streets of north Aiken, arriving at Pinecrest Cemetery shortly after three. The hearse led the funeral parade under the arch and through the gate on Florence Street. Two massive deodar cedars spread their evergreen arms, offering their silent blessing to the solemn occasion. The cortege came to a stop just yards beyond. A few steps off the divided path through the cemetery stood a green and white canopy. Green tarpaulins covered a mound of freshly unearthed Carolina red clay. Twenty folding chairs were aligned under the canopy, facing the gravesite, awaiting the mourners.

Reverend Pope assisted Minnie from her car and walked her over to the middle chair in the front row. The children followed. Alex, Ben, George, Cleo, Phoebe and the Page children took seats on both sides of Minnie. Lester and Jonah overflowed to the second row with the other relatives.

The sprays of gladiolus were draped over the twin headstones. The flower van had pulled around behind the mound of clay and the attendants hurriedly arrayed the floral tributes around the grave. The pallbearers removed Sam's casket from the hearse and gently sat it on the frame spanning the yawning grave. Reverend Pope indicated for everyone to be seated.

"We are gathered here on God's bright, sunshine filled day under His bright, blue heaven to commit the earthly remains of our dearly departed brother to the earth from which God molded him. However, this earthly vessel before us was only a repository for the soul of this beloved man. That soul has now departed and resides in heaven. This earthly repository has served its purpose. We now return Sam's ashes to ashes and his dust to dust. As Shakespeare's Hamlet said in his famous soliloquy, 'Sam has shuffled off this mortal coil,' for he has no more use for it. However, the vessel remains behind to remind us of Sam and the life he lived. This will be a place to come, to visit, to reflect on his life. This will not be a sad place but a place to rejoice in Jesus' promise of life everlasting, a place to commemorate Sam's life and to rededicate our own.

"Whenever we come to walk these hallowed grounds we will be reminded of the life Sam Devereux lived. We will look around at all the other departed saints and say 'This is a good place. This is God's place.' We shall rejoice in the knowledge that the souls of all these empty vessels now dwell on the right hand of God. We can look forward to that glorious day when we too 'shuffle off our mortal coil' and go to join the saints in heaven. Shall we pray?

"Our Lord and Father, Redeemer of our souls, the Alpha and the Omega of all life. Grant this family peace and comfort. Be with them in their goings out and their comings in that they shall dwell forever in the house of the Lord. Protect all who gather here. Pour out Your tender mercies upon them. Accept our beloved Sam into the company of Your angels. We ask this in the name of Your Son, Jesus Christ, amen."

"Now Mr. Miller if you will please commit Sam to the earth from which he came."

The funeral director led his assistants in lowering the casket into the grave, pulling the straps from underneath it when it had found purchase at the bottom. He removed the catafalque frame that had held Sam's casket.

"Miss Minnie," Reverend Pope said, "will you please come forward to initiate the final rites?"

With Alex and Ben on either arm, Minnie arose and walked over to the graveside. She took the small shovelful of dirt proffered to her by an attendant and let it slide into the open grave. The sound of red clay hitting the wooden casket released the pent up pool of Minnie's tears. She sagged into the arms of her sons who helped her back to her seat. Two white clad figures materialized from behind the tent and ministered to their bereaved sister.

Minnie regained her composure as the rest of the family came forward to pay their final respects to their patriarch. All but Jonah, who had slipped away from the group and was smoking a cigarette behind one of the deodars.

Now all the other mourners came forward to honor Sam. A knot of well-wishers gathered around the family, shaking hands and offering condolences. Ben stood at the edge of the crowd. A movement across the path from the cortege caught his eye. He recognized Simon Pettigrew.

17

Quincy, Redux

Simon motioned for him to come over. Ben looked around to ensure no one saw him. He started toward Simon as he slipped behind one of the massive live oak trees dotting the cemetery.

"What are you doing here, Simon! If Alex sees you there'll be hell to pay."

"Didn't nobody see me Ben. I was careful. I came to tell you 'bout Quincy."

"What about him? I slipped off to see him two days ago and he was doin' fine."

"Well he ain't no mo. I seen him dis mawnin' and the nurse say he ain't gonna make it. He said he wanted to see you befo' he goes. I tol' him I'd try to let you know."

"Thank you, Simon. I'll try to sneak away and git over there tonight. He in a lot o pain?"

"Naw, they got him all doped up. He kinda go in an out when you is talkin' to'im. If you sees 'im, let me know. I gonna be at *The Black Cat* late tonight."

"I will if I can. We hafta be careful."

"All right then. I done what Quincy asked me. I's goin' now. I gonna wait til you gits back over to the crowd. If anybody asks jest tell'em you was takin' a leak."

"Thanks, Simon. See you later."

Ben hurried back to the tent. The crowd had begun to disperse. No one seemed to have missed him. He let out a sigh of relief. It was premature.

"Where have you been?" Alex demanded as he walked up from behind. "We are about ready to head back to Miller's."

"I just needed to relieve myself. I went behind that big old oak tree over there."

"Okay, let's get the family into the cars now. Have you seen Jonah? Keep him away from George."

"He left while we were at the grave side. I seen him takin' a smoke down by them cedar trees."

The funeral party bundled back into the limousines for the ride back to Miller's chapel. A few attendees who had carpooled over to Pinecrest were reclaiming their nearby cars and buggies for the trip home.

"Miss Minnie," said Clarice Stallings, the church secretary, "I want you to know you can call on me anytime if you need a hand. We loved Mr. Sam. It ain't gone be the same without him. I don't know who gone take care of that old cantankerous boiler downstairs. He the only one who knowed how to make it work. I guess maybe Ben can do it. He pretty handy with tools and such. You take care now. We'll see you at church."

"Bye, Clarice. Thank you for all the kind words. You come a callin' any time. I can sho use the company now with Sam gone. I'll talk to Ben 'bout the boiler."

The long day was over at last. Cleo and Jonah had packed the two sleepy kids back into the car and headed for home. Phoebe and Lester had a bite to eat with the boys and left. Finally, it was time for George and Mary to leave.

"George, it was a blessin' you comin'to yo daddy's funeral. I's glad we got through it without no blowups. You be careful drivin' back to North Augusta. Ain't no tellin' what's goin' on in the Valley on Saturday night.

"Mary, thank you for gittin'im here. Come back to see us now, you hear. I'm glad somebody is lookin' out for my boy. You seems like sech a sweet girl. You gotta be careful, bein' white like you is. They's lotsa crazy white folks 'round these parts what don't cotton to whites and blacks mixin' and they ain't gone ask what color you is fo they hurts you. I reckon I be preachin' to the choir. You been round long 'nough to know what goin' on. Jest you take care."

"Thank you, Miss Minnie. I'm very fond of George. I'll see to it that nothing bad happens to him. It was a great pleasure meeting all of you under such trying circumstances. I wish I had known Mr. Sam. He must have been a fine man. George won't admit it but he thought the sun rose and set with his father. It's unfortunate that things got crossways between them. Thank goodness that's all over now."

Alex listened to the conversation from his perch on the back porch swing. Despite Mary's optimism, he harbored serious doubts about it being all over. Jonah's actions of the day did not bode well for the future. He only hoped Cleo could keep her husband under control.

George and Mary waited until it was dark before braving the passage home through the Valley. Minnie gave Mary one of her shawls,

"Drape this over your head," she said. "It might help. Won't do no harm."

"Can you drop me up by Gaston's on the way out," Ben asked George. "I told Mr. Sims I'd check on the horses tonight."

"Sure thing Ben, hop in."

The old Reo sedan sputtered and spewed black smoke as it chugged up the street.

"George," Ben said as they approached Park Avenue, "I

jest 'membered I'm s'posed to pick up sumpin' in the Alley for Mr. Sims. Jest drop me off downtown. I'll walk on back to Gaston's."

Ben watched as George's borrowed car hiccupped, emitting a cloud of dense blue smoke before it headed west on Richland. When it was out of sight, he struck out on foot for the hospital.

The nursing night shift for the critical patients ward had just changed. Two of the nurses met him coming down the stairs. The duty nurse was engrossed in several patient's charts as he approached her desk. She looked up as he approached.

"I'm a friend of Quincy Patterson. I was with him when Doc Johnson cut off his leg. Hear tell he ain't doin' so good."

"You heard correctly," the matronly nurse said, looking imperiously down at Ben over the half-glasses sitting on the tip of her nose. "His infection had spread beyond the lower extremities before the amputation took place. He's in and out of consciousness now and the drugs don't seem to be having much effect. I'm afraid the doctors have done all they can. He's in the hands of the Lord now."

"Can I see him?' Ben asked.

"We're not supposed to allow any visitors, especially this late, but since it won't make any difference considering his prognosis, I guess it won't matter. You can go in for a few minutes. I will need your name for the records."

"I'm Benjamin Devereux."

"Was it your father they buried today?"

"Yes ma'am."

"I'm sorry for your loss. Losing your dad and your friend at the same time must be kind of hard."

"Yes, ma'am, it sho is."

"You can go on in now, but limit your visit to five minutes please. He's down the hall in the Negro section at the back, room 222."

"Yes ma'am, I jest wants to say goodbye befo he gone."

Ben tentatively pushed on the door to room 222. The same putrid stench that had filled the bedroom on Ravenel assaulted his nostrils. He forced himself to approach the bed. Quincy was asleep, obviously in a narcotic haze. His bedclothes were soaked through with both his sweat and his blood. Ben touched him on the arm. A slow moan gurgled up from deep inside Quincy's chest.

"Quin, it me, Ben."

Quincy slowly turned his head toward the voice, struggling to open his eyes. In his morphine-induced state, he had difficulty recognizing Ben's face. The fog slowly lifted. His eyes opened wider. Ben's face came into focus.

"That you Ben."

"Yeah Quin, it me."

"I done 'bout give up on seein' you again," rasped Quincy, his voice cracking. "I reckon the nurse done tol' you."

"Yeah. She say they done 'bout all they can do. Simon, he come by the cemetery durin' the funeral for Pa. He say you ain't gonna make it and that you wanted to see me."

"Ben, I ain't wantin' to go 'thout sayin' how much I 'preciate you bein' a friend to me. They ain't been nobody in my life like you been. You done been a friend when I ain't had none. I jest wanted to tell you to keep on goin'. You a good man. You gone be all right. Alex gone understand me and you and how you come along when I needed a friend, after Simon done treated me so bad."

Ben leaned over, put his arms under Quincy's shoulders, and lifted him. He embraced his friend. A torrent of bitter tears cascaded onto the sweat-soaked gown. He released Quincy gently onto his pillow, his salty tears mingling with the perspiration on Quincy's face. There was a knock on the door. Ben jumped back, expecting the door to open.

"Ben your five minutes are up." The nurse's voice filtered

through the door. "You'll have to leave now."

"Yes ma'am. I'll be out directly."

Ben squeezed Quincy's hand and turned to leave. Quin held it tight.

"Jest remember Ben, I gone be waitin' for you. Say bye to everbody for me."

"I'll never forget you Quin. Dyin' ain't gone change that none."

Quincy released Ben's hand. Ben moved reluctantly toward the door, never taking his eyes off Quincy. The last memory he had of his friend was the broad smile and the river of tears.

Ben leaned against the wall in the corridor. He took a few seconds to gain control of his emotions before he walked back down the hall past the nurse's station.

"Goodnight Ben. I'm sorry about your friend. Do you wish to be notified when he passes?"

"No ma'am. His friend, Simon Pettigrew, say he gone let me know."

"Very well, then. Good night."

"Good night, ma'am. I thank you for lettin' me see 'im"

"You're quite welcome. Be careful going home. It's mighty dark outside."

It was nearing eleven when Ben got back to Charleston Street. He took his shoes off and stealthily entered the house. He was almost to the bedroom hallway when a voice from the darkened parlor spoke.

"It's mighty late to be tending to horses Ben."

"Alex! What you doin' up? You nearly scared me to death."

"I'm just curious as to what needs doing at a livery stable at this time of night."

"I told you. Mr. Sims asked me to check on them new horses what come in today."

"Ben why do you feel you have to lie to me?"

"What you mean!" Ben said fierily.

"I walked over to the stables after you left. There was no one there."

"I forgot I had to pick up sumpin' for Mr. Sims in the Alley. I asked George to drop me off downtown."

"Ben, I can't imagine there was anyone working in the Alley stables after nine. I stayed at Gaston's for over an hour. You never showed up. Were you at *The Black Cat?*"

"Naw, Alex, I swear I won't!"

"Go on to bed Ben," an exasperated Alex said, "we'll finish this in the morning."

Alex slept later than he had planned. Minnie was already washing the dishes from Ben's breakfast.

"Sorry I overslept Mama. Yesterday plumb wore me out."

"Me too Alex."

"Has Ben already gone to work?"

"I reckon he left 'bout twenty minutes ago.

"What time you boys go to bed last night?" Minnie asked. "I thought I done heard voices bout midnight." "Ben got back late from Gaston's and we were just talking about Pa and the funeral. It hit Ben pretty hard."

"It done hit us all hard. I finds myself startin' to call out to Sam and then I know he ain't there no more. I jest cain't get used to it. It gone take me a while I reckon."

"It's going to take us all a long time Mama. Things will settle down after a while. What are you going to do now that you don't have to take care of Pa? You think you'll want to go back to work? You're still pretty young."

"I don't know son. I ain't give no thought to it. I been so busy with Sam. I could sho use the money, what with all the expenses lately. That $250 for the funeral gone pretty nigh use up our savings."

"That reminds me," Alex said, springing from his chair,

"I'll be right back."

He ran to his bedroom and opened the chifforobe where his suit was hanging. He retrieved the envelope that Tommy Hitchcock gave him after the funeral and took it back to the kitchen.

"Here Mama," Mr. Tommy handed this to me outside the church and asked me to give it to you. It's probably a letter of condolence from his parents."

Minnie took the letter and carefully slipped the edge of a paring knife under its flap, slicing it open. It was a letter from Miss Lulie — but there was more. A small piece of paper fluttered to the floor as she unfolded the pages.

"Here Alex, read it to me. I don't see so good no more."

She handed the letter to Alex as he was reaching to retrieve the paper that had fallen. He put the slip of paper on the table and began to read.

> *"Dear Mrs. Devereux,*
>
> *I know how devastated you all must be over Samson's death. I remember all his kindnesses during his tenure with Tante Celestine. He was always there to help when we needed someone, as were you. Our thoughts and prayers are with you during this trying time.*
>
> *Tommy told me he saw Alexander. He said that he looked wonderful and had finished his studies at Howard University. I know my aunt would be so proud. It was her dream that Alex come back to Aiken to practice law.*
>
> *I know that Tante left some money for you, but these last few months must have been a real financial burden. I hope the enclosed will help to defray your expenses and cover some of Alex's costs as he embarks on his legal career.*
>
> *With kindest regards,*
> *Louise Hitchcock"*

Alex picked up the piece of paper from the table.

"Ma, it's a check for $500!" he exclaimed.

Minnie grabbed her apron and covered her face as she burst into tears.

"Ain't nobody in this whole wide world been so good to us as Miss Lulie and Miss Celestine," Minnie blubbered through several eye-wipings and nose-blowings. "Thank the Lord. We gone be able to pay all them debts and have some money left over. Halleleujah! The Lord, He done blessed us for sure."

"That's great Mama. If anybody in this world deserves it, it's you."

"Oh Alex, this takes sech a load off my mind. You gone be able to use this money to pay Mr. Poole some of his expenses. Maybe it gonna help you git them papers sooner."

"Thank you Ma. I'll be going in to his offices next week. He wants to help me get up to speed on South Carolina law. It differs in so many respects when compared with other state laws. I've been trying to read those legal articles he gave me, but I've still got a lot to learn."

Ben returned from work late that Sunday afternoon. Alex was waiting for him on the front porch. Ben avoided his eyes and headed inside.

"Ben," Alex said calmly, "we have some unfinished business. Come sit with me under the pecan tree."

"Alex, I don't wanna talk about it no more. Sides, it ain't none of your business where I was or what I done last night."

"I beg to differ with you Ben. Anything that affects Ma and the family is my business, and I think whatever was going on last night falls into that category."

"Why you using all them big words and high-falutin' talk? You acts like you's better'n us now you done got all that book learning."

"Don't change the subject Ben. We're going to talk about this whether you want to or not. Now come on."

Alex settled into the rickety Adirondack chair by the tree. Ben sat on the old nail keg his father had brought home from *The Cove.* He looked as if he would rather be anywhere else in the world right now than here with his brother.

"Okay Ben," Alex began, "I know you weren't at Gaston's and you swear you were not at *The Black Cat,* so where were you for over two hours."

"If you must know, I went to the hospital to see Quincy."

"Why last night Ben?"

"You remember when you won't able to find me at the funeral?"

"Yeah?"

"Well, Simon Pettigrew done sneaked into the cemetery. He waved to me. He was hidin' behind one of them big ol' oak trees. He waved to me to come over there. He say Quincy in real bad shape and he bout to die. He say Quincy wants me to come to see'im in the hospital. I knowed you'd be mad if I went, so I sneaked off."

"Oh Ben, if you'd just be honest with me. I know Quincy's your friend. I would have told you to go. I have to ask you again, was there more to your friendship than you're telling me."

"No, Alex. I know what you been thinking. It won't like that. Quin needed a friend at a bad time in his life. I felt sorry for him, but I didn't never do nothin' with him and that's the truth. I jest happened to be round when he needed somebody. If that's a sin then I don't know sinnin'."

"Look, Ben, tomorrow's Monday. I want you to go over to Friendship and talk to Mr. Pope. Maybe he can help you to sort out your feelings. If you don't, sooner or later you might give in to the temptations. Then it's all going to come out into the open and there'll be all hell to pay. You know it'd kill Ma. She's already half-crazy with Pa dying. This would just drive her over the edge. Will you do that Ben?"

"All right Alex. I'll go by on the way to Gaston's. I'm sorry I lied to you. It been botherin' me ever since I done it."

"Do you want me to go with you?"

"Naw, I spec it better if I go by myself."

18

The Intervention

Ben arose earlier than usual that Monday and slipped out of the house before anyone else woke. He went by Friendship and asked Miss Clarice if he could see Reverend Pope at noon. Then he went straight to Gaston's to get his chores done early. He was going to ask Mr. Sims for an hour off before noon.

"You're in mighty early Ben," his boss said as he entered the double doors to the carriage lift.

Ben looked up from his kneeling position at the foot of the huge timbers supporting the lift. He was squirting oil onto the mechanism that allowed the iron counterweights to raise and lower the heavy lift and its cargo.

"Yassuh. I knowed I needed to git all my work done early. I need to ask you if I can git an hour off fore dinner. I needs to git sumpin' for Ma over to the shoe shop on York Street."

"I guess, seeing how you've got everything under control. There's not a whole lot going on this morning anyway. You need to be back before two. We've got to get a bunch of those polo ponies over to the depot and load 'em up for their trip back to New York."

"Yassuh. I'll be back in time for that. Thank you, suh."

Ben bustled around to finish feeding and grooming the horses. He moved two of the carriages used during the polo meet into storage on the second floor. He oiled the tack used the day before and hung it on the appropriate pegs by the stalls. When Sims left for the Alley, Ben headed toward Friendship.

"Come in Ben, I've been expecting you," Dr. Pope said in answer to the soft knock on his office door. "Clarice said you came by this morning that you wanted to see me."

"Yassuh. Alex says he spoke to you bout me."

"He did, Ben and I think it shows a great deal of love for you that Alex would do that. Come on in and have a seat. Clarice is whipping up some dinner for me in the kitchen. I told her to make enough for you."

Thank you, suh."

"Alex didn't say what it was you needed to discuss with me but he did say you had been frequenting *The Black Cat* recently so I have some idea what it's about. I'm quite familiar with the type of clientele that place attracts. It doesn't have a great reputation. How is it you came to start going there?"

"Well, when Pa got real sick and started staying home, I jest couldn't take it. Pretty soon he jest be laying there moanin' and sleepin'. Ma had to look after him all the time and I jest wanted to git away from it. One of the men who worked at the Gaston told me 'bout it and I jest went over there one Saturday night."

"Did you have any idea what went on there?"

"Naw suh! I jest thought it was a bar and pool hall where folks went to have fun."

"Didn't you notice that only men came in there, no women. Were you aware at the time of such a thing as homosexuals?"

"Naw suh. I ain't heard that word til Alex tell it to me."

"Didn't you find it strange that all the men seemed to pair up and go off together?"

"Yassuh, but I met this boy name Quincy and we kinda hit it off. He was there with a boy named Simon. He said him and Simon had been together lak that. I asked him what that meant and he said, 'you know, we does it together.' "

"Do what I said, and he said, 'we sleep together.'"

"What was your reaction to that?"

"It kind of scared me. I said I ain't never heard of that before and Quincy said they's a lot of queers in Aiken. He say thats what they calls folks like him — queers. I started to leave and Quin grabbed my arm and said to stick around for the show. 'What show I said'?"

"Bout midnight some of the "girls" dresses up and puts on a show."

"What girls?" I said. "They ain't no girls in here."

"Jest wait," he said. "You'll see."

It was after eleven, so I decided to stay round. Well by twelve everbody was pretty likkered up. The door to the toilets in back busted open an' these men dressed up like women comes out and starts a shimmyin' an a shakin'. They comes out into crowd and starts kissin' and foolin' round. I ain't never seen sech. I told Quincy I had to git home and I left. He come by the stables that week and asked me to come back on Saturday. He said he done broke up with his man Simon and he jest needed a friend. I won't gone do it til Saturday, bout three. Pa was in a bad way and Ma said I oughta go out. Won't no place for me to go, so I went back to the *Cat.*"

"Did you understand what was going on when you went back?"

"Yas suh, I kinda asked round the stable bout sech things. One a the older grooms what come by from *Nandina,* he take me outside and tell me all 'bout queers and sech. He said he been up to New York wit Mr. Baltazzi. Him and some others would go to black night clubs what had bunches of queers hangin' round. He asked me why I wanted to know. I told him 'bout the *Black Cat* and he said, 'Boy you best stay way from that place before you gits your head bashed in. They been some bad things happen round there."

"Wasn't that enough to discourage you from going back?"

"It shoulda been but I got curiouser and curiouser 'bout whaut was goin' on and they won't no other place to go so I jest went back. I reckoned I's big enough to take care of myself if one of them "girls" starts messin' round."

"What happened then?"

"Me'n Quin jest got along like regular friends. Didn't nobody mess with us when we's together. "

"Did he make advances on you?"

"They was a coupla times when he got a little feisty and I say 'Quin, I ain't like that' an he left me alone. They a couple others tried to git me to do it but I run 'em off."

"Why do you think Quincy kept on with you?"

"He jest lonely. Him and Simon done broke up. I think Quin was wondrin' bout what he was doin' and was jest lookin' to git out. He jest needed friends to help him out. I kinda felt sorry for him."

"When was this?"

"Bout two months ago."

"How many more times did you go there to see Quincy?"

"Four, maybe five times."

"And what was Quincy's response?"

"Lak I say, he done broke up with Simon and I don't think he had nobody else."

"Alex told me about Quincy getting tetanus and losing his leg. He says you went to see him in the hospital."

"Yas suh. See, me'n Quin was good friends no matter whut he done. I owed it to him to go. He'd a done it for me. I seen him Saturday night, jest fo he passed away. I'm goin' to his funeral next Saturday."

Dr. Pope leaned back in his swivel chair and smiled.

"You're a good man Ben Devereux. We can all love the lovable. It's more difficult to love the fallen. Christ gave us examples of agape love. His parables about the beggar, the blind man, the leper and the prostitute were meant to guide our approach to people who are hurting or down on their luck. I can't fault you for what you did, but I need to know if you are through with that life now."

"Yas suh, now that Quin done gone, they ain't no use in me goin' round the *Cat* no more. It ain't no place fo me."

"Good, Ben. Let's see what Clarice has whipped up for us so you can get back to work. He led Ben into the church kitchen. After two helpings of pork chops and mashed potatoes, the reverend pushed back from the table.

"Ben, Clarice tells me you used to help Samson around the church. She also says you used to sing in the choir."

"Yas suh, I did."

"It would be good to have you back up there on Sunday mornings. And, we could sure use some handyman help around the church. Think about it. If you agree, I'll ask the deacons if we can spare a little change for you. You could come by on weekends or after work."

"Yas suh, I will. That sounds real good," he said.

Ben's step returning to Gaston was considerably lighter than when he left.

"Did you see Reverend Pope today?" Alex asked Ben as he plopped down in the back porch swing.

"Yeah, I did."

"And?"

"We done got it all worked out. I ain't gone go back to the *Cat* no mo and he asked me to come back to sing in the choir. He said they'd pay me some to help out round the church when things need fixin'.

"That's great Ben. I'm glad it's settled. From what you told me Quincy just got into a situation he didn't understand. I imagine that Simon character could be very persuasive. I'm sorry you lost your friend, but I'm glad that affair is all over."

"Me too, Alex, me too."

19

Mr. Poole

It seemed impossible that only a week had passed since Alex first visited the offices of Esquire Frampton Poole. The cascading series of events — Sam's death, the trip to see George, the shooting, Quincy, the funeral, Ben, — all ran together in his thoughts as he dodged the piles of debris still littering the roadsides. He clutched the papers Mr. Poole had given him on that first visit. Papers he had pored over at every opportunity. The list of questions they raised filled several sheets of a legal pad.

"Good morning Miss Rhodes," Alex said, bracing himself for an icy blast in return. She greeted him instead with an almost beatific smile as she walked around her desk to welcome him.

"Good morning Alex. How nice to see you again. Mr. Poole asked me to bring you in as soon as you arrived."

Alex couldn't know what had transpired in the conversation between Mr. Poole and Miss Rhodes after he left, but whatever it was he certainly welcomed the change in her attitude. The knot in his stomach that started forming the night before began to relax.

"Young Alex Devereux is here Mr. Poole," Ida said as she pushed the office door open.

"Wonderful. Thank you Miss Rhodes. Come in Alex. Have

a seat.”

"Can I get you something to drink?” she asked.

“No ma’am. Thank you. I already had too much coffee at breakfast.”

“All right then. I’ll leave you gentlemen to your business.”

The look on Alex’s face amused Mr. Poole.

“Alex you look puzzled.”

“A little,” Alex confessed. “I’ve been dreading coming back. Miss Rhodes was so intimidating last week. I don’t know what you said to her but I sure appreciate it.”

“I just told her that you are now a lawyer just like I am and that you should be accorded the courtesies befitting your position. I told her you would be working here and that she needed to establish a good working relationship with you. I also filled her in on some of the details about the relationship you had with Miss Eustis. It was that last part that won the day. Ida idolized Miss Eustis. I think she concluded that if Miss Eustis put that much stock in you then you had to be all right, no matter the color of your skin.”

“Thank you sir, that will certainly make it easier for me to work here,” Alex said as he handed the sheaf of papers to Mr. Poole.

“I brought back all the papers you gave me. I studied them as much as I could during the past week, but there was so much going on I probably didn’t absorb many of the details.”

“That’s all right Alex, there’s a lot of meat in there. Was there any particular treatise that got your attention?”

“Yes sir, the article on the effect of poll taxes on minority voting. I hadn’t paid much attention to voting before, but it struck me that the poll tax was one of many tools used to discourage minorities from voting. My mama said she and Pa never voted. First of all, she said they couldn’t afford the tax and those who did vote often lost their jobs. I suspect that if you check the voting records you won't find many votes cast by minorities."

"I'm sure you're right. Most of those barriers were erected after Reconstruction when the white ruling class realized that freed blacks outnumbered the whites in the state, and that if they became organized they could take over the government. The Carpetbaggers had taken advantage of their power after the war to install illiterate blacks into various government positions and then proceeded to manipulate them for their own personal gain. When Reconstruction ended, those puppet blacks were thrown out of office and replaced with whites. Many of them feared persecution and moved north."

"The poll tax is still in effect in South Carolina," Alex said. "That's one of the things I'd like to see changed."

Mr. Poole leaned back in his swivel chair and steepled his fingers. He gazed at Alex with an unyielding look.

"You'd best be careful Alex. Some of your people have protested against the tax and were then hassled by white supremacist groups like the KKK. However, there's a new organization that was formed a few years ago in Aiken called the National Association for the Advancement of Colored People. You might want to look at working through them to avoid being singled out."

"Speaking of that," said Alex, "there's something else I wanted to ask you about."

"What is it Alex."

"When I was on the way home from your office the other day, I ran into my brother Ben. We walked on home together. He asked me how things were going with the bar exam and I told him what you had said about being careful. He got this strange look in his eye and he said I had to watch out. I asked what he meant, then he told me about how the sheriff was shot and how three young coloreds were dragged out of jail and lynched for it. I hadn't read anything about it in the Washington papers and Mama didn't write about it. What really happened?"

Frampton Poole's face turned ashen, as if a ghost had entered the room.

"Alex, that's one of the saddest episodes in Aiken County's history. I didn't want to get into it knowing how concerned we both are about the exam."

"What do you mean? What does the bar exam have to do with that?"

"When the three children were first brought to trial, the judge asked me if I would represent the girl since she couldn't afford a lawyer. I said I would. There was very little time before the trial because the whole town's blood was up and they wanted to see the sheriff's killers tried and executed. Revenge was more on the mind of most people than justice was. The facts in the case were so muddled and confusing that I petitioned the judge for a stay until I could do a proper investigation and trial preparation. He informed me that he was powerless to intervene, there were too many influential interests pressuring him for a speedy trial, not only in Aiken but from Columbia as well.

"Because of my petition, word went around that I was favoring the "niggers" and then there were threats on my life. I got telephone calls in the middle of the night, scaring my family to death. I went ahead as best I could, but the lack of all the facts and the rampant bloodlust were more than I could overcome. All three were found guilty—in less than an hour. I was able to convince the judge to spare the girl's life; both the boys were sentenced to the chair.

"I was back in court a year later when the South Carolina Supreme Court reviewed the case and ordered a new trial. They brought the defendants back to Aiken and the new judge immediately vacated Demon Leeman's conviction and ordered a new jury impaneled for the daughter and nephew. As soon as word got out, the whole town was up in arms. The new sheriff re-arrested Demon on some bogus charge and threw him back in jail.

"I had some former clients in the Valley that I had gotten off on liquor running charges. One in particular hadn't been able to pay me all his fees. He called me up and said he had some information I would like to have. I asked him 'What information?' and he said he'd give it to me if I'd forgive the remainder of his debt. It wasn't a large amount so I said I would. He said 'Mr. Poole, they's gonna be a lynchin' tonight.' I asked him how he knew, but he wouldn't tell me. I went to the lawyer that was representing the boys and told him. He just brushed it off and said there was no truth to it. Then I called the sheriff, and he told me to mind my own business, that he was in charge at the jail and no lynching was going to take place on his watch.

"God help me Alex, I just let it go, and three people died a horrible death that night. I don't know what more I could have done to stop it. By the time someone called me early that morning, it was too late. When I got to the place they took them, the two boys were already dead and that poor girl was crawling around on the ground with her dress on fire screaming for mercy. Someone stepped out of the crowd and shot the poor thing in the head. Someone was trying to beat out the flames with his hands. That image has haunted me ever since. The smell of burning human flesh is something that never leaves your nostrils.

"There was a state investigation but no one was ever arrested, much less indicted. A reporter from New York claimed he had uncovered the names of 17 perpetrators, but the list was never published. The sheriff and the state authorities ultimately clamped a lid on everything and to this date, no one has been implicated or punished for such a monstrous miscarriage of justice.

"I not only have to live with what happened out there in those pines, but I have to live with the continuing recriminations from certain citizens of Aiken who resent what I did—and what I tried to do—for the defendants. My law practice has suffered from that."

Alex observed Mr. Poole's mounting agitation and changed the subject.

"I'm sure you did everything that could be expected. Who knows, the real truth may yet come to light.

20

The Bar

"**M**eanwhile, what should I be doing to prepare for the bar exam?"

Light returned to the vacant eyes that had been staring beyond Alex at a remembered horror.

"Oh! I wrote to the Secretary of State and requested the forms we need to fill out and for any other requirements the licensing board may need. I should have his reply within a couple of weeks. You will need to have certified copies of your degree from Howard, and letters of recommendation from two sitting South Carolina lawyers, and a letter from the Aiken police department certifying that you are an upstanding citizen of South Carolina with no criminal record. Of course, mine will be one letter and I'm sure Julian Salley will give you one as well, and the letter from the police is *pro forma* and shouldn't be a problem. Assuming all this comes together, we should be able to submit your application in early September. Barring any hang-ups in Columbia you should be cleared to take the exam in October."

"I'm really looking forward to it. I'd like to get started as soon as possible. I was wondering if your court case been scheduled yet?"

"Yes, as a matter of fact I got the notice from the clerk-of-court this morning. We're scheduled for opening arguments on the fifteenth of September."

Mr. Poole reached behind and took a stack of manila folders from his credenza.

"Here, this is the brief I have prepared for the case. You can't take it home but you can use my conference room to read it over. I'd like to see if you have any questions or suggestions."

"Thank you, I don't need to be home until later today so if you don't mind I'll get started on it now."

"By all means, go ahead. Miss Rhodes will get you pencils and a pad for notes. If you'll leave your questions from the other cases I'll look them over and we can discuss them later."

Alex sat at the far end of the conference table, surrounded by floor-to-ceiling shelves of leather-bound law books. He began to read the brief. As he finished each section, he spread the trial's opening arguments on the table. Page one was a stipulation of the charges. The defendant, Arbutus Jones, was indicted by a grand jury for shooting his neighbor, Malcolm Mitchell, in the entry hall of his home in the Salley community. The state charged that Mr. Mitchell was unarmed and had not threatened Mr. Jones in any way.

Mr. Poole's defense argued that, in fact, Mr. Mitchell had threatened Mr. Jones the previous day for allowing the Jones cattle to roam onto the Mitchell farm and destroy his crops. Mitchell had demanded restitution of fifty-dollars, which my client refused.

Mr. Jones states that he saw Mr. Mitchell drive into his yard early the next morning and exit his pickup truck. He crossed the yard toward his front door with a club of some sort in his hand. When Mr. Mitchell burst through that door, Mr. Jones assumed the worst and fired his shotgun, killing Mr. Mitchell instantly. The sheriff states that he found no weapon of any sort at the scene and declared that Mr. Mitchell was unarmed and therefore posed no serious threat of bodily harm to Mr. Jones, and that the slaying was an extreme overreaction on Mr. Jones's part.

Mr. Poole's counter argument posited that the threats made by Mr. Mitchell the previous day, and the appearance of a weapon in his hand as he exited his truck, was just cause to fire his gun. In addition, Mr. Poole invoked the "man's home is his castle" doctrine. Legal precedents have long established the unassailable right to defend one's home and hearth from intruders.

Furthermore, subsequent searches of the front yard at the Jones house had turned up several items that Mr. Mitchell may have brought with him as a weapon but for some reason decided to drop on his way to the front door.

In any case, according to the Poole brief, there are multiple defenses to invoke justifiable homicide.

Alex continued to plow through the document. The remaining sections simply elaborated on the opening premise and provided numerous legal references that supported the Poole defense.

The case fascinated Alex. This was his first exposure to the real-world legal process, in a trial that held life-and-death implications for the defendant. He felt a certain tingle and a rush of anticipation. The last seven years of his life were preparation for this moment.

Alex pulled a gold watch from his pocket, a gift from his father upon his departure for Howard. He had been engrossed in the brief for hours. He gathered the papers and his notes and returned to Mr. Poole's office.

"I was going to interrupt your assessment of my brief, but you were so engrossed I decided to leave you alone," Mr. Poole said. "What's your opinion?"

"Based on my reading of the law, I believe you have laid out a very valid defense of Mr. Jones. I jotted down a few things where I was not entirely clear on the legal points, but all-in-all I don't see how the prosecution can possibly overcome your arguments."

"Thank you Alex for your vote of confidence, but don't underestimate the abilities of the prosecutors. They have many more resources at their disposal to pursue their position than I do, and believe me they will employ them all. I have received all the bits and pieces of discovery, but old Abner Peabody always has a few tricks up his sleeve. He's been doing this a long time and his record of convictions runs pretty high.

"I briefly read over your observations on the poll tax, and you make some good points. I'm tied up for the balance of today but next time you come in we'll discuss them as well as your notes on the Jones case."

"Thank you Mr. Poole. I'm really enjoying my introduction to the legal system in South Carolina. I can't wait until I can fully participate as a licensed lawyer."

"I admire your enthusiasm Alex." He paused thoughtfully before adding, "I think you'll make a fine lawyer."

"Thank you, sir. I promise I will work as hard as I can to justify your faith in me — and Miss Eustis' as well."

Alex found Ben waiting for him on the porch when he returned home. Ben was beaming from ear to ear.

"What's up Ben? You look like the cat that ate the canary."

"I don't know 'bout that Alex, but Reverend Pope stopped me on the way to work and asked me to look at overhauling the furnace at Friendship. He say it been helt together with bailin' wire for years and did I think I was up to the job?"

"I said 'Sho nuff Reverend. When you wants me to start?' and he say 'Right away.' He gone pay me fifty dollars if I finish it before the first frost. I'm gonna start Saturday. Moses Henry, he the blacksmith over to Gaston, he say he gone help me if I needs some parts made. Ain't that sumpin' Alex?"

"It sure is Ben. Let me know if I can help you. I don't know much about mechanical things but I'll try."

"Thanks Alex. It sho make me feel better 'bout things."

"I'm glad things are looking up for you Ben. Make the most of it."

"I sho plans on it, Alex, I sho do."

"Come on, let's see what surprise Ma has for supper."

Mr. Poole received the necessary forms from Columbia the next week. He filled them out immediately. When he had the letters of recommendation prepared and the police department certification of good character in hand, he sent for Alex to sign the forms. True to his word, he mailed the packet to the South Carolina Secretary of State on September 8. Now they could only wait. Meantime they were a week away from the Jones trial.

The oppressive heat of August relented. The George Funeral Home fans were in less prominence than normal as the jury pool filed in for the selection process. Alex nervously took his seat at the far end of the defendants table. Every eye in the chamber watched as he sat next to Frampton Poole. Most in attendance were not aware of Alex Devereux and his unique position in today's court proceedings. A pronounced buzz flowed through the crowd. Mr. Poole had been careful to apprise Judge Lester Fairbanks of the expected presence of his new protégé. The judge was taken aback initially, but he relented upon hearing the whole story. The crowd settled down and jury selection began.

Each side exercised three peremptory challenges as the

prospective jurors were called to the stand. Four other candidates were found to be related to either the defendant or the victim. As the courthouse clock struck noon the twelve jurors along with two alternates were impaneled. The judge declared a recess for dinner.

"All persons having business before this court in the case of the State versus Arbutus Jones will reconvene here at 1:30 p.m. sharp. Court is recessed."

Mr. Poole walked Alex over to the Willcox Hotel where he ordered a plate lunch for him. The dining room was off-limits to blacks. Alex was served his meal on the back porch of the Willcox residence next door where several black members of the kitchen staff joined him. Alex introduced himself.

"You Samson's boy?" one asked.

"Yes sir, I am."

"I knowed yo daddy. I worked some at the Hitchcock's when they had some big parties. I sho liked Mr. Sam."

"Thank you. That means a lot to me. We're all going to miss him."

"I hear tell you done gone to law school up north."

"Yes sir, I just got back a few weeks ago, just before my father died."

"What you gone do?"

"I've applied for a license to practice law in South Carolina. If I get it, I'll be working with Mr. Frampton Poole. That's why I'm here today. I'm sitting in on one of his cases over at the courthouse. We're on dinner break now."

"Lawsy me," another diner said. "You gone be a lawyer in Aiken. Now don't that beat all."

Alex finished his pork chops and peas then waited for Mr. Poole. The lawyer came out at 1:15 and the two headed back to court.

"Hear ye! Hear ye!" barked the bailiff, "This court is now in session, Judge Lester Fairbanks presiding. All rise.

The judge emerged from the anteroom door behind the bench in his black robe and gaveled the chamber to order.

"You may be seated. Is the prosecution ready for their opening remarks?"

"We are your honor," said Abner Peabody. "It is our aim to prove to the jury assembled that Mr. Arbutus Jones did, with premeditation and malice aforethought, cause the death of Mr. Malcolm Mitchell."

The prosecutor spent the next fifteen minutes summarizing the evidence he planned to present against Mr. Jones and why that evidence would prove his culpability in Mr. Mitchell's death.

"Thank you Mr. Peabody. Mr. Poole, is the defense ready with its opening remarks?"

"We are your honor."

"Please proceed."

Alex sat, his head forward, his eyes closed, listening intently to Mr. Frampton Poole lay out the case for finding Arbutus Jones innocent of murder against Malcolm Mitchell. He ticked off each of the substantive points Alex had read last week in the Poole conference room. He was impressed with his mentor's delivery and the comprehensiveness of his position. His admiration for the man grew with each point presented.

"And that, gentlemen of the jury, is how we plan to refute the claims of my esteemed opponent, Esquire Abner Peabody, and thus prove, without a shadow of a doubt, the innocence of our client, Mr. Arbutus Jones."

He turned to face the bench.

"With your indulgence your honor I would like to introduce the young man sitting at the defense table."

"By all means Mr. Poole, go right ahead."

"Thank you, your honor. For those in the chamber who

knew the late Samson Devereux, this young man is his son Alexander. Alex returned to Aiken just days before his father's death, having completed seven rigorous years at Howard University in Washington D.C. where he received his *Juris* Doctor degree, *summa cum laude*. His education was encouraged and underwritten by the lady deemed founder of the Winter Colony in Aiken, Miss Celestine Eustis. Her only condition was that young Alex Devereux come back to practice law in his hometown. She recognized in him a brilliant mind and a compassionate heart — qualities that she felt were needed by his community in Aiken. She asked me if I would sponsor Alex if he succeeded in achieving this goal. I promised her that I would. Alex has submitted the necessary papers to sit for the South Carolina bar in October. When he successfully completes that task, he will become a member of my firm in accordance with Miss Eustis' wishes. I appeal to the community to welcome him with open arms. Thank you."

Frampton Poole sat down, listening intently for any reaction to his speech. None came. He didn't know whether that was good news or bad — or whether Judge Fairbanks stern countenance forestalled any outburst. Whichever it was, he was pleased that the moment was over. Now his task was to work for Alex's acceptance in both communities — black and white.

The trial was into its second day and the jury seemed swayed by the state's presentation. Alex anxiously searched Mr. Poole's face for any sign of concern.

"It is well past eleven," Judge Fairbanks said glancing at the clock over the jury box. "We will resume deliberations at 12:30. Mr. Poole are you prepared to present your defense?"

"Yes, your honor. The defense is ready."

Poole looked distracted as he walked with Alex to the Commercial Hotel for their noon meal.

"Is there a problem sir?" Alex asked.

"I'm not sure. I feel I can counter every argument the prosecution made but one. I was watching the jury during their presentation on the "phantom" weapon Mr. Jones swore he saw. I thought I could convince them that Mitchell had just thought better of his intentions and dropped it in the yard. Now I'm not sure."

"Sir, if I may, I think I can help you with your argument."

"How's that Alex?"

"I took the liberty of going out to Salley yesterday to see the crime scene for myself. There was no one home so I went up on the porch and looked out over the yard. It faces due east and slopes down to a creek, beyond a large field. You can see the Mitchell house in the distance. Someone sitting at the Jones breakfast table would see a vehicle pulling into the driveway. However, if he got up to go to the door his view would be blocked by the heavy curtains as he passed through the parlor. They were drawn to keep out the morning sun. Mr. Jones testified that he sat down to breakfast at six that morning and that the weather was clear with not a cloud in the sky. He said when he saw Mr. Mitchell drive up and get out of his truck with a club of some sort, he walked through the front parlor and took his shotgun from over the mantel. He would have lost sight of the front yard due to the heavy curtains over the parlor windows. When he stood in that hallway and Mr. Mitchell burst through the door, he was looking directly into the morning sun, which rose at 6:16 on June 21. That means he would have been blinded by the sun and could not see if Mr. Mitchell had a weapon in his hand or not. He would likely assume that if Mr. Mitchell left his pickup with a club in his hand then he still had it."

Frampton Poole stopped in the middle of Chesterfield Street and looked at Alexander Devereux in utter amazement.

"Alex, I can't believe you took the initiative to do that on your own. I am totally flabbergasted. I went out there with the sheriff to survey the scene in mid-July and neither of us ever thought about sun-angles and weather on the day of the shooting. That's amazing. I think you just assured Arbutus Jone's freedom."

"I didn't think much about it until you mentioned the juror's uncertainty about the club. Then it dawned on me that Mr. Jones would have only seen a silhouette of Mr. Mitchell coming through his front door."

"Well, I'm sure glad you did. You're going to make one helluva lawyer young man, with instincts like that. Let's grab a quick sandwich. I want to get back to prepare the argument you just made. I also want to call an associate. I need him to bring over some props."

"Hear ye! Hear ye! All rise. This court is now in session, Judge Lester Fairbanks presiding."

"Please proceed with your defense Mr. Poole," the judge said as he settled in behind the bench.

"Thank you, your honor."

For the next two hours, Frampton Poole elaborated on the points he had raised in his opening remarks. He saved Alex's revelation until the end.

"Gentlemen of the jury, I know some of you may have reservations about how threatening Mr. Mitchell seemed when he barged into the Jones house at 6:20 a.m. on June 21st of this year. Especially since the sheriff has testified that there was no obvious weapon in that front hallway, and despite my client's testimony to the contrary. I repeated the date and time of the shooting for a specific purpose. With the court's indulgence, I will now recreate that most unfortunate encounter when Mr. Mitchell entered the Jone's home."

"What do you have in mind Mr. Poole?" the judge asked.

"It is crucial to my client's case that we know exactly what he saw when Mr. Mitchell came through that door. I believe I can reconstruct a near-facsimile of the scene that will corroborate my client's statements."

"I object," Abner Peabody interrupted, "I don't see the relevance of this charade and besides, the defense has given no prior notice of these shenanigans."

"Mr. Poole, what specifically do you hope to prove by this reenactment?" Judge Fairbanks asked.

"I will demonstrate that Mr. Jones had every reason to believe he was in imminent danger of bodily harm, right up to the moment he pulled the trigger on his shotgun."

"I will allow it Mr. Poole, but I warn you, I will not allow my courtroom to become a sideshow."

"I assure you Judge Fairbanks that what I am about to unveil is very serious. I respect the sanctity of your courtroom and I would never bring dishonor to it.

"Very well then, objection overruled. Proceed Mr. Poole."

The rear doors to the courtroom swung open and John Wiggins, Mr. Poole's investigative associate, trundled a cart down the aisle. It was laden with various pieces of electrical equipment, which he proceeded to unload in front of the jury box. When he had finished assembling the apparatus, a large klieg light on a heavy metal tripod stood fifteen feet in front of the jury box. A heavy electrical cord from the lamp was attached to a battery. Mr. Poole whispered to Mr. Wiggins then turned back to the bench.

"We are ready Judge," Mr. Poole said.

"Go ahead," the judge said tentatively.

"Turn it on John."

An intense light flooded the jury box. The jurors shielded their eyes as the sulfur arc-lamp crackled and hissed. The lawyer then stepped in between the light and the jury and walked toward them. He stopped at the rail.

"You may turn it off now, John."

"My question to the jury is this, What did you see? I contend that all you saw was a silhouette of my body and nothing else. If I was holding anything in my hand, you could not identify it because of the blinding light of a mid-June sunrise. This is exactly what Arbutus Jones saw when his front door burst open — blinding sunlight and the silhouette of Malcolm Mitchell. He had no way of knowing if Mr. Mitchell was brandishing a weapon or not. He testified that he saw a weapon when Mr. Mitchell exited his truck. What happened to it between the truck and the door is a mystery. As far as my client is concerned it still resided in Mr. Mitchell's hand and it represented a mortal threat to him. He shot Malcolm Mitchell in self-defense. End of story. The defense rests your honor."

"Has the jury reached a verdict?"

"We have, your honor."

"How does the jury find?" Judge Fairbanks asked, handing the paper verdict back to the bailiff.

"Not guilty, your honor."

"And do you all so say?" he asked the other eleven.

"We do your honor."

"Mr. Jones, you are free to go. Thank you to the jury for your diligence and respectful deliberation."

With the crack of his gavel on its walnut plate, Judge Fairbanks adjourned the court.

"Frampton, that light thing was a stroke of genius," Abner Peabody said as he stuffed his trial papers into his briefcase. "How did you come up with it?"

"I must confess that I didn't. It was my young colleague

here," he said, nodding toward Alex.

"My goodness," the prosecutor said. "If he's that brilliant now, I just hope I don't come up against him after he's licensed."

"I came up with the theory," Alex said "but it was Mr. Poole who thought of the theatrics. Now that's what I call genius. I believe it was an ancient Chinese philosopher who once said, 'a picture is worth a thousand words.'"

"In any case, you two make a formidable pair. Frampton you had better hang onto Alex lest someone steal him away. Good luck to you boy."

With that Abner Peabody returned to his offices on Fairfield Avenue.

"Alex, it's been a long day. I think I'll head for home and a good, stiff shot of Tennessee sour mash whiskey. I'll be glad to drop you at home. I owe you that much at least."

I'd appreciate that Mr. Poole. I sure did enjoy this experience. It just whets my appetite to get involved."

"You surely understand that not every case that comes down the pike is as exciting as today's. For every one of these, there's a hundred routine, mundane responsibilities you have to attend to. But, I must admit, cases like today's sure do get the old juices flowing."

21

The Barriers

The burgundy LaSalle pulled into the Charleston Street driveway of Minnie Devereux.

"Good-bye Mr. Poole. Thank you for a great experience."

"No, thank you Alex. I haven't relished a trial like this in years. By the way, will you stop by my office on Monday?"

"Yes sir, I will."

Puzzled, Alex walked inside. Minnie was standing behind the parlor curtains, staring out the front window.

"Boy, that's a mighty fine car you jest got out of. Was that Mr. Poole?"

"Yes ma'am. The trial wrapped up this afternoon and he gave me a ride home."

"How'd it go?"

"We won, and the good thing is I helped to win it."

"What you mean?'

"I mean I had an idea that Mr. Poole used to help win acquittal for Mr. Jones."

"Go on! What you do?"

Alex related his inspiration for the sun theory to his mother. He delighted in the newborn respect he saw in her eyes, and for that brief moment, everything was right with the world.

"Come in Alex," Mr. Poole said. "I'm glad you came. Have a seat.

"Mr. Jones came by this morning to pay my fee for representing him. You may not know that he is one of the most successful farmers in Salley, and he was more than willing and able to pay my $1000 fee."

Alex was bowled over at the large amount.

"I can see you're surprised, but when your life is on the line, $1000 can seem insignificant in the overall scheme of things. I wanted you to come by today so that I could give you your share."

"I don't understand."

"I probably would have won the case in any event, but your contribution sealed the deal. Here."

Alex reached across the desk for the piece of paper tendered him.

"One-hundred dollars! Mr. Poole, I can't accept this."

"Sure you can. It's for services rendered. I hope it's the first of many. Welcome aboard."

Alex almost ran into a lamppost as he made his way up Laurens Street. He stared at the check, half expecting it to disappear in a puff of smoke. Finally, convinced that it was real, he stopped by Hahn's and bought a large beef roast—and a box of chocolates for Minnie. He also stopped at the hardware store on Park and bought a set of mechanic's tools for Ben.

The first day of October came and went with no response from the Secretary of State's office concerning Alex's application to take the upcoming bar examination.

"I don't understand it Alex." Mr. Poole said as he hung up the phone after the third attempt to find out what was holding up the application. "That was some low-level functionary. He would only reiterate the same old excuses. He recommended I call the head of the examining board directly. I've tried that and got no response. I get the feeling that we're getting the runaround by someone who doesn't want you to sit for that exam."

"But why?" asked Alex. "Do you think it's because I'm black? There's nothing in the application that applies to race. How would anyone there know I am black?"

"The fact that your diploma comes from Howard University is a dead giveaway. Someone higher up has made sure that the approval is delayed until it's too late for the exam. I have one more contact in Columbia who may be able to help us."

Poole lifted the phone from its cradle.

"Hello, Sam, this is Frampton Poole over in Aiken, how are you doing? Great and how's your family? Good. I know I haven't spoken to you in a while, but there's a delicate situation I need you to look into for me, if you'd be so kind.

"I have a young man in my office who has applied to sit for the bar exam in October and we've been getting the runaround from the Secretary's office. I was wondering if you could nose around to see who's sitting on his application. The applicant is Alexander Devereux. He's a Negro. He graduated from Howard University with highest honors. I can vouch for him without reservation. It would be a travesty if he's denied his license because of his race, and I suspect that's what this is all about. Wonderful, Sam. I surely appreciate that. You can imagine that time is of the essence since the exam is coming up in two weeks.

"Thank you, give my best to Emily and the boys. I look forward to hearing from you soon. Bye-bye."

"Sam won't be able to get back to me for a day or two. Why don't you go on home and I'll come by when I hear something. Now, don't you worry, we'll get to the bottom of this thing."

"Thank you Mr. Poole. It's discouraging to think that there are people high up in our state government still with so much prejudice toward black people. I thought that war was over, but

Jim Crow keeps raising his ugly head."

"I know Alex and I apologize on behalf of my race. It's not fair but it's a fact we have to live with. It seems anything worthwhile in society takes forever to evolve, but evolve it eventually does."

Two days later the burgundy LaSalle pulled in front of the Devereux home. A despondent Frampton Poole emerged with drooped shoulders. He walked slowly up the driveway and knocked on the screen door. Minnie answered.

"Mr. Poole," she said while anxiously twisting her apron, "is they sumpin' wrong?"

"I don't know Minnie. I just heard from my friend in Columbia concerning the bar exam. He had disturbing news. I need to talk to Alex about it."

"He sittin' on da back porch. Come on in. I gone fetch 'im for you."

"Mr. Poole," Alex said as he came down the hall, "Did you hear from your friend in Columbia?"

"I did Alex, and I'm afraid the news isn't good."

"What do you mean?"

"The man holding up your application is an influential member of Governor Richard's administration. He's connected to the late Senator Tillman whose old associates still carry a lot of weight around the capitol. He's a known bigot, in the mold of his former mentor. No one in the administration will buck him. Someone in the secretary's office alerted him to your application. He walked over to the office and put a hold on it. No one has dared to question it, so there it sits. I don't know what to do next."

"What's his name?"

"DeWitt Andrews."

"What does he do for a living?"

"He's president of the Edgefield Bank and Trust."

"I have an idea." Alex said. "May I make a phone call from your office?"

"Certainly, I'll drive us back."

Alex opened his wallet and removed a tattered, yellow scrap of paper.

"Operator, will you please place a call to New York City. The number is Murray Hill 222. Please call Mr. Poole back on this number when you reach the party. Thank you."

"Alex, are you going to tell me what you're up to?"

"When Tommy Hitchcock was at Pa's funeral he said if there was ever anything he could do for me I should call him at this number. I never thought I'd have to use it, but if ever I did, this seems like the time."

The phone jangled in the outer office. Miss Rhodes could be heard answering, her voice audible through the closed door.

"The Poole Law Offices," she said.

Moments later, she popped her head in with a startled look.

"It's Mr. Tommy Hitchcock — from New York."

"Thank you, Miss Rhodes, I'll take it," Mr. Poole said, picking up the phone.

"Mr. Hitchcock, how good of you to return our call so promptly. Alex Devereux is here. He would like to talk to you."

"Tommy, its Alex. How are you? Good. I didn't want to bother you, but you said I could call you if I needed help. Well, I need help."

For the next few minutes, Alex related the entire sorry saga at the licensing office.

"Do you think there's anything you can do? I thought maybe you might have some influence in Columbia. Thank you. That'll be great. I look forward to hearing back from you. By tomorrow! About ten a.m. Wonderful! Good-bye."

"Alex you've got some pretty powerful friends. I hope Mr. Hitchcock can help. I'm afraid Andrews is beyond my reach."

"I know he'll help if at all possible. I'm leaving now, but I'll be back in the morning in time for his call."

"Good afternoon Alex. Let's hope for the best."

Alex sat across from Miss Rhodes desk. He was on tenterhooks, nervously awaiting Tommy's call. He thumbed through a legal magazine, never actually seeing a single word on the page. Finally, the clock over the desk chimed ten just as the phone rang. Alex's nerves were so taut he jumped as if shot.

"Yes sir, I'll let him know right away."

Miss Rhodes scurried to the inner office door, bursting in without a knock.

"It's Mister Hitchcock sir."

"Thank you Miss Rhodes. I'll take it from here. Please send Alex in."

"Mr. Hitchcock, this is Frampton Poole. Thank you for your prompt response. Alex is right here. I'll put him on."

"Good morning Tommy. Yes, they're all fine thank you. Were you able to do anything?" Alex listened intently. "You did! And what did they say. That's wonderful! I don't know how to thank you. Will I see you this fall? Around Thanksgiving. I look forward to it. Maybe I'll have my license by then. Once again, thank you. Good-bye."

Frampton Poole stared at Alex as he dropped the handset into its cradle.

"Well, are you going to tell me?' he asked.

"You're not going to believe this. It turns out the Hitchcock's control a bank in New York that holds a mortgage on the Edgefield Bank and Trust property. It seems the bank took out a loan to expand their business and the loan was later bought by the Hitchcock bank. Tommy had someone from their bank call Mr. Andrews to remind him that they held the note and that it was callable with ninety days notice. He strongly suggested that if my application were not approved immediately the ninety-day clock would start ticking. He was quickly assured that all barriers to my application would be removed immediately."

"I'll be damned," Poole said.

"I guess it's back to the books for me,"Alex said. "The exam is less than three weeks away. The closer it gets the scarier. Do you think there'll be any other problems?"

"I believe Mr. Hitchcock has put the fear of God into Mr. Andrews. You won't hear any more from that quarter. I wouldn't be surprised if he hasn't already instructed the examiners to just stamp your application as approved. No, you have nothing more to worry about on that account."

"Mama," Alex yelled as he entered the kitchen," I've got great news. Mr. Hitchcock was able to get my application approved, and I'll be going to Columbia to take the bar exam on October 15th."

Minnie grabbed Alex. She burst into tears.

"Them Hitchcocks jest keeps on being a blessin' to this family. I want you to write a letter to Mr. Tommy and Miss Louise tellin'em how much we 'preciates all they been doin' for us."

"I will Mama, I will. Is Ben home yet?"

"He say at breakfast he gone stop off at the church on his way home to take a look at that ol' boiler."

"I think I'll walk over there and see how he's doing. We'll be back before dark."

Alex walked in the back door of Friendship to find Miss Clarice Stallings standing at the top of the basement stairs yelling down at Reverend Pope.

"Mr. Pope there's a phone call for you from Reverend Forest over to Second Baptist. He sounded mighty urgent."

The disembodied voice of Reverend Pope floated up from below.

"Tell him I'll be right there as soon as I can wash this soot off my hands."

Clarice saw Alex as she turned to pick up the phone.

"Mr. Alex!" she exclaimed. "You gave me a scare. I didn't hear you come in."

"I'm sorry, Miss Stallings. I just wanted to stop by and see how Ben is doing and see if I might help out."

"You just go on down to the basement. Ben and Mr. Pope are down there messing around with that old boiler."

"Thank you," Alex said, "I'll try to stay out of the way. I don't know a lot about mechanical stuff, but I thought I could offer a little muscle if needed."

"That's mighty kind of you. We can use all the help we can get. I don't want to go through another winter having to wear an overcoat in the office."

Alex met Reverend Pope on the stairwell.

"Hey Alex, it's good to see you. Me'n Ben were just sizing up the problems with that old boiler. Looks like one or more of the valves are sticking. I know I had to come down here last year and bang on them to get it going again."

"I'll just watch over Ben's shoulder," Alex said. "He's the mechanic in the family. You go on up and take that call. We'll talk later."

Ben was up to his waist inside the boiler. A clangorous din poured out the furnace door as Ben hammered on something inside. Alex reached down and touched him to announce his presence. Ben jumped. A sharp cry of pain replaced the banging.

"Who that?"

"It's just me Ben," Alex said. "I came over to see if I can help. You all right."

"Yeah, 'cept I gone have a big knot on my head where I hit that pipe when you goosed me."

"I'm sorry Ben. I guess you can do without that kind of help."

Ben squiggled backwards out of the furnace, his face and

upper body covered in soot.

"Ben you're black all over. Folks could mistake you for that tar baby in Uncle Remus."

"I know," Ben laughed. "It's mighty dirty in there, but I think we done figgered out what's wrong."

"Yeah, I met the reverend on the way down. He thinks it's the valves."

"I reckon that be right. This furnace so ol' I don't know if them valves be available no more."

"How about that blacksmith over at the stables. Do you think he can repair them or make replacements?"

"I don't know. I gone take one out an let'im look at it tomorrow."

"You through for the day?'

"Yeah, I'm gonna head on home an' take a bath."

"Okay, I want to have a few words with Reverend Pope. I'll see you at home."

"Alex you gone talk about me?"

"I just want to get his feel for your state of mind after Quincy's death. I'm not prying. Besides, he won't discuss anything the two of you talked about. Look Ben, I just want the best for you, believe me."

"Okay," Ben said hesitantly, "I'll see ya at supper."

"No Alex, I think Ben has been able to take in everything that happened with Quincy and is moving on. I believe he allowed himself to get into that situation because his desire for friends outweighed his concerns about Quincy and his way of life. As a matter of fact, his renewed interest in the church and especially the choir is very encouraging. I never knew what a wonderful baritone voice he has. He came to choir practice and our new choir leader was so impressed he asked Ben to sing a solo next Sunday. I hope you'll come."

"I had no idea! Certainly I'll come! You don't know what a

relief it is to hear this. Thank you Reverend."

"Give my best to Miss Minnie. Tell her we'll be expecting the whole family on Sunday."

"Yes sir, I will."

Alex got word to Cleo, Phoebe and George that Ben was singing a solo next Sunday at Friendship.

"Miss Eustis done give a whole lotsa money to Samson and Miss Minnie. I got it on good word. It s'posed to be for the whole family and I wants you to get your fair share," Jonah ranted at Cleo as she dressed the kids for church.

"I cain't believe you got all that from two old women talking in a stable. I'm gonna ask Ma about it at church."

"You don't think she gone tell you? Her and them boys is holdin' onto it for theyselves. 'Sides, I heard it from more'n one place. It true. I know it true. Why you think George come home. It won't cause his pa died. He come to git his share of that money. Mark my words, they's cheatin' you an' Phoebe cause you got menfolks a workin' and they thinks you don't need it."

"Jonah, you always lookin' out for the worst from folks. Me an' the chilren goin' to Ma's for dinner after church. You come if you want. I ain't fixin' nothin' here."

Cleo left Jonah in a smoldering rage. He headed for the kitchen where he pulled a bottle of moonshine from behind the firebox.

22

The Solo

Minnie was first to spy George and Mary as they came down the side aisle.

"Alex, look, George and Mary's here. I sho won't 'spectin' them to come.

"George, Mary, I's so glad you done come to hear Ben sing. He been so nervous 'bout singing by hisself. He sho gone lak seein' you."

"I remember when I first started singing in Savannah how scared I was," Mary said, "and how much I appreciated seeing my mother sitting in the front row. I had to come for Ben."

Reverend Pope began the services with a prayer. The congregation sang two hymns then the pastor read a passage from Job. He closed the bible and paused to look out over the congregation before gathering himself.

"It gives me special pleasure this morning to introduce the newest member of our excellent choir. Benjamin Devereux has been coming to Friendship all his life. Lately, he has been helping around the church with our maintenance. He spent last week struggling with that old boiler downstairs. I know sometimes he felt like cussing that rusting old relic but instead he would sing while he was working. I stood at the top of the stairs marveling at the majesty and power of his voice. I asked him to join the choir and he accepted. This morning he is going to sing "*Swing Low Sweet Chariot,*" a song that he says has special meaning to him in the days since his father passed away. Ben, the floor is yours," he said, raising his eyes to the choir loft.

Ben rose from his seat at the back to stand at the rail by the organ. Mrs Treadway began to play the introductory chords. Ben cleared his throat as the notes soared toward the opening chorus,

> *Swing low, sweet chariot,*
> *Coming for to carry me home.*
> *Swing low sweet chariot,*
> *Coming for to carry me home.*

He then launched into the first stanza,

> *I looked over Jordan, and what did I see*
> *Coming for to carry me home?*
> *There was a band of angels coming after me*
> *Coming for to carry me home*

The deep baritone voice floated over the balcony rail like a mellow cloud and enveloped the rapt audience. The old Negro spiritual had never sounded so powerful or so emotional.

Minnie bowed her head and thanked the Lord for Ben's gift while Alex entertained thoughts of how close Ben had come to ruining his own life and bringing disgrace to his family.

> *Swing low, sweet chariot,*
> *Coming for to carry me home,*
> *Swing low, sweet chariot*
> *Coming for to carry me home.*

The chorus swelled behind him and Ben, having survived the first stanza, warmed to the occasion. He launched into the second with a newfound confidence in his ability. There was an imperceptible catch in his voice as he reached the line in the third stanza that declared,

When Jesus washed my sins away,

There were only two other people in the building who understood the deeply felt meaning of those words.

Ben finished the last stanza with a flourish and then accompanied the choir for the final chorus. The last notes had not faded into the soaring vault above when the customarily reserved congregation leapt to their feet and burst into wild applause. Amens and hallelujahs rang out from every corner of the sanctuary.

Mary Waters was the first to greet Ben at the foot of the choir loft stairs at the conclusion of services.

"Ben I never knew you had such a voice! George never even mentioned it. I've listened to a lot of men singers in my time and none of them can hold a candle to you."

"Thank you, Miss Mary," Ben stammered. "I don't know what to say. I sings some at the stables, but I don't get a whole heap of applause from them horses."

Mary's eyes flashed and she grabbed Ben's hand excitedly.

"I've got an idea. We don't have anybody lined up to perform next Saturday night. I'm supposed to sing, but it would be wonderful if you'd come over and join me. I know Mr. Pollard won't mind. He might even pay you a little something."

"I don't know Miss Mary. I ain't never sung to no crowd like that. I don't know none of them kinda songs."

"Don't you worry Ben. Just come over early and we'll

practice a couple for you to sing. Maybe we'll even do a duet. What do you say?"

"Well, I reckon I will if you be sure it all right."

"I'll call the church tomorrow after I talk to Mr. Pollard. I'm sure he'll approve. Just stop by on your way home and ask Mrs. Stallings. I'll leave a message with her."

Mary was quickly jostled aside by a horde of well-wishing parishioners, each eager to heap their praises on top of hers.

Dinner at Minnie's was more festive than ever that Sunday. Everyone gathered around the big kitchen table. The excited conversation picked up where it had left off at the church. Minnie had laded the table with her Sunday best victuals.

"Everbody be quiet now." she said. "This been a real special day for me. Ben done made us all so proud. The whole congregation be singin' his praises. Now it time to thank Jesus for all his blessings. Miss Mary would you say grace."

Mary had not been especially religious in Savannah and she and George did not attend church in North Augusta. She summoned up old memories from her childhood.

"Lord we thank you for the blessing of Ben's voice today and for this family that loves and supports him. We thank you for this food as we prepare to partake of it. Amen."

Mary's words were brief but seemed to satisfy everyone at the table, especially the children, who were famished from running around the churchyard.

Mary continued.

"Miss Minnie I've asked Ben if he'll sing with me at Carolina Springs next Saturday."

The table chatter ceased as all eyes turned to their matriarch.

"Ben what you think?" she said.

"I don't know Ma. I ain't never sung befo no crowd like that, but Miss Mary say she gone teach me some songs. And, she say Mr. Pollard might gone pay me sumpin' so I reckon it be all right."

"What 'bout you George?" Minnie asked. "You gone be all right with it?"

George sat sullenly at the far end of the table, upset that Mary hadn't consulted with him before announcing the invitation.

"If Mary thinks it okay, I reckon so," he submitted.

"Well then, I reckon Ben's gonna sing for his supper at the Springs," Minnie pronounced with a proud grin. "Now everbody dig in."

23

The Exam

The fragile wire-mesh mantle of the Aladdin lamp sitting on the Devereux kitchen table burned brightly until well past midnight. It was the second week of October. Amid a crescendo of preparation, Alex crammed for his upcoming trip to Columbia. The stack of legal documents on his bedside table grew thicker by the day and despite the repeated assurances of Mr. Poole, he wanted to leave nothing to chance.

The final South Carolina lawyer's examination for 1927 was scheduled for Saturday morning at ten. The burgundy LaSalle pulled up in front of the Devereux house at six a.m. Alex, scrubbed, shaved and dressed in his starched collar and blue serge suit, bounded down the front steps. Mr. Poole had insisted that his driver ferry Alex to Columbia and then bring him home at the conclusion of the exam.

The ten apprehensive applicants had exactly three hours to demonstrate their grasp of the law. The distillation of years of study would soon be embodied in the scant few pages they presented to the examiner. Alex scanned the room as he entered, taking note that his was the only black face.

He chose a desk near the rear of the room. The proctor entered promptly at ten. He walked among the desks depositing a sheaf of papers on each.

"Gentlemen, you now have three hours to demonstrate your grasp of the federal and South Carolina legal statutes. Please begin."

Alex opened the test papers and began to read the first question. It dealt with federal interstate commerce law. He was comfortable with the subject and moved smoothly into a delineation of the legal precepts. His confidence rose with each problem presented. In most instances, he was able to recall the actual cases and their arguments.

The clock at the front of the examining room crept ominously toward one. Feet began to shuffle. The first applicant to finish handed in his papers. Alex was completing his essay on a South Carolina divorce law question as time elapsed. He signed and dated his application before submitting it to the proctor. His fate was now in the hands of the examining board. He could only wait and pray. Results were to be mailed to each applicant the following Friday.

Mr. Poole's car dropped Alex off at three-thirty. The Mitchell car was in the driveway. The Devereux clan was gathering for their pilgrimage to Carolina Springs. Minnie, Phoebe and Lester were in the kitchen.

"How'd it go son?" an apprehensive Minnie asked.

"I think I did all right. I knew most of the subjects they tested us on pretty well. We'll know in a week or so." He looked around. "Did Ben get off early?"

"He caught the trolley to North Augusta 'bout ten this mawnin'. He was wound-up tighter'n a drum. I jest hopes he settles down some befo tonight."

"I'm sure he'll be fine," Alex said. "Miss Mary will take him under her wing. Ben's smart."

"I know he smart," Minnie said, "but smart don't take no notice of nervous. I hope you right."

"Lester how are things with you?" Alex asked.

"Oh, I cain't complain none. Mr. Clark been plantin' a heap more trees and flowers. He keepin' us real busy."

"How about you Phoebe?" Alex asked. "Things going well at the hotel?"

"I ain't never seen so many folks comin' to town this early. Ever room done filled up. I been ironin' sheets all week."

"I reckon that means this will be a good year for Aiken's business community," Alex said.

"I spec so."

"It looks like everybody's ready to go over and hear Ben sing tonight. Have you heard from Cleo? Is she going?"

"She asked me'n Lester to drive you and Miss Minnie over to her place to pick her up. She say Jonah ain't goin.' He stayin' home wit da chilren. Ain't no love lost 'tween him and George noways. She say it better he don't go."

"I suppose she's right. I wish the two of them would work out their differences. It would sure make things a lot easier for all of us."

"What time you think we oughta leave, Alex?" Lester asked.

"Mary said they would start singing about eight and Ben would be finished with his part before nine, so probably 6:30 or so. Lester can you fit Ben in for the trip back?"

"It gone be a little tight," Lester said, casting an eye toward Minnie, "but I 'spec we can."

24

The Debut

There were fewer cars in the parking lot than on a normal Saturday evening when the names on the marquee out front were more prominent than Mary Waters and Ben Devereux. Alex recognized several vehicles from Aiken. Word of Ben'a appearance had spread during the week. Upon entering the building, he recognized several members of the Friendship family as well as others from among the Winter Colony servant community. He smiled as he observed his mother brighten and preen with pride. She had not smiled much since the funeral.

Mary greeted them at the entrance and escorted the family to a table near the stage.

"I'm so glad all of you were able to come. Ben is a bundle of nerves, but he'll settle down after we begin. I'm going to sing a duet with him first to allow him time to adjust to performing before a strange crowd. He did really well in rehearsal, so I don't think he'll have a problem with the lyrics."

George came over from the bar area to welcome the family.

"I won't real taken with the idea of Ben singin' here at first, but seein' him rehearsin' with Mary done changed my mind. He gone do good. I gotta git back to the bar now. They gone need my help soon. I gone see you when the show be over."

"I ain't gone drink nuthin' since I's drivin'," Lester said, "but ya'll go ahead if you wants to."

"I think I'll have a beer," Alex said. "I know Mama doesn't drink, but how about you girls?"

"I don't drink any at home," Cleo said," because of the children, but I think I'll have a beer too."

"Me too," Phoebe echoed.

Alex waved to a waiter to come and take their order. Minnie asked for some iced tea. The drinks came, and the table lapsed into silence with nervous anticipation.

Suddenly, spotlights flooded the stage as Mr. Abe Pollard parted the curtains and walked to the microphone. His recent investment in an amplifier system permitted his voice to reach the far corners of the hall.

"Ladies and Gentlemen," the emcee proclaimed, "we are privileged tonight to have our own Mary Waters performing for you accompanied by the incomparable Carolina Spring's orchestra. As a special treat this evening, Mary will introduce to you a fantastic new talent from our own community. I was privileged to hear this young man sing for the first time in rehearsal with Mary this afternoon. I think you will agree with me that he has an amazing voice. I predict a great future for him.

"And now I invite you to welcome to the stage the Pride of Savannah, Georgia, Miss Mary Waters."

Polite applause, encouraged by a blinding spotlight, welcomed Mary as the curtains parted and she crossed the stage. She was dressed in a stunning, off the shoulder, floor length dress of blue silk. The sequined bodice accentuated her slim waist. The skirt swathed her sensuous curves. It's cascading folds of iridescent blue plunged to the floor in a bouffant swirl. It was a new fashion statement inspired by women who tied their skirts before ascending in open cockpit airplanes.

There was an audible gasp from a table near the stage. Alex could only stare, mouth agape, at the vision in blue. He closed his eyes and saw Betty Carlton wearing a dress of that same hue when he saw her off at Union Station in D.C. It was the last time he had seen her. She was off to New York and a new life in show business. His heart skipped a beat. He suddenly realized how much he missed her.

Betty Carlton's past could be a mirror image of Mary Waters's: white father, fair-skinned mother, discrimination, impoverishment, struggle. Betty too could have passed, but like Mary, she chose not to. She was proud of her parents and the life they had created for themselves despite being shunned by Charles Carlton's prominent Baltimore family.

Charles' bohemian, spinster Aunt, Maggie, who lived in Greenwich Village, had rescued him from his grim predicament. She vehemently disagreed with her brother's treatment of his son. Her monthly stipend allowed Charles to begin his own small business and to afford Mary's tuition at Howard.

Mary's resemblance to Betty was not confined to her physical beauty. Her voice brought back memories of their walks through Rock Creek Park where she practiced her solos on the squirrels and the pigeons.

"This next number I dedicate to Miss Josephine Baker," Mary Waters said. "She will always be identified with this song in my mind. She first sang it on Broadway. *Bye Bye Blackbird.* I hope you enjoy it"

Even the waiters and ushers stopped to listen as Mary reached for the high notes. There was absolute silence as she trilled the last line,

Now my dreams will come true.

Slowly at first, then in a deafening roar, the audience leapt to its feet and the applause rolled on and on.

"Thank you so much. I love doing that song. Now, my next number is a tribute to one of my favorite songwriters. His songs were such a great inspiration to our soldiers in the war. However, the one I'm going to do was written almost by accident.

"Miss Belle Baker had been plugged into a one night performance in the new show *Betsy* by Rodgers and Hart. The problem was she didn't have a new song to sing. In a state of panic, she phoned an old, dear friend.

"Irving, I've been written in for a song in *Betsy* for tomorrow night, and I don't have any new material. Help!!!"

"Belle, I don't really have anything new right now."

"Irving you've got to help me!"

"Tell you what. I've got an old, unfinished tune sitting in my trunk. I'll haul it out and see if it'll do."

"It'll do, Irving, It'll do."

"It's not finished, Belle."

"Well, finish it."

"I've got the first and last sections done, I just need a "bridge," I'll call you in the morning."

"Irving finished his "bridge" at six the next morning and rushed it over to Miss Baker. She took the song to Mr. Ziegfeld, producer of the show, and he gave it his blessing. Belle sang it that night and it brought the house down. When she was called back for an encore, the words escaped her. At that point Irving Berlin jumped up from the audience and finished his song for her. Ladies and Gentlemen, I give you *"Blue Skies."*

Again, she had the crowd mesmerized. Again, a standing ovation, wild cheering and repeated shouts from the balcony.

"Now I know how Belle felt when she was called back for her encore. However, instead of an encore of *Blue Skies* I'd like to bring you another selection by songwriters of equal fame. This song, written for the musical *Oh, Kay* languished while its lyricist was bedridden with appendicitis. While lying flat on his back he realized that he and his brother were using the wrong tempo for the song. Immediately after escaping his sick bed the duo rushed through the song just in time for the show's opening. It is destined to become a standard in every songbook in America. *Someone to Watch Over Me.* by George and Ira Gershwin.

By the time Mary refrained the last line, *Oh how I need someone to watch over me,* every man and boy in the audience was ready to obey her wish and vault onto the stage.

"Thank you, thank you so much," she said as the applause finally died down. "I love that song. I'm sure glad they got the tempo right.

"Mr. Pollard teased you at the beginning of the show that we had a special guest tonight. Well, I'm going to bring him out now, and we're going to sing a duet. He's a little nervous so this will let him ease into the performance. We're going to perform another song that I associate with Miss Josephine Baker. It is from the first Broadway show in which she appeared, *Shuffle Along.* The song is *Love Will Find a Way* written by Eubie Blake. Please join me in welcoming Aiken's own, Benjamin Franklin Devereux. Come on out Ben."

Nervously, the young man strode across the stage to the welcoming applause.

"I hope ya'll won't mind that I brought the sheet music out with me. I never sung this song til Miss Mary showed it to me today. I sho don't wanna mess up in front of all ya'll folks."

A titter arose then quickly subsided as the orchestra played the opening bars. Mary pulled Ben closer to the microphone as the notes began to soar. She sang the first few bars before Ben came in on the chorus. He then sang the second stanza and she joined in for the chorus.

> *Love will find a way*
> *Will love find a way*
> *Love will find a way*

The plaintive question was asked and answered, and the audience knew that love would indeed find a way.

Mary curtsied. Ben bowed, as she had taught him. The nervousness gone, he beamed at the applause.

"How about that voice? Didn't I tell you?"

Mary waited for the applause to fade before announcing the next number.

"There was another new talent in that chorus along with Josephine Baker in *Shuffle Along*. I recently heard him perform the new hit from Jerome Kern's smash Broadway production, *Showboat*. If you've ever heard Paul Robeson sing you probably still have goose bumps. I predict you'll have the same response to Ben Devereux's rendition of *Ol' Man River*. In solo, Ben Devereux."

Ben stepped to the microphone and waited as the orchestra ran through the introductory bars. He licked his lips, closed his eyes, said a small prayer, and waited for the cue note.

> *Here we all work 'long the Mississippi*
> *Here we all work while the white folk play*
> *Pullin' dose boats from de dawn to sunset*
> *Gittin' no rest till de judgment day*

Just as the lyrics of *Swing Low* had transfixed the congregation at Friendship, Ben's *Ol' Man River* riveted the patrons at Carolina Springs. There was no tinkling of ice, no shuffling of feet, no clank of fork; just rapt attention as his rich baritone held his audience spellbound.

> *Ol' man river*
> *Dat ol' man river*
> *He mus' know sumpin'*
> *But don't say nuthin'*
> *He jes' keeps rollin' along*

There was hardly a dry eye in the room as Ben finished the last plaintive notes of the chorus. The tragic lyrics of Ol' Joe on that Mississipi dock just as easily applied to the long, dusty rows of Carolina cotton. Once more the crowd was on its feet bellowing its approval of this new, homegrown talent in their midst. There was a recognizable pride in the raucous response. One that might have escaped the ear of a visiting performer.

George and Mary stood by the car as the Devereux family prepared to leave.

"Ben, Mr. Pollard grabbed me just as you finished your solo. He said he wants you to come back and perform again. Maybe next month. He told me to tell you he'd pay you ten dollars a night. What do you think?'

"I don't know whut to say. I don't make that much money in a week at Gaston's. Sho nuff I'll do it. Jest let me know when."

Laughter and chatter flowed out the open windows of Lester's old Model-A on the ride back to Aiken. Everyone was overwhelmed with the success of Ben's debut as a professional singer. Alex admonished everyone to lower their voices as they passed through the Horse Creek communities. The memory of his last trip through here was still very fresh in his mind. Fifteen minutes later, they were home. Alex stepped down and helped Minnie from the car. She was stiff from having been wedged between her two sons in back.

"Thank you for driving us over tonight, Lester." Alex said. "It was a great show. I couldn't be more proud of my little brother," he said, giving Ben a slap on the back.

"You welcome. Me'n Phoebe sho enjoyed your singin' Ben," Lester said. "I cain't wait to go back over there agin'."

"I sho enjoyed it too," Cleo said. "I just wish the young'uns coulda heard you singin.'"

"Maybe next time, Cleo, maybe next time." Ben said.

Minnie watched Lester's tail lights disappear around the corner.

"Ben you sho done us proud tonight. I gotta thank Miss Mary for givin' you the chance to sing over there. She a real blessin' to this family."

The three Devereuxs strolled up the driveway.

"It done been a blessed day."

25

The Surprise

Alex was at loose ends all week anticipating the letter from the examining board. He hoped it would arrive by Saturday, but in his heart he knew it would be sometime next week. He was tempted to call Columbia but thought better of it. Better to let sleeping dogs lie, lest you get bitten.

He spent most of the week at the law office reading the treatises recommended by Mr. Poole. It amazed him the span of legal subjects a small law office was expected to handle: wills, divorces, real estate, legal notices, lawsuits, criminal defense, the list went on.

Each day when the mail came, Alex waited expectantly for news from Columbia, having listed the Poole office for his return address. When it had not arrived by Friday he accepted that his earlier prediction was correct. Nervous energy was driving him to distraction.

"Ben, how would you like to go over to see the show at Carolina Springs with me tomorrow night?" Alex announced at breakfast on Friday. "I hear there's a new band in from New Orleans. I need to get my mind off the bar exam for a while."

"Sho Alex, that sound good to me. Reverend Pope done paid me for the boiler work so I gots some money. What you think Ma. You gone be all right here by yo'self."

"Lawsy chile, I done been by myself so many times it don't matter none to me."

She sat under the bare light, struggling to thread a needle. The darning egg waited for its sock on the table beside her.

" Here Ben, thread this here needle for me. I jest cain't see so good no mo'."

She slid the frayed sock over the clear glass egg and waited.

"Ya'll go on and have yo'selfs a good time. How you gonna git there?"

"I thought we'd catch the trolley over," Alex said. "I understand the last one leaves Augusta at ten. We'll see the first show at eight and catch the last trolley. Should be back before eleven."

Ben handed the threaded needle back to his mother. She pushed her glasses up on her nose and stared at the frayed sock.

"Ya'll jes' be careful. 'Member them "lint heads".

"Yes ma'am. We'll be careful."

A new marquee greeted Alex as he drove up to the casino.

Doc Rivers and his Band

———

The Toast of the
New Orleans Music Scene

———

Featuring
Miss Betty Carlton,
Chanteuse Extraordinaire.

Alex stopped dead in his tracks, staring up at the marquee. This was impossible. Betty couldn't be here. Her last letter said she was happy and doing well in New York. Surely, she would have told me if she was coming to South Carolina. Maybe she didn't know I had come home. There must be some mistake. Maybe there's another singer named Betty Carlton.

The Doc Rivers band, started just a few years earlier in New Orleans, had caught fire with its flapper-centric style of syncopated jazz. Rivers came from the King Oliver school, and had adapted much of his mentor's approach to his own music. Miss Carlton had joined his ten- piece orchestra when it played at the *"81" Theater* in Atlanta. She was coming off an engagement with Virginia Liston's *Seminole Syncopators* at that same venue. The *Syncopators* had completed their gig and were returning to New York. Betty told Miss Liston she had no desire to go back with them. At Betty's urging, Virginia recommended her to Mr. Rivers, and he took her on. This information Alex had gleaned from the young man he buttonholed outside the box office. Bobby Clampett was an assistant manager in charge of acquiring new talent for Carolina Springs.

Alex, pale and shaken, purchased two tickets and led Ben into the theater.

"What's the matter Alex? What that man say? You whiter'n a sheet."

"Come on in and let's find our seats. I'll tell you later."

Several rows of seats rose up from the main floor at the rear of the room. Their seats, the least expensive in the house, were in the top row, farthest from the stage. It was a good vantage point however, and one almost needed binoculars to recognize faces on stage. Alex reflected that if it was truly his Betty, being back so far wasn't necessarily a bad thing. He had to be certain it was her before he did anything rash and embarrassed himself.

"I haven't told anyone but Mama," he whispered to Ben as they settled into their seats, "but I was seeing a young lady at Howard. She was also named Betty Carlton. She left for New York a year or so before I finished. She was a singer and worked on Broadway and in Harlem. I really liked her and I thought she liked me. We wrote to each other fairly regularly, but I haven't heard from her in a few months. I can't believe this is the same Betty. Why would she leave a promising music career in New York to come down here?"

"You gone find out soon 'nough," Ben said. "The show's startin'."

The green velvet curtains parted revealing ten musicians, five arrayed on either side of a small stand. Doc Rivers stepped from the shadows and mounted the stand, cornet in hand.

"It sure does feel good to be here in South Carolina. I been talkin' to a whole bunch of folks down in New Orleans who have performed here, and I heard nothing but good things about Carolina Springs. Everybody on the Chitlin' Circuit says the same thing. My old boss, King Oliver, has played here and he said, 'Doc you gotta go up there to Augusta and play.' Well, I took him at his word, and here we are. Welcome to the show."

Rivers turned to the band, waved his horn up and down three times and the orchestra took off with their arrangement of *"Dippermouth Blues,"* a King Oliver composition inspired by Louis Armstrong's exceptionally large mouth, the result of his many years of trumpet playing.

The second number was another song made famous by Louis Armstrong, *"West End Blues."* Rivers led the band through several bars before he called on the trumpet, the clarinet and the saxophone for solos. He brought the tempo down and turned to the audience.

"Please welcome our featured vocalist, fresh from her sold out performances in Atlanta at the *"81"* Club. I give you, Miss Betty Carlton."

Alex could not breathe. She *is* here!

"Is that her Alex? Is that her?" Ben asked impatiently.

"I can't believe my eyes Ben. It's her. It's Betty Carlton from college."

"What you gonna do now?"

"Wait until the show is over and go backstage to see her. I have to know why she came here without telling me."

"I spec she got some good reason. She sho pretty Alex. She look a lot like Mary."

"She certainly does Ben, she certainly does."

Betty stood at center stage with the spotlight on her and sang *"Some Day Sweetheart."* It was a song written by Johnny Mercer. Mary, being from Savannah like Mercer, recommended the song to Betty. Alex had the strange feeling that she was looking directly at him as she sang. The lyrics were a lament for the lover that had done her wrong.

The orchestra waded through another half-dozen jazz and blues numbers before Betty came back on stage to sing *"I'm Crazy Bout My Baby."* The lyrics were the polar opposite of *"Some Day Sweetheart"* as she waxed ecstatic about how happy she was and how she was ready to marry this guy. Maybe the choice of songs and their lyrics had nothing to do with her love life, but he had to know.

Betty came back later to sing a sultry version of *"Frankie and Johnny"* a tune Alex had heard many times before without paying much attention to the lyrics. Now he hung on every word. Frankie had found her unfaithful lover in a honky-tonk bar and shot him dead. Now we were back to the mournful tone of the first song. It had to be just musical coincidence. After all, nearly all blues songs boiled down to spats between lovers.

Two lively Jazz standards later, Betty was back for the finale. To everyone's surprise, she was joined onstage by Mary Waters. The band struck up its boisterous rendition of *"Yes Sir That's My Baby"* and the two girls launched into the raucous lyrics with gusto. Halfway through, they invited the audience to stand and join in the popular new dance, *"The Charleston."* Ten minutes later, everyone exhausted, Doc Rivers rang down the curtain on the evening. He introduced the band members to loud applause, before calling Betty out for her bow. Now everyone was on their feet. The opening night performance for Doc River's band was a huge success – and Betty Carlton was the hit of the evening.

Alex and Ben circled around the dance floor and headed for the bar area. George was carrying a large tray of dirty glasses back to the kitchen when he saw them approach.

"What you boys doin' here?"

"We just came over to see the show. We heard about the new band and didn't have anything better to do.

"George what do you know about Betty Carlton?" Alex asked.

"Not much. The band jest got here today. They been rehearsin' mos' the day. Mr. Doc, he come back and asked Mary if she wanted to sing with their girl and Mary say sho."

"You didn't meet her then? She doesn't know your name is Devereux?"

"Naw, lak I say, I ain't met her yet. Why you ask?"

Alex told George about his and Betty's relationship and his surprise that she came to town without contacting him.

"Mary say she been over to Atlanta for a while. Say she come from New York. That bout all she 'low."

"George will you go back to the dressing room and ask Mary to come out; before Betty does?"

"Sho Alex. I'll be right back."

Within seconds, George reappeared with Mary in tow.

"What a surprise seeing you two here tonight. George is acting awfully mysterious. What's up?"

Alex re-told the saga to Mary.

"My goodness what a story! That's really something, Alex, I haven't talked to Betty very much since she got here, we've been so busy. Do you want me to get her out here?"

"Would you please, but don't tell her why. I'll wait over by the stage. Thanks Mary."

The look of bewilderment on Betty's face turned to shock when she saw Alex.

"My God, Alex, what are you doing here?"

"You *must* remember that I come from Aiken?"

"I remember you saying that but I had no idea where Aiken is. I didn't know you were anywhere around. I thought you were still in Washington."

"No, I finished school a few weeks ago and came home for my father's funeral."

"I'm sorry Alex. I didn't know."

"How could you? I haven't heard from you in a while. Last time you wrote you seemed happy in New York."

Betty averted her eyes and stared at the floor.

"I was in a new play that was supposed to open at the Pantages two months ago. During rehearsals one of the producers asked me out. We went for dinner a couple of times, and then he got very serious. I wasn't ready for that, so I told him no. He got very angry and threatened me. I thought he was going to hit me. Instead, he went to the director and had me fired from the show. I went to all the other directors in town and no one would hire me. This man had blacklisted me. No one dared cross him. He was too powerful.

"Finally, I got a job with Virginia Liston's all girl band, up in Harlem. When she got the job in Atlanta she asked me to come with her. When that engagement was over, she headed back to New York. I was scared to go back, so I signed on with Mr. Rivers. When his contract was up in Atlanta, he asked me if I would like to travel with him. I didn't have anywhere else to go, and the pay was good, so I said sure; and here I am.

"What about you Alex? What are you doing?"

"I told you in DC about my agreement with Miss Eustis. Well, after a lot of thought, I knew I had to honor it, so I'm staying in Aiken. I'll know next week if I passed the South Carolina bar exam. If I did, I have a position waiting for me with one of the white law firms in Aiken.

"I didn't mean to spring all this on you tonight. My brother Ben and I came over to see the show and visit with my brother George and his girlfriend Mary Waters. "

"George is your brother!"

"Yeah, small world ain't it," he said with a big grin. "Come on over and meet my brothers.

"Betty Carlton, this is my older brother George. He works here as you know, and this handsome fellow is my younger brother Ben. Turns out you two have a lot in common. Ben made his debut here last week. We discovered that he's been hiding his light under a bushel all this time. He has a voice to rival the best."

"Hello George. Hello Ben. It's so good to meet you. Alex used to talk about this big family of his in Aiken. I never dreamed I'd get to meet you, especially not under such strange circumstances."

"Well, we're certainly glad you did," Mary said. "How long is the band's contract with Carolina Springs?"

"I think we'll be here through next weekend."

"Then what?" Alex asked, dread in his voice.

"I don't know for sure. I think we're scheduled to go to Savannah after that."

Alex looked crestfallen. Now that she'd come back into his life he didn't want to lose her again, but what could he do?

"Betty, it's 9:30 and Ben and I have to catch the last trolley to Aiken at 10:00. Where is the band staying? I want to come back over tomorrow and see you."

"The Richmond Hill Hotel has a separate building where their colored performers can stay. They let the folks appearing at the Springs stay there too."

"I've got to run, but I'll catch the trolley over tomorrow morning," Alex said. "I have to see you."

"Okay, but I have to be back here at three," Betty said.

"That's great. I'll see you then.

"Come on Ben, we have to hurry if we're going to catch that trolley."

"Ben, what am I going to do?" Alex asked as they settled into the trolley seats. "Now that Betty's here, I can't stand the idea of losing her again."

"I don't know Alex. Maybe she don't wanna stay here. She seems to be doin' fine with that band."

"I have to find out Ben. I have to."

The trolley car rumbled across the Valley toward Aiken, taking Alex away from the woman that he was now certain he loved.

25

The Reunion

"How'd you boys enjoy that show over to the Springs last night?" Minnie asked as Alex stumbled in to breakfast.

"Mama you're not going to believe who showed up there last night."

"Who?"

"You remember the girl I told you about at Howard that I was dating."

"Yeah."

"Her name is Betty Carlton and she's the singer for the band that opened last night."

"My Goodness! See, I told you so. Funny things can happen when you's in love. What'd she say?"

"She came down to Atlanta with an all-girl group and stayed to join the band she's with now. She had a bad experience in New York and wanted to get out of town. She didn't know I was back in Aiken. It was a complete surprise for both of us.

"I'm going back over to see her today. I really do like her Ma. I'd sure like to find some way to convince her to stay here."

"You know what they say 'where there's a will, there's a way'."

"I hope you're right Mama. I sure do."

The grand Richmond Hill Hotel sat at the apex of the hill overlooking the Savannah River in North Augusta. The dormitory for black performers was down the slope behind a tall stand of cedars. Alex stepped into the reception area and asked the clerk for Miss Carlton.

"She came by a few minutes ago on the way to breakfast. She told me to send you in when you got here. The dining room is right across the lobby behind those double doors.'

"Thank you, Miss."

"Good morning," he said as he approached her table.

"Good morning, Alex," Betty said brightly, "I slept in a little this morning. I was really tired after the bus trip from Atlanta and the show last night."

"Well you look great. No worse for the wear."

"I still can't get over our meeting like this. What are the chances?"

"Yeah, it's kind of amazing.

"Betty, I know when you went to New York there were no promises, but I think you knew that I really cared for you, and now that you're here, I can't bear the thought of you going away again. It seems like fate has thrown us together for a reason. I don't know what it is, but I'd sure like you to stay here so we can find out."

"Alex, leaving you was very hard for me, too. When I got to the city, I thought I could start another life, but all I could think of was you. When I went out with that producer guy, I thought I might be able to forget you and start a new life. Obviously, that didn't work out. Maybe, in the recesses of my mind, when I decided to come south, I was really looking for you. In any case, call it what you will—fate, kismet, fortune—here we are."

"I don't know if you are aware that Mary's story is similar to yours. She grew up in Savannah – white father, black mother, tough childhood. She had to leave Savannah and came here. George helped her to regain her bearings and they became very close. Why don't we go over to the Springs and talk to her and George. She's a very savvy lady. Maybe she can help us figure this out, that is if you'd really consider staying here."

"Oh Alex, I don't know. The way of life here is so different. Even from Baltimore. I'd like to have some time to figure things out. I don't know if that's possible in a week, but I'm willing to give it a try. Come on, let's go see Mary."

Mary was onstage with the house piano player rehearsing a new number when they came down the aisle.

"Eddie why don't you take five," Mary said, "Two of my favorite people just came in and I need to talk to them."

"Good mawnin', good mawnin', you two. I stayed up half the night talking George's ear off. I said 'George those two are just meant for each other'. I mean, the way you looked at each other, you can just tell. You couldn't keep your eyes off each other."

Betty blushed and Alex kicked at the floor.

"Don't deny it. The minute I heard the details, I knew it was meant to be. They ain't no other reason in the world that the two of you showed up here last night. I don't believe in coincidences. It was just meant to be."

"Mary I just got through telling Betty that I don't want to lose her again and that if anyone can help us figure things out, it's you. She left New York with very little money. She saved a bit in Atlanta, but she still needs to work. Doc Rivers has asked her to go on to Savannah with him next week."

"I don't know if Mr. Pollard could use her here at the Springs. He might fit her in with me when we don't have performers from out of town. I'll ask him."

Mary walked over and sat on the edge of the stage. She stared off into the distance for several minutes.

"I've got an idea. I know the club manager over at Richmond Hill. He told me that their lounge singer is getting married and moving to Charleston. He's going to need a replacement. The pay's probably not as good as the band but you get free room and board. I might even get Mr. Pollard to use Betty on some of her free weekends. Whaddaya think? Is it worth a try?"

"Gee Mary, I don't know," Betty said. "It would be such a big change."

"Just think about it Betty," Alex pleaded. "We've got a week to decide. You know I want you to stay, but this is a decision you have to make. Go over with Mary and talk to the folks at Richmond Hill. Find out if there's really an opportunity. If there is, then you can decide,"

"Okay, Alex, I'll do it. If there is, then we'll take it from there."

"Great, that's all I can ask. I know you girls have to get ready for tonight so I'll get out of your hair. I'll try to get back over here before Wednesday. If so, I'll see you at the hotel Betty. I'll keep my fingers crossed."

26

The Esquire

Alex was in the Poole offices bright and early on Monday. He sat in the conference room poring over an article of arcane court rulings by the South Carolina Supreme Court while keeping one eye peeled for the mailman, who normally came around ten.

"Good morning, Miss Rhodes," he heard before he saw the carrier enter. Alex waited an appropriate time before casually strolling into her office.

"Miss Rhodes, did there happen to be a letter to Mr. Poole from the Secretary of State's office."

"Let me see," she said as she thumbed through the pile of envelopes. "Why yes there is one."

"Would you mind if I take it in to him?"

"Why not at all," she said, suppressing a smile, "Here!"

"Mr. Poole, I think this might be the results of my exam," he said as he burst into the office. He handed him the letter.

"So it seems Alex. Go ahead, you open it."

With trembling hands, Alex opened the envelope and extracted the letter within.

"Dear Mr. Devereux.

It is with great pleasure that I inform you that you have passed the examination that allows you to practice law in South Carolina. The enclosed certificate permits you to establish a law practice within the state. I offer my sincere congratulations and wish you well as you embark on your career.

Edward Markham
Secretary of State
State of South Carolina

Overcome with emotion, Alex plopped down in the chair with a thump. He struggled to hold back the tears of joy. The long and arduous struggle had finally paid off.

"Congratulations Alex, and welcome to the firm. We'll have to get you a proper shingle to hang outside—Alexander Devereux, Esquire—that has a very distinctive ring to it.'

"Thank you, sir. If you don't mind I'm going to run home and tell Ma. She's been on pins-and-needles for a week. She'll be almost as happy as I am."

"Sure, Alex. I won't dock you for the time off," he said with a chuckle. "Come in tomorrow and we'll decide how we're going to make this work."

Alex was out the door like a shot. He ran down Park Avenue and past the depot on Union Street before settling into a fast walk.

"Mama, Mama, it came. I have my certificate to practice law in South Carolina. The faith you, and Pa, and Miss Celestine had in me has finally paid off."

"Lawsy, me." She said, gathering her apron for the onrush of tears. "I never did think one of my chilren was gonna go off to college, much less git to be no lawyer. Samson be so proud if he could see you now. I spec he noddin' his head and smilin'.

Maybe him and Miss Celestine doin' a little jig bout now. I so proud of' you boy. The whole family gonna celebrate this."

The entire congregation at Friendship Baptist gathered around Minnie and Alex after Sunday services to congratulate him on his great achievement. Several of the local businessmen said they had pending legal matters that they would be glad to move over to the Poole offices. Alex was overwhelmed with gratitude for the instant acceptance he received. He prayed that he was up to the task. He was sure that under Mr. Poole's tutelage he would be able to succeed.

Alex was in the office before eight on Monday and anxious to get to work. He was brought up short when told that he had to apply for a license to practice law in Aiken. Mr. Poole escorted him across to city hall and introduced him to the clerk.

"Miss Busch, this is Alexander Devereux. He has just received his law certificate from the state and would like to apply for a business license to practice law in Aiken."

"Certainly, Mr. Poole. If he'll just fill out this form and give me a check for twenty-five dollars we can issue it today. Is he going to be working with you?"

"Indeed he is, Miss Busch. He's already been helpful in one of my cases and I expect him to be participating in many more. He has been welcomed with open arms by the colored community and I expect he'll be getting several new clients for the firm."

"Look Miss Rhodes." Alex crowed as they re-entered the office, "I'm now a full-fledged attorney, authorized to practice law in Aiken and all of South Carolina."

"Congratulations Alex. I know you'll be a real asset to Mr. Poole. I look forward to working with you."

"Thank you, that means a lot to me."

"Now Alex, we have to see to an office for you." Mr. Poole said. "I had a junior associate that moved to Greenville last year. He had a small office around the corner from mine. We should be able to fix that up for you. Miss Rhodes can you see to that?"

"Certainly, I'll have it all prepared when you gentlemen get back from your lunch hour."

"Mr. Poole I know I just started," Alex said on their way back from the Willcox, " but if it's okay, I need to run over to North Augusta on Wednesday. It's a personal matter that I need to take care of."

"Alex you do realize that your earnings will depend on billings for services and billable hours to your clients. Your time will be your own to allocate as you see fit. As you add more clients you will find that time management becomes a major part of your job. It'll probably start out slowly but you'll be surprised how you run out of hours before you run out of work. That will be a good thing for you but also frustrating at times."

"I look forward to having such a problem. I've been living off the generosity of others for a long time and I look forward to being able to support myself."

"We haven't discussed the terms of your employment, Alex. Typically, you will set a fixed hourly rate for your general legal services. For routine functions such as real estate closings, you will charge a standard fixed fee. Miss Rhodes has a list of those. The firm expects to receive twenty-percent of those routine functions and thirty-percent of your billed hours. This will cover your use of office space and Miss Rhode's services as well as other incidental expenses. Does that seem fair to you."

"I guess so. I don't have any experience in such things."

"Those were the terms with Mr. Blodgett, your predecessor, and they seemed to work well for both of us. Miss Rhodes will draw up a contract for you to sign.

"Now, I have several cases coming up for docket in the next four weeks. I'd like you to look at them and give me your opinion as to how you would proceed with them. There's nothing like jumping in with both feet to get a feel for the work. You okay with that?"

"Yes sir. Just point me in the right direction."

"I've already given a list to Miss Rhodes. She'll sign them out to you this afternoon and you can get started on a review.

"By the way, there are a few loose ends with your father's estate that we need to tie up. It sounds like the rest of your week is going to be pretty busy. Do you think you can bring your mother in to the office next Monday?"

"Yes sir, I can arrange that. Are there any papers we need to bring?"

"No, there are just some things we need to complete," he said with an enigmatic smile.

Alex spent Monday afternoon and Tuesday reviewing the five cases. He gave his prepared comments along with several questions to Miss Rhodes for typing before leaving on Tuesday.

"Miss Rhodes, I'll be out tomorrow, but I'd appreciate it if you could get these comments to Mr. Poole tomorrow."

"Certainly Alex, they'll be on his desk before you get back."

"Thanks, I'll see you Thursday morning."

27

The Plans

Alex caught the nine o'clock trolley and was in North Augusta before ten. A brisk twenty-minute walk took him to the Richmond Hill Hotel. The desk clerk in the dormitory rang Betty's room and ten seconds later, she came bounding down the stairs.

"My, aren't you all perky and spry this morning," he said bussing her cheek.

"I feel perky and spry," she said, "because I've got great news. Mr. Rogers has given me a two-week trial at his supper club here and I start next Friday night. Mary has also convinced Mr. Pollard to use me in support of her on my off nights. Between the two jobs, I'll make almost as much as I did with the band. All I have to do now is convince both men that I can do the job."

"Wait until they see the audience reaction. They'll be begging you to stay. If the rabbits and squirrels in Rock Creek Park stopped when you sang, there's no doubt the folks here will too."

"That's sweet of you Alex, but you've got to admit you're a little bit prejudiced."

"Well, just a little bit.

"You're not the only one with good news," he said. "My law certificate came on Monday. I'm now a fully licensed lawyer in the state of South Carolina. Mr. Poole has already given me several cases to look over for him."

"That's wonderful Alex," she said, squeezing him in a big hug. "That means we're both gainfully employed; at least for a while."

"What say we have some lunch and then go over to the club?" Betty said. "There are several things I need to discuss with Mr. Pollard and Mary and I need to go over several numbers we'll be performing."

"Sounds good to me. I want to spend some time with George. We haven't had a lot of time alone to catch up since the funeral."

"Good, you can do that while Mary and I rehearse."

The couple strolled hand-in-hand along a river path on their way back to Carolina Springs. Flights of warblers skittered about in the tall pines, gorging themselves on the plentiful river insects, preparing for their long migration south. Betty stopped at a steep turn in the path and looked up into Alex's eyes.

"Alex I'm so glad we found each other again; here in South Carolina. I had no idea when I left New York that I'd run into you here, much less in a supper club. I almost gave up hope when I couldn't find a job after I'd been banned from working on Broadway. I just couldn't go back to Baltimore after all the sacrifices my family had made for me to get an education. Aunt Maggie would have supported me, but I told her I needed to make my own way. I think Mary and your mother are right. It was just meant to be."

"Ma talks sometimes about her grandmother Hattie, when she lived on the plantation up in Edgefield where she grew up. Hattie came to this country on a Portuguese slave ship with her parents at thirteen. She was sold on the auction block in Charleston. She never saw her parents again.

"Ma said Hattie had learned conjuring in Ghana. Her tribe practiced Macumba, a type of Voodoo religion. Her mother, who was a high priestess in the Ashanti culture, passed on her skills to Hattie. Mama swears that her grandmother could cast spells and tell the future. She told my mother that she would move from Edgefield and marry a pirate. The family laughed at her. There were no pirates in South Carolina. Turns out though, she married my father who was a pirate's grandson. My great-grandfather sailed the Caribbean with Jean Lafitte. His grandson, my father. came to Aiken with Miss Celestine, the woman who paid for my schooling.

"He met and married Minnie Hillman, my mother, after she moved to Aiken. Her family had taken the name of the plantation owner, Frederick Hillman.

"Hattie was never legally married, since it was prohibited by law for slaves to marry, but she had several children, mostly from the same Negro slave she lived with. Mama says no one will swear to it but she thinks that, because of her skin color, that her father was one of the Hillman sons. It was a common practice in the day. So, it turns out that two of my grandfathers were white.

"Anyway, old Granny Hattie may still be conjuring from somewhere up in Ashanti heaven and she decided we should get back together. I guess that makes as much sense as anything."

Betty continued up the path, trying as best she could to stifle a laugh.

"That's the funniest thing I've heard in a long time. However, if it was Granny Hattie that got us back together, I guess I'll have to learn an Ashanti prayer so I can thank her."

Mary was already on stage running through her songs when Alex and Betty arrived.

"Come on up Betty and we'll go over these songs that Doc wants to play this weekend. He's picked out three duets for us. I really love singing with you. I hope you'll stick around after Doc leaves."

"I've got good news on that score," Betty said. "Your friend Mr. Rogers is going to give me a tryout at his club. I start Friday of next week. If it goes well, I'll sing four nights a week. The pay isn't as good but I get to stay at the hotel and best of all, Alex and I will have time to figure out where we're going."

"And for me, that's the best part," Alex chimed in.

"Great, I'm so happy for both of you," Mary said.

"I'm going back to visit George while you two rehearse", Alex said. "We've got some catching up to do."

"Do you know where George is?" Alex asked the bartender.

"Last I saw him he was out back unloading ice from the delivery truck."

"Thanks, I'll go on back if it's all right."

"Sure, just go through those doors back there." he said indicating two double doors into the ice house.

George was guiding the last 300-pound block of ice through the back door with a baling hook. He looked up in surprise when Alex called his name.

"Alex, I didn't know you was here. How you doin'?"

"I'm fine George. The girls are rehearsing so I thought we could spend some time together. We haven't had a lot of time alone since I got home."

"That's the truth. If you don't mind I needs to take care of this ice."

"Sure, go ahead George. I'll just sit over here."

George took an ice pick and separated the large block of ice into three 100-pound pieces. The blocks were scored into three sections by the ice-forming machine and came apart easily when George's icepick found the seams. He slid the blocks across the floor to the sawdust-insulated icehouse and shoved them through the door.

"That's six hundred pounds. Oughta hold us through the weekend."

"George, I was wondering what really happened with you and Papa that got you so riled up? Mama won't talk about it much. She says it has to do with Jonah."

"Yeah, it had a lot to do with Jonah. He was treatin' Cleo sumpin' awful and we got in a big fight 'bout that. Pa kinda took Jonah's side sayin' it was a man's right. Me'n him got into it then and I left. I think Pa changed his mind some after that but I was gone by then. Me'n Jonah ain't had much to do with each other since that day. When I seen him that last time at home he say, 'George I knows 'bout that money Miss Eustis done give to the family and I wants Cleo to git her share.' I tol' him 'I don't know nothin' bout no money' but he don't believe me. He say, 'George, if Cleo don't git some of that money they's gone be hell to pay.' I ain't seen him since."

"I can't imagine what money he's talking about. Miss Lulie sent $500 dollars to Ma to help pay Pa's final expenses. Mr. Hitchcock handed the check to me at the funeral. There hasn't been anything else that I'm aware of."

"I'll ask Cleo about it when I get back to Aiken, maybe she knows what put this burr under Jonah's saddle.

"George it's good to see you doing so much better. You seem to be getting around more easily, and the stutter is mostly gone. How about the seizures?"

"They don't happen so often nowadays. Useta be once, twice a week. I ain't had more'n two or three since Mary come. She make sure I takes my medicine like I sposed to. I don't know why she took up with me but she sho been a blessin'."

"You've got a good heart George Devereux. Mary saw that. Pa always said that. I know he'd be glad to see you back in the fold. Why don't you come on back to Aiken?"

"Naw, Alex, me'n Mary, we happy here and we gits by on what we makes. They some other things what went on 'bout the time I left that I cain't talk 'bout. It jes be better if I stay here."

"What things George?"

"I best not say. You might want to talk to Ben 'bout that."

Alex mulled over George's comments and decided to let them go. He shifted to another subject.

"Tell me about your work here George."

"Oh, I mos'ly be sure they plenty of ice in the bar. I help in the kitchen some, washin' dishes and such. In the summers, I work some 'round the pool. They's always things to do."

Betty and Mary came back to see what the boys were doing after they finished running through their song list.

"You boys caught up with everything now?" Mary asked. "Betty needs to get back over to the hotel. Eddie said he'd run her over. You want to go along Alex. He can drop you off at the trolley station on the way back."

"Sounds good to me," Alex said. "I'll see y'all Saturday night. Ben said he wants to come back with me."

"Good, maybe I can get Doc to listen to Ben sing. If he likes what he hears he might let him sing a song or two."

"I'm sure he'd like that,' Alex said. "Hey. Maybe you and Betty can ask Mr. Rogers to give Ben an audition after she gets established. That way we can keep it all in the family."

"Sounds like you've got this all figured out Alex Devereux," Mary said laughingly. "Get us all working over here and you can become our legal advisor."

"I hadn't thought about that," Alex laughed, "but it's not such a bad idea."

"I'll see you Saturday Betty," Alex said as he opened the door to the hotel. "It's been a wonderful day. I'm so glad you're going to be around—at least for a while."

"Me too, Alex, me too." She gave him a peck on the cheek and ran inside.

"She's mighty pretty Alex," Eddie said, "and smart too. Better hang on to that one."

"I'm trying Eddie, I'm trying."

28

The Gun

The trolley ride back to Aiken was decidedly pleasant. Things were looking brighter by the minute. Ben was home from the stables and sitting on the back porch swing with a glass of tea.

"Ben I saw George today and I asked him about the fight with Jonah and Pa. He just repeated what you and Mama told me. When I suggested that maybe he should come back to Aiken, he was evasive. He said he was happy there with Mary and he thought he should stay. Then he said something that was completely out of left field. He said Jonah claimed that the family had gotten some money from Miss Eustis and he wanted Cleo to get her share. He said he told Jonah he didn't know anything about any money. Jonah called him a liar and threatened him. Do you know anything about that?"

"Yeah, George told me the same thing. I asked Cleo 'bout it and she say Jonah say he heard Miss Iselin talkin' bout it. I ain't heard nothin'. George so worried Jonah gone do sumpin' to him he asked me if I might know somebody what could git him a gun. I said 'Quincy told me one time he had a gun and I'd see if he'd sell it.' Quin didn't want to sell it then but back when he started gittin' real sick he told me to meet 'im at the pool hall. We sat down in the back and he shoved this shoebox cross the table at me. 'What this Quin?' I say. He say 'this that gun you asked 'bout while back. I don't want Simon gittin' aholt of it'. 'I say 'Quin where you git this gun?' He say, 'You 'member when them Leeman folks got killed over to Crosland Park. Well me'n Simon goes over there next day jest to see what happened. That place way off in the woods. It was all chewed up with tire tracks and sech and they was blood all over the place. We was walkin' round and kickin' up the dirt when I saw sumpin' stickin' up out the mud. Well, I pick it up and it was a pistol. I stuck it in my pocket real quick so Simon don't see it and I don't tell 'im 'bout it. I took it home and cleaned it up. It was a revolver with three bullets still in it. It had a ivory handle with two silver initials set in it. 'I says 'What was the initials?' He say, 'E on one side and C on 'tother'. We both knowed they won't but one man in Aiken what got a pistol lak that, Mr. Eric Caldwell. He was the chief deputy sheriff. He musta dropped it in all the ruckus and it got buried by all them folks tramplin' round. We seen his car back out there and we reckoned he lookin' for it. Quin say he was too skeert to say nothin' bout it. He say I oughta give it to George an git it outtta town. So thats what I did. I told George where it come from and he oughta git rid of it or hide it real good."

"My God Ben! You know this directly implicates the sheriff's department in those killings. Everybody always thought they were involved, but no one there that night ever talked. If the coroner recovered the bullets from the Leemans, *and kept them*, they'll surely find a match for the rounds left in that pistol. If Caldwell finds out George has that gun he'll be in real danger. Do you know what he did with it?"

"He say he was gonna keep it cuz he still worried 'bout Jonah comin' over there. He won't say where he put it, he jest say it in a safe place."

"Ben have you told anyone else about this?"

"Naw Alex, you'n, me and George the onliest ones what know."

"Make sure it stays that way. If word gets back to any of those men out there that night, George's life won't be worth a plugged nickel."

"You think he oughta chunk it away?"

"No, not yet. There may be some way to use this to get at the truth of what happened in Monetta and at Crosland Park. I'll talk to George this weekend when I go back over there and we'll decide how to handle it. Just keep quiet. Don't even tell Ma. Especially don't tell Ma."

"Mr. Poole, can I talk to you in private – off the record?" Alex asked when he came into the office on Thursday morning.

"You mean like an attorney-client privilege thing?" Poole asked. "That only applies if I am representing you legally."

"No sir, just something that's come up that I don't quite know how to handle."

"Alex, I expect we're going to be working together for a long time. If we can't start off trusting each other then it won't work. I assure you that anything you tell me in confidence will be held in confidence and I assume vice-versa. What's bothering you?"

"If a person comes across something that could be incriminating evidence in a crime what should they do?"

"If that person is an officer of the court, as you and I are, they are bound by law to bring the evidence forth to the proper authorities."

"What if that evidence might incriminate one of those same authorities?"

Poole swiveled around to face Alex and sat up straighter in his chair.

"Let's stop beating around the bush, Alex. Tell me what this is all about?"

"I can't tell you everything I know, but someone has come forward with information that one of the guns used to shoot those three Leeman children in Crosland Park has turned up."

The blood drained from Poole's face. His knuckles turned white from gripping the chair arms. He was at a momentary loss to respond to Alex's revelations. His jaw muscles finally relaxed enough for him to say, "Alex you are aware that, if what you just told me is true, whoever has possession of that gun is in mortal danger."

"I realize that. That's why I was so reluctant to tell you."

"How many people know about the gun?"

"Just three. Me and two others."

"You, the man with the gun, and one other."

"Yes sir."

"Can that third person be trusted to keep his mouth shut?"

"Yes sir."

"Do you know the person who has the gun and how he came to be in possession of it?"

"Yes sir, I do."

"Do you know where it is?"

"No sir, not exactly."

"What do you mean not exactly?"

"I know the building it is in but not where the gun is."

"Does he know whose gun it is?"

"He believes he does."

"We'd better stop right there. Any further knowledge and I might not be able to plead deniability—if it comes to that."

"What do you think I should do?" Alex asked.

"I don't know. If the gun ultimately winds up in a court of law, then whoever has it—and whoever found it—is going to be forced to testify. Once those names become public, it'll be impossible to protect them. Several people, including other inmates, who were in a position to know what happened at the jail that night, have just disappeared.

"If it were me, I'd be tempted to throw it in the river. On the other hand, if the gun is destroyed, whatever chance there may have been to achieve some degree of justice for the Leeman children will be lost."

Poole relaxed a bit and leaned back in his chair.

"Why don't you just sit tight and let me nose around a bit. It's been over a year next month since the killings occurred. Things have quieted down considerably and the people responsible may not be as cautious as they were. They may think it's all blown over. I'm sure the majority of the white citizens of Aiken would just as soon see it go away. It's been a trying time for the entire community. There's little doubt in anyone's mind that the KKK was behind the lynchings, and many are fearful of what they may do if things start up again."

Alex was still uncertain of what to advise George as he rode over to North Augusta on Saturday afternoon. He was afraid of what might happen to his brother if the authorities found the gun. He was also torn about asking him to dispose of it. He began to think long and hard about the future of black people in Aiken.

If my reason for being back in Aiken is to see justice done, then I can't ignore what happened to the Leemans. No matter what the original motive for the raid in Monetta, there could be no justification for what was done to them. At least five people were dead and there were many more whose lives were forever changed.

* * * * *

Sam Leeman, the father of Demon and Bertha, served all but 72 days of a sentence for bootlegging. Evidence against him had been a single bottle of moonshine found buried in the backyard of the home where his wife and the sheriff had died. Few doubted that the evidence was planted. Upon his release Sam said, "I'm moving north to Philadelphia. I can't live among these people anymore."

* * * * *

No! Someone has to make a stand, and it might as well start with me. I'm going to ask George to give me the gun so I can make sure it gets to someone in authority who is not tainted by the events in Monetta or in Crosland Park.

29

The Murder

There was a single car parked out front when Alex walked up the hill to the club. He recognized the car as belonging to Jonah Page. He rushed inside, his pulse quickening. Out front, the club was eerily silent. He walked toward the bar area. Through the door to the storage area and the ice room, he could hear the muffled sobs of a woman. He ran behind the bar and shoved the door open. Mary Waters was leaning over the prostrate, unconscious body of George Devereux, her white skirt covered with blood.

"Mary! What happened? Is George hurt?"

She looked up at Alex, her face distorted by fear and anguish

"No," she cried, "but he seems to have had a seizure."

"Where did all that blood come from?"

"Oh, Alex, it's awful!"

She pointed toward a heap of boxes in the far corner of the room. Alex walked toward them apprehensively. There, lying on the floor in a pool of blood was Jonah Page, a baling hook protruding from his skull.

"My God! What happened Mary?"

"I don't know," she cried through her sobs. "I was out front on the stage when I heard someone shouting, 'Where the hell is it George? I know you got it.' Then I heard a big crash. When I got in here, I found George lying there. I didn't see any blood on George but I saw a trail of blood leading across the room to those boxes. I ran over there and found Jonah. After he was struck he must have stumbled and fallen behind those boxes. Alex there was blood all over the place. What are we going to do?"

"First, we have to call the police. Will you run out front and call them? I'll see if there's anything I can do back here."

Alex went to Jonah and felt his neck for a pulse. There was none. He grabbed a bar towel on the way across to George and wiped the blood from his hands. George's eyes were open and rolled back in his head. This was a typical symptom of his seizures. He felt for a pulse in George's throat. It was weak but steady. He ran for some water and lifted his brother to take a drink. George spluttered and coughed before sitting up. He looked dazed and disoriented.

"George, what happened?"

George rubbed his eyes and shook his head to clear away the cobwebs.

"I heard a noise. I was in the bar. I came back here and found a man poking around through my stuff and I said, 'What you doin'?' He whipped around and said, 'Where the hell is it George? I know you got it.' Then he came at me and I passed out. That's all I know."

"You know Jonah is dead?"

"What! No! Why Jonah here? I don't know nothin' bout that."

"Well he is! He's lying over there behind those boxes with a baling hook stuck in his head!"

"My God, Alex! You don't think I killed Jonah, do you?"

"George I don't see anyone else here, and you've got his blood all over you. It doesn't look good. Do you keep a baling hook back here?"

"Yeah, they's one I use to drag them big blocks of ice round with. I keep it stuck in the door frame by the back porch."

Alex looked over to the rear door.

"It's not there now, George. Did you have it when Jonah came in?"

"Naw, Alex! Lak I said, I didn't never see no Jonah. I ran over to the man who was pokin' through my stuff. He come at me and that's the last thing I remember."

"Did you know the man?"

"Naw, I never seen him before. He was white, scrawny looking, bout twenty-five or thirty I reckon. He had on Bib overalls and a red flannel shirt. And one of them felt hats you see them lintheads wearin' over to Graniteville. That's bout all I 'member befo I blacked out."

Mary came running back in, ashen and out of breath.

"I spoke to the police in North Augusta. They said they'll send someone right over. George, are you all right. I thought you were dead."

"I'm okay Mary. I jest don't know what happened. Lak I told Alex, I was standing there and he came at me. That's when I passed out."

"Mary said the same thing you did George. She was on the stage and she heard someone say, 'Where the hell is it George? I know you got it,' then she dropped what she was doing and ran back here. Did you hear or see anything else Mary."

"I saw a man going out the back door and the sound of a car driving off. I didn't go to see who it was. I was too worried about George. That was before I saw the blood and found Jonah."

The sound of sirens drew near. Seconds later two uniformed members of the North Augusta police department rushed through the door.

"Are you the woman who placed the call," the senior cop asked, looking at Mary

"Yes I called you." Mary said.

"Who are these other people?"

"This is my friend George Devereux and his brother Alex."

"Where is the dead man?"

"He's over there, behind those boxes," Mary said, pointing.

The two policemen approached the scene cautiously, peering over the tops of the boxes.

"You sure he's dead?"

"Yeah, I checked for a pulse," Alex said. "There was none. It's pretty obvious the hook went through his brain. He must've died almost instantly."

The other cop kneeled down by Jonah's body and stared into his open eyes.

"You think old Pete Conrad will mind if I close his eyes?" he asked.

"Naw, it won't hurt nothing. Pete won't care." Pete Conrad was the Aiken county coroner.

"Okay, who wants to tell me what happened here?" the lead officer said.

George related his story of finding the intruder and confronting him and then having a seizure.

"Who discovered the body?"

"I did," Mary said. "I was out on the stage when I heard the shouting and noise. I came running back and I found George unconscious and Jonah dead."

"Jonah? You know the victim?"

"Yes sir," Mary said. "He's married to George's sister Cleo."

"And who are you again?" he asked turning to Alex.

"I'm George's brother."

"And what's your business here?"

"I came over to see George and to meet my friend Betty Carlton. She and Mary will be performing here tonight."

"Tell me what you know."

"When I came in Mary was kneeling over George. She was crying and shaking George, telling him to wake up. George has epilepsy and is prone to seizures. There was blood on her skirt and I asked her if George was hurt. She just pointed toward those boxes. She could hardly speak. I went over, followed the trail of blood, and there was Jonah's body. Like I said, I checked his pulse and couldn't find one. Mary said she had gone over to check him also and that's when she got the blood on her. I asked George what happened and he said he was in the bar area when he heard someone back here. He said that when he came back he saw this man rifling through his belongings. George confronted the man. That's when he came at George and that's when George fainted. He said when he started to wake up Mary was there and he doesn't remember anything else.'

"I see," said the officer. "And this other man, can you describe him?"

"Yeah," George said, "he was white, bout twenty-five or thirty, red, checked, flannel shirt and Bib overalls. Oh yeah, and he had a mustache and a short beard."

"What do you think he was looking for?" the man asked.

"I don't know," George said. "Just before I passed out he said, 'Where the hell is it George, I know you've got it?' "

"So this stranger knew you by name, but you didn't know him?"

"Yes suh, that's right."

"That hook sticking out of his head, do you know where it came from?"

"It looks like the one I use to drag ice blocks around with."

"Did the man have it in his hands when you approached him?"

"I don't know," George said.

"Why was Jonah, here?"

"I don't know that either," George said.

"Did he come over here often?"

"Naw suh, this the first time I seen him here."

"Do you have any idea why he came over here today?"

"Naw suh I don't. Lak I say, I didn't even know he was here

'til Alex come in."

"Miss Waters, when were you first aware that something was going on back here?"

"Like I said, I was out on the stage when I heard a loud noise and shouting from back here. Then I heard a man yell, 'Where the hell is it George? I know you've got it.' When I got back here, I found George lying on the floor. I saw a man going out the back door and heard a car driving off."

"Did you go to see who it was?"

"No sir, I was too worried about George and then when I saw blood all over the floor and went to see where it came from, that's when I found Jonah. I checked to see if he was alive and couldn't find a pulse. Then I came back to check on George. A few seconds later Alex came in."

"What about you boy?" the officer asked Alex. "Did you see anyone else back here?"

"No sir."

"Did you hear a car driving off?"

"No sir, the only car I saw was Jonah's old Model-T out front. I thought that was strange, so I hurried back to see what was going on. I must've been running through the club when the other car drove from around back."

"I'm going to call the coroner and the Aiken County Sheriff now. This club is outside the city limits so they have jurisdiction here. We'll hang around until they get here. I suggest all of you wait in the bar. Don't touch anything else and don't change any of your clothes. Officer Melton will stay with you."

Officer Melton leaned against the bar drinking a Coca-Cola. Alex, George and Mary were sitting several feet away. Alex leaned over and whispered to Mary.

"Are you certain you heard another voice besides George's and then a car driving off?"

Mary looked at Alex in wide-eyed disbelief.

"Alex, how can you ask me such a thing? You think George did this? Why would I lie to you?"

"You've got to admit things don't look good. Jonah is dead and the murder weapon belongs to George. There's no physical evidence that anyone else was here. Everyone knows about the fight George and Jonah had before he left home and came over here."

"But Alex, that's no reason to kill him, just because they had a disagreement."

"Did George tell you that Jonah had threatened him after Pa's funeral?"

Mary looked at George quizzically.

"What's he talking about George?"

"I didn't want to git you all upset. Jonah claimed he heard somebody say that Miss Eustis done give the family some more money. It was to be paid out when Alex got his law papers and come back to Aiken. She wanted to be sho he done lak he was sposed to. I didn't never hear bout no sech thing. Jonah think we all got a chunk of it but Cleo didn't. He was hoppin' mad and he said if she didn't get her share they was gone be hell to pay. He say he gone make sho we all gives her some of what we got. I reckon he thought I'd be the easiest to git it from, bein' crippled and all."

"You see, that's what worries me, Mary," Alex said. "When you heard a man's voice say, 'Where the hell is it, George. I know you have it,' the first thought I had was that Jonah was looking for money that he thought George had."

"George, that might explain why somebody broke into our place last week!" Mary said. "It must have been Jonah looking for money. When he didn't find any there, he figured you had it somewhere here at the club."

"You didn't say anything about that to me George!" Alex said.

"They won't nothin' took. We reckoned it was jest some

kids in the neighborhood messin' round. I didn't think no mo bout it. I put some new locks on the doors and screens."

"Did you call the police?"

"Naw, I didn't want them nosin' round none. Sides, lak I say, they won't nothin' missin'."

"When did the break-in happen?"

"It was last Saturday night while we were at the club," Mary said.

The police officer finished the Coke and came over.

"I need to go powder my nose, if you don't mind," Mary said to him.

"Go ahead Miss."

Three sheriff's deputies were coming through the club when Mary returned.

"Hey Melton," one of the men said, "what we got here?"

"Roy is in the back. He'll fill you in. Just go through them doors behind the bar over there."

"Thanks."

An hour later, the deputies and Officer Ron Branch emerged from the backroom. They crossed to where the three were seated.

"We're going to need the three of you to come with us to the sheriff's office in Aiken so that we can get your written statements," Deputy Shackleford said.

"But we have a show to put on this evening," Mary protested.

"Little lady, they ain't gonna be no show here tonight. This whole place is a crime scene. Until we get through with our investigation, this place is shut down. Just follow us and we'll get started."

The sheriff's car was exiting the driveway when Peter Conrad arrived in his ambulance. He stopped and rolled down his window.

"Hey Shack, you boys done in there?" he asked.

"Yeah, we done collected all the evidence we need. The only thing left that's important is the murder weapon. When you git that baling hook outta that boy's head just bring it over to the office. Try not to touch the handle on it. They may be some fingerprints we need. Con Massey is still in there. He'll stay until you finish up."

"Okay Shack. I'll see you back in Aiken," the crusty coroner said. He'd seen a lot of killings in his tenure as coroner but never one with a baling hook.

Chief deputy Eric Caldwell sat across the room from Con Massey and Ezra Shackleford as they took the statements. Each of the three witnesses were brought in separately and asked to give their version of what happened. When they had all finished they were required to sign the statements. Afterwards Massey took them to a waiting room.

"Bring those statements into my office," Caldwell said. "I want to go over them. When I'm ready, I want to question them myself."

"George Devereux, come with me," Deputy Massey said.

George followed the deputy across the hall and into the sheriff's office. Eric Caldwell was sitting at the sheriff's desk with his feet propped-up on an open drawer.

"Sit down," he commanded.

"Boy, you expect me to believe this cock-and-bull story about some mysterious white boy coming in and scaring you to death and then him just disappearing into thin air. You wanna tell me what really happened? I hear tell they was some bad blood between you and your brother-in-law Jonah Page. I been asking around ever since the boys called and told me what happened."

George began to sweat profusely. He realized that all the

evidence in that storage room pointed directly at him as the killer of Jonah Page. On the face of it, his story that an intruder had committed the murder lacked any credibility.

"I been telling the truth. Everthing he wrote on that paper be the gospel truth bout what happened. They was a man what was goin' through my things. When he come at me I had one of my seizures. They happens most when I gits nervous lak that. I didn't even know Jonah be there til I woke up. You can ask Mary. She heard the same man yellin' at me. She seen him run out the back door and heard him drive off."

"I know what she says she saw and heard. It looks to me like she's just covering up for you. I understand the two of you live together. I think she's just trying to protect your black ass. In the absence of evidence to the contrary, we must assume that you killed Jonah Page. The only question I have is why he came over there today and what he was looking for in your belongings. Unless and until we find that out we're going to have to hold you for his murder."

"What you mean? You gonna lock me up? I swear I's tellin' the truth. I didn't kill Jonah."

"Well it sure looks like you did and we're going to hold you until there's been a full investigation."

"Con, Ezra," Caldwell shouted, "come in here."

"I want you boys to take this nigger to a holding cell while I get the proper documents drawn up to charge him with the murder of Jonah Page. On your way out send that other boy and the girl in here.

"We're charging George Devereux with the murder of Jonah Page," Chief Deputy Caldwell said to Mary and Alex. "The two of you are listed as material witnesses. I'm releasing you for now but don't you leave the area. George will be arraigned first thing Monday. You might want to see about gittin' him a good lawyer. He's sure gonna need one."

30

The Suspect

"What can we do Alex?" Mary sobbed as they stumbled down the steps of the sheriff's office.

"First thing we have to do is get over to Cleo's house. Poor Cleo. She's going to be completely devastated over this. Not only is her husband dead, but her brother is charged with his murder and she's left with two little children to raise."

"What about George?" Mary asked. "Do you still think he killed Jonah?"

"I don't want to believe that after what you and George both told me, but it's going to be hard to prove otherwise. You've got to know now, that it was Jonah that broke into your house looking for money. And when you heard him say 'Where the hell is it George?' he must have been talking about the money he thought George had gotten from Miss Eustis. Whoever killed George knew his name. If it was just some intruder, he wouldn't have known him.".

"Alex I swear to you, the voice I heard was not Jonah's. I've only been around him a few times but it's hard to mistake his voice. The voice I heard was high-pitched and twangy. I just can't believe it was Jonah. George is right. There was another man in that room when he fainted and I believe Jonah was already there, lying behind those boxes with that hook through his head. George found the white man going through his things. Then George confronted him before fainting."

"Mary, put yourself in the place of the sheriff and look at the known facts. There is no physical evidence that there was any other person in that room when Jonah died. If you and George are right, we've got to have evidence to prove it in a court of law, and right now I don't have a clue as to how to do that."

"There must be a way," she said as they stumbled along a darkened Richland Avenue toward the Page home. "Jonah was clear on the other side of the room from where George was lying, and hidden from view. Not more than thirty seconds passed between the time I heard that voice and I entered the room. If George was having a seizure after hitting Jonah with that hook, he couldn't have moved to the other side of the room. I think Jonah was already dead when George went back there and saw the other man. He said he didn't even know Jonah was there. He ran over to see what was going on and that's when the man said 'Where the hell is it George?' He couldn't have known about any money George was supposed to have! He was looking for something else Alex! When he heard me coming, he took off out the back door. I saw the door closing."

Alex slowed his pace. Suddenly, it all made sense. Whoever killed Jonah was not after money. He was looking for Eric Caldwell's revolver. But, how could he know about the gun. Besides me, only George and Ben knew it existed. If he was looking for the gun, someone had spilled the beans. But who, and why?

Cleo lay prostrate on the sofa in the front parlor of the small bungalow on Marlboro Street. The racking sobs had subsided only to be replaced by sporadic wails of anguish. Mary dabbed at Cleo's face with a cold cloth. She had closed the door to the children's room, hoping they wouldn't wake.

"Why, Alex, why?" Cleo managed between gasping breaths.

"Why George hafta kill Jonah? He won't gone hurt'im none. He always athreatenin' to do sumpin' but sides hittin' on me some he ain't never hurt nobody. Why he ain't never even laid no hand on the chilren. It jes don't make no sense."

"I don't know Cleo. I guess George was so threatened he felt he had to do something to protect himself. Did Jonah say anything more about the money he thought George had?"

"He was always grumblin' about how it won't fair but he ain't said nothin' mo about it to me."

"Did he tell you he was going over there?"

"Naw, he ain't said nuthin to me bout it."

"Do you know of anything else Jonah might have had a grievance with George about?"

"Naw, it was jest the fight they had and the money Jonah reckoned George done got."

Alex began to wonder if Jonah had found out about the gun some way. But, even if he had, what good would it do him to get his hands on it? No, there has to be more to it. He walked out onto the front porch, signaling Mary to follow.

"Mary, can you stay with Cleo tonight?"

"Certainly Alex. She's in no condition to be left alone. I'll see to the children as well."

"Thanks Mary. I'm going over to Mr. Miller's and have him pick up Jonah's body at the coroner's office then I'll go back over and pick up Jonah's car. I'm not going to tell Ma about all of this until I get back. The last thing she needs tonight is to hear there's another death in the family."

All the lights were out at the Devereux household at ten-thirty when Alex drove up. He took his shoes off before entering the house. There was no sense in getting Minnie and Ben all roused up tonight. Tomorrow will be sufficient unto the day.

Alex slept until eight. He heard his mother in the kitchen. He dressed hurriedly and joined her there.

"Alex, whut Jonah's car doin' in our yard?"

Alex's plans to ease gently into an exposition of the events of the previous day were thrown into a cocked hat.

"Sit down Ma," he said.

The expression on his face told Minnie everything she needed to know.

"What done happened now!" She blurted out.

"Ma, Jonah has been killed. It happened over at Carolina Springs. We think he went over there to get money from George. He had this crazy idea that Miss Celestine had left more money to the family and he thought Cleo should have gotten part of it. We didn't say anything to you because we thought his obsession about it would go away. Apparently it didn't. Mary found him with a baling hook imbedded in his head and George lying on the floor with one of his seizures.

"My Lord, Alex, say it ain't so!"

"I wish I could Mama but it is.

"They both swear that Jonah was killed by someone else. George, when he woke up, said he didn't even know Jonah was there. He said he went to the back when he heard noises. He said there was a young white man digging around in his things and that he demanded to know where "it" was. We assume it was money. Mary said she heard the same thing while she was out front on the stage. She says that when she got back there she saw George lying on the floor and someone was going out the back door. She swears the voice she heard was not Jonah. She said it was a nasal, twangy voice. Something you might expect to hear in the Valley.

"Jonah's body was found on the other side of the big storeroom with a baling hook imbedded in his head. There was a large amount of blood trailing across the floor to where Mary found him behind a stack of boxes.

"We called the police from North Augusta. They came and immediately called the Sheriff since the Springs are in the county. Several deputies came over to investigate. They took us to the sheriff's office and wrote down our sworn statements.

"Based on all the evidence, they assumed that George had killed Jonah, and they put him in jail."

Minnie crossed her arms on the table and rested her head.

"Oh Lawd, ain't I done got more'n enough crosses to bear already? Now you done put this on me too."

She began to cry.

"Whut we gone do Alex?"

"I'm not rightly sure Ma. It doesn't look good for George. They know about the bad blood between him and Jonah and they know about the threats. All the physical evidence points toward George, but both he and Mary swear that there was another man in that room. The sheriff's men think Mary is just covering for George and so they don't believe either of them."

"What about Cleo? She know?"

"Yes ma'am. Mary is with her and the children. We went there from the sheriff's office. She took it mighty hard but seemed to be calm when I left.

"I called Mr. Miller to pick up Jonah's body from the morgue and then I went back over to The Springs and got his car. I didn't tell you last night. Both you and Ben were asleep and it wouldn't have served any good purpose to have everybody up all night."

"What they gone do with George?"

"He's charged with capital murder so they probably won't allow bail. He'll have to stay in jail until the trial."

"Alex, you gone defend George?"

"I need to talk with Mr. Poole. I hope he'll help me with George's defense. I think he will. The fact that it's a black-on-black crime will make it easier for him to do so. If the victim had been a white man, it would make it more difficult for him because of what happened during the Leeman trial. Many folks in town still resent the position he took.

"By the way, I forgot that he wanted me to bring you into the office on Monday. He said it had to do with Pa's estate. When I asked him what it was he wouldn't say. Now we'll have two things to discuss with him."

"I reckon so," Minnie said. "Alex I wants you to go fetch Cleo and the chilren. She oughten to be left alone in that house. Bring Miss Mary too. They can stay here while this all gits straightened out. You and Ben'll hafta share a room again lak you did befo."

"Okay Ma. I'll go over right after breakfast. I'll go by Gaston's and let Ben know what's going on, too. I guess you and Cleo and I will need to go over to Miller's and to Friendship church to make funeral arrangements as well."

"I reckon so. I figgered I was done with funerals for a long time. It jest show how the Lawd got special plans for us."

31

The Trust

The sun was beginning its lazy descent when the family returned from the dismal task of arranging Jonah's funeral. The spare arrangements reflected both the family's diminished funds after Sam's funeral, as well as Jonah's standing in the community. Certainly there would be an outpouring of support for Cleo, Minnie and the family. Little would be focused on Jonah himself however. He was estranged from his family in far-off Florence and few Page family members were expected to make the arduous journey to Aiken.

"That gone bout use up all the money Miss Louise give us for Sam's funeral."

Minnie struggled up her back steps and plopped down in the swing as the back door swung open. Phoebe emerged carrying little Maggie with Toby clinging to her skirt.

"How the chilren doin?" Minnie asked.

"They be fine," Phoebe said. "Toby, he seem to unnerstan his pa is gone, but I'm not sure Maggie do. They took a long nap and they's been playin' in the yard. I reckon they'll be plenty tuckered out and go to bed early.

"Cleo, how you doin'?"

"It don't seem real somehow. I knows he gone but it ain't sunk in good yet. It gone hit me hard when I gotta go back to that empty house."

"You ain't gotta go nowhere girl." Minnie said. "You's welcome to stay with us long as you want. Fact be, if you cain't manage over to Marlboro, you'n the young'uns can move in with us."

"Thank you Ma, but I'm gonna try to make it by myself for a while. Things get real bad then I might hafta."

"Alex'n me don't mind sharin' a room Sis. You stay long as you wants. Be good havin' the young'uns around," Ben said.

"Girls we best git the house straightened up. They gone be lots o folks comin' round after church tomorrow," Minnie said. "Lawsy mercy me, I sho won't spectin' to be doin' all this agin so soon. I reckon the good Lord'll git us through it."

With that, she went into the kitchen to stoke the fire in the wood stove. Suppertime was coming no matter what, and folks gotta be fed.

Once again, pew number six at Friendship Baptist Church was draped with black bunting. The members of the Devereux household passed through the sad gauntlet of well-wishers on their way down the aisle. Cleo wore Minnie's wide-brimmed black hat with the black veil.

Reverend Pope opened his remarks with condolences for Cleo and the children and reminded the congregation of their Christian duty to support the family through their bereavement and in the coming weeks and months as they adjusted to a life without a father and husband.

"It has been such a short time since we gathered here to mourn the passing of our dear brother Samson Devereaux. Now we gather again to remember another of our own. One who has passed away far too young. Let us remember Jonah Page as we pray for his eternal soul."

Cleo lifted her veil and dabbed at her eyes. Her thoughts

drifted to the difficult times she and Jonah had struggled through in their marriage. Nonetheless, she had loved him, despite all his faults, and she would miss him in her life. If nothing else, he had left her with Toby and Maggie and that would atone for many of the troubles he had visited on the family.

"…and let us not forget about our brother George Devereux. We can't know all that happened on Friday over at Carolina Springs, but whatever the circumstances that provoked such a tragedy it is our duty to support Brother George and to hope that he will be exonerated of the charges against him."

The dining table in Minnie's kitchen once again groaned under the weight of all the dishes delivered to the Devereux family. Dozens of friends called during the afternoon to repeat the time-honored rituals surrounding southern funerals, especially black southern funerals.

The women gathered inside to offer solace to the widow and children. The men gathered outside to console the men and to banter with each other in that good-humored way that helped to take the sharp edge off their grief.

Stories about the events at Carolina Springs were rampant in the Aiken black community. Wild variations emerged with each telling until the truth became lost in the rumor. Most knew the history between George and Jonah and were dubious of his claims of a mysterious assailant. Most agreed that the best George could hope for was to convince the jury that it was an unpremeditated crime of passion and to throw himself on the mercy of the court. Twelve white jurors were likely to be merciful to a stuttering, physically challenged, black man if he appeared contrite and remorseful.

The last visitors departed shortly after dusk and the family gathered in the kitchen for supper. There was scant conversation.. The events of the weekend, following so closely on Sam's death, left everyone exhausted and drained of energy. By eight, the children were bedded down, with the adults following shortly thereafter.

Cleo scheduled the funeral for Friday. She just wanted the pain to be over. So much was going on. She asked Reverend Pope to keep the church service brief and to dispense with a graveside ceremony.

A flock of chickens, scratching about the yard for food, scattered in a flurry of feathers as Jonah's old car sputtered and backfired. Alex reminded himself to ask Ben to take a look at it later. He hoped it didn't have any major problems which were beyond Ben's limited automotive skills.

Mr. Poole was already at his desk when Alex and Minnie made their way up the stairs. He wanted to clear his desk of pressing Monday morning work prior to their arrival. Miss Rhodes came out of his inner office with a sheaf of papers and a handful of scribbled notes he had dictated.

"Good morning Alex," she beamed. "this must be your mother, Mrs. Samson Devereux. I remember you from several years back when you came in with Mr. Devereux."

"Thank you for rememberin' me, but please, jest call me Minnie. Everbody else do."

"Very well, Minnie. Mr. Poole said to give him about five minutes and then he'll be out. Just have a seat. Would either of you care for some coffee or water?"

"No ma'am." Alex said. "We just finished breakfast a short while ago."

"Very well then. If you don't mind, I've got a lot of Monday morning work to get to so just make yourselves comfortable. Mr. Poole will be out shortly."

Minnie sat and stared at all the framed documents amd photos attesting to Frampton Poole's elevated standing in the community. She recognized a picture of Mr. Jimmy Byrnes. She had served him many times at the Hitchcock's. There was a photograph of Mr. and Mrs. Julian Salley. They too, had been frequent visitors to *Mon Repos.*

Alex thumbed through a copy of the *South Carolina Law Review.*

The door to Mr. Poole's office opened and he stepped out to welcome them.

"Mrs. Devereux, how nice to see you again. I was so sorry to hear of Sam's passing. I thought a great deal of him. I must say the two of you have raised an extraordinarily bright and capable son. I can't tell you how impressed I am with his knowledge of the law. I predict he'll go far in the legal world."

"Thank you Mr. Poole for them kind words. We mighty proud of Alex."

"Come on in," he said, "and have a seat."

"Before we get started Mr. Poole," Alex said, "I wonder if you've heard about the tragedy over at Carolina Springs over the weekend?"

"You mean the murder. Yes I heard about it, but I don't have any of the details."

"Well, as I told you before, my brother George works over there. It appears that my sister Cleo's husband, Jonah Page, went over there and he and George got into some kind of argument and Jonah wound up with a baling hook in his head."

"My Lord, I didn't know any of your family was involved. What has happened since?"

"It appears they'll be charging George with murder. He's being held at the county jail."

"Is it conclusive that your brother killed Mr. Page?"

"Both he and his girlfriend, Mary Waters, insist there was another man there and that he's the one who killed Jonah. The police think that Mary is just trying to cover up for George. Mary swears that the voice she heard before she ran back to the murder scene was not Jonah's voice. She claims it sounded like someone from the Valley, a white man. George says the same thing. He says he came upon this man rifling through his effects and confronted him. The man went at George and then George had one of his seizures. He doesn't remember anything else until he woke up, after Mary and I got there. Mary said she saw a man leaving through the back door and then she heard a car drive off. Jonah's body was clear across the room, hidden, and lying in a big pool of blood.

"I think I told you before that there was some bad blood between George and Jonah and that's why George left home. Jonah had this crazy idea that Miss Celestine had left some more money to me and the family. He thought Cleo should have part of it. We think he broke into George's apartment last Saturday. When he didn't find the money there, we assume he went to The Springs looking for it."

"How much credence do you give to George and Mary's story?"

"I must admit it doesn't look good for George. There's no physical evidence that there was anyone else in the room. However, I have a great deal of respect for Mary. I don't think she would lie about this. Nor would George.

"Another thing, George was lying clear across the room, toward the back door when I came in. Jonah was on the far side of the room behind a stack of boxes. If George was going to faint after striking Jonah with the baling hook, wouldn't we have found him close to the body, and wouldn't there have been a lot of blood on him? The only blood was that which Mary transferred after checking Jonah to see if he was alive. Those things don't add up, but I don't know how to prove differently."

"This is ironic." Poole said. "The reason I asked you to come in today was to tell you that Miss Celestine *had* left you some more money. She opened a trust for you, the payout of which was contingent on your getting your degree and returning to

Aiken to practice law. She swore me to secrecy. If you hadn't returned to practice law here, the funds would have reverted to the family. With accumulated interest, the trust is now worth $12, 233 and 35 cents. So, if Jonah found out about it, I don't know how."

"Jonah worked for Miss Iselin at Hopeland as a groom. He told my sister Cleo, his wife, that he overheard Miss Iselin talking to another woman in the stables. It appears that Miss Eustis may have confided in Miss Iselin about the trust and that's how Jonah found out. None of us knew anything about it. That's why we thought Jonah was acting so crazy. He became obsessed with what he felt was unfairness to him and Cleo and threatened George if he didn't give some of the money to him. Obviously, George didn't know anything. None of us did."

"That would explain Jonah's motives, but it doesn't explain the disparities you've noted nor the story both George and Mary have related about there being another man."

"What that mean Alex? A trust?"

"It's assets someone places in reserve to be dispensed upon the occurrence of certain events."

"Boy, don't you go spoutin' them big words at me. What do it mean?"

""It means that I will receive that money per the directives in the trust."

"Exactly," Poole said. "You will receive it in equal installments over the next five years. The first will occur this week. It will be deposited in an account opened in your name, next door at the Farmer's and Merchant's bank."

"That means we can afford to pay for your services in defense of George," Alex said.

"It certainly does Alex, but I will be glad to offer my services to you and your family *pro bono.* "

"What that mean?" Minnie demanded.

"It means he'll help me defend George for free. Thank you

sir. That's very kind of you."

"Kindness has nothing to do with it," Poole said smiling. "I expect to extract my foregone fees and much more from you in the years to come. You're going to have to sing for your supper."

"It will be my pleasure sir."

"The Good Lord, He close one door and then he open another one," Minnie said as they clattered down Park Avenue. "That money gone hep you git George off. I knows it is."

"Now Ma, don't get your hopes up too high. The evidence pointing to George is pretty overwhelming. It'll be up to me and Mr. Poole to try to find something to support what George and Mary have said. It won't be easy. It may be that the most we can do is to try to create enough reasonable doubt in the minds of the jurors to force a hung jury or for them to convict him on a lesser charge, one that carries a shorter jail term."

32

The Search

"So Jonah be right all the time," Cleo said. "I thought he was jest crazy. No wonder George was so mixed up. He won't knowin' nothin' 'bout no money."

"No Cleo, Jonah was sure, from what he heard at Hopeland, that you were being cheated. He assumed the money was to be paid to Ma for the benefit of the entire family. Whenever he talked to anyone in the family about it, and they denied any knowledge of it, he was sure they were lying to him

"I want you to know that I will stand behind you and support you through all this. Don't worry about the funeral expenses, just take care of yourself and the kids.

"I'm convinced now that George and Mary are telling the truth about what happened Friday.There were just too many inconsistencies at the crime scene. There was someone else in that room and he was looking for something besides money. I think I may know what it is. Finding it was important enough to them to kill Jonah for it, and I think he would have killed George if Mary hadn't barged in. George is the only one that can identify him and that puts George in jeopardy. I'm going to talk to Mr. Poole about this. Maybe he can help assure that George is protected."

"Mr. Poole, I think I know what that man was looking for when Jonah was killed?"

"What?"

"I think it was that gun I told you about."

"But, you said only two other people knew about its existence and neither one would give it away."

"I know, but somehow, someway, this man found out about it and went to Carolina Springs looking for it. I believe when he yelled, 'Where the hell is it George? I know you have it!' he wasn't talking about money, he was talking about the gun."

"So it was your brother you were talking about before."

"Yes sir, he had the gun. My other brother, Ben, gave it to him for protection. George was worried about Jonah."

"And you're sure neither of your brothers has told anyone else of its existence?"

"They swear they haven't."

"Where did your brother get the gun?"

Alex explained the Ben and Quincy relationship and how Quincy had found the gun at the scene of the shootings in Crosland Park.

"Do you think this Quincy boy told someone else about finding it?"

"Ben says he was so scared once he found out whose gun it was he just wanted to be rid of it. When Ben asked him to get a gun for George, Quincy saw an opportunity to get rid of it and to help out a friend."

"How did Quincy know whose gun it was?"

"When he got it home and cleaned it up he discovered that the gun had ivory handles with silver initials set into them."

Frampton Poole stood and began to pace the room, obviously agitated that this was more information than he had bargained for.

"What the hell," he said, throwing caution to the wind, "in for a dime in for a dollar. What were the initials?"

"E.C."

"My God Alex! You know what this means?"

"Yes sir. That gun ties the sheriff's department directly to the killings of the Leemans."

"If Eric Caldwell has found out in some fashion that his gun was found at the scene of the killings he will stop at nothing to get it back – or to make sure that whoever has it never testifies against him."

"What can we do?" Alex asked.

"I told you I was going to do some snooping around. I nosed around the courthouse and the sheriff's department and I found out that Caldwell has taken a brief leave of absence from the Sheriff's department. I didn't think anything of it, but it all makes sense now. Somehow, he found out about the gun and who had it. He wouldn't have been stupid enough to try to go after it himself, but he certainly may have put someone else up to it."

"Is there any way to find out who?"

Poole paced back and forth, eyes closed, his face wreathed in deep concentration.

"Alex, did you say that George's girlfriend Mary heard someone shout at George?"

"Yes sir."

"Did she say she heard the same thing George said he heard?"

"Yes sir, she said it was a high pitched, nasal voice. George confirmed that. He said the man was no older than thirty, dressed in Bib overalls, a flannel shirt, and an old felt hat like the mill workers wear. Oh yeah, he also said he had a short beard and a mustache."

"That makes sense. Caldwell lives in Warrenville. He used to work in the mills. It stands to reason that he would choose an accomplice from his own neighborhood, someone he knew and could trust."

"If this is true, is there any way to find out who?"

"I don't know but I'm going to get John Wiggins to have some of his people snoop around the bars and juke joints in the valley to see if he can find anything out."

"Mr. Poole, if we don't find anything, how long will it be before George goes to trial?"

"Typically, capital murder cases take about three months to schedule. It depends on how much time the prosecutor feels he needs to investigate. I'm sure Abner Peabody thinks this is such an air tight case that he won't ask for any delays. I'd guess we're looking at early to mid-February."

"So we don't have much time to come up with evidence that would support George's story."

"That's true. Like I said, I'll get John on this right away. Maybe he can dig up something. That seems to be the most promising alternative at the moment. Meantime, I want you to go back and grill both your brothers just to see if there might have been some slip along the way that got back to Caldwell.

"I'm going to talk to some friends at the courthouse and see what kind of security there is for prisoners in George's cellblock. I'll talk to him and tell him what we're doing and what we suspect. He needs to be aware when anyone comes into his area. I don't think Caldwell would be so brazen as to try to kill George there, but we need to know if he's going to be moved. That's when accidents happen to prisoners. I have a contact in the sheriff's office who will alert me of any such move so I can make sure nothing untoward happens en route.

"One other thing Alex. You need to get George to tell you where that gun is. We don't want Caldwell sending his man back over there again to look for it. If we ever want to tie him to the murders we need to have that gun. We need to keep it in a safe place. Bring it in and I'll put it in my safe deposit box."

33

The Slugs

The sunny and cool days of mid-November gave way to December's early chill. The Gingko trees lining Laurens Street acquired their brilliant saffron hue in anticipation of a late December leaf drop. Alex settled into a work routine at the law firm, mostly consisting of legal research to support positions Poole took in defending his clients. He even sat second chair for a few cases, cases that were not fraught with any whiff of a racial nature. Many Aikenites were still not ready to have a black lawyer participate in any criminal litigation affecting a local white man. To be effective, Poole needed to be very careful to protect his image in the community.

The funeral for Jonah on Friday was low-key and devoid of any pomp. Besides the Devereuxs and a few close friends, the sanctuary was almost empty. As expected, no one came from Florence.

Respecting Cleo's wishes, Reverend Pope kept the ceremonial aspects to a minimum and sent Jonah off to meet his maker with a very brief sermon. The bleak comparison to Sam's funeral did not go unnoticed.

Poole delegated many of the more mundane duties associated with the office's day-to-day activities such as real estate and tax preparation to Alex, who enjoyed the opportunity to delve into the inner workings of Aiken's upper classes, especially when it involved members of the Winter Colony.

Still, the dilemma facing George and the Devereux family weighed heavily on him. Alex visited George the night after Mr. Poole asked for the gun. When the jailer left them alone for a few minutes, Alex leaned close to the bars and whispered.

"George, Mr. Poole says we need to get hold of that gun and place it somewhere safe. He's afraid Caldwell might send someone else over there to search for it if they think it's still there."

"I reckon he right 'bout that. They's a big ice box in the store room. I's sho you seen it. It's walls is filled with sawdust to keep the ice froze. Round back, they's a loose board. I done prized it open and stuck that gun in the sawdust. I wrapped it in a towel. You'll see where the sawdust done leaked out. It 'bout two feet off the flo."

"Thanks George. I'll drive over there tomorrow and get it. I'll come back by and let you know if everything went okay. You still don't have any idea how somebody might have found out about the gun?"

"Naw Alex. Ben and me's the onliest one's what knowed about it. Ben ain't said nothing has he?"

"No. He says he never told another soul. I keep wracking my brain but I can't figure it out."

Alex pulled slowly into the parking lot. There were only two cars at the club. He recognized the one belonging to Mr. Pollard. The other wasn't familiar. He entered the club to find Pollard in the back talking to a bartender.

"Hank, I think we're going to need some more gin and bourbon. I already cleared it with the police. A large donation to the police league will help them look the other way. I suspect there is a direct conduit from the police league to the police pockets. Those guys don't make a lot of money. I'm sure this helps them provide for their families. I guess I look at it as a form of charity," he snickered. "In any case, call up Charlie Duvall down in Charleston. He's expecting an order from us."

Alex coughed to announce his approach. He didn't want to know any more than the little he heard walking up.

"Mr. Pollard, you may not remember me. I'm Alex Devereuax, George's brother."

"Oh yes Alex, I do remember you. How's it going with George? Such an ugly situation. Any more on his claim that someone else killed his brother-in-law?"

"No sir, we're still looking but so far, no luck."

"That's too bad. I hope something turns up. George was a good worker. I'd like to get him back. So, what can I do for you Alex?"

"George says he left some things in a box that he'd like to get back. He told me where he kept it and asked if I'd come over and pick it up for him."

"I guess that'll be okay. I keep that room locked since the killing. Hank, go back and let Alex in then lock up when he leaves."

"Yes sir, Mr. Pollard."

This was a complication that Alex hadn't counted on. How could he walk behind the cooler and retrieve the gun with Hank standing there?

Hank opened the lock and let Alex in. Alex walked over to a stack of boxes near the ice-house and looked inside. Sure enough there were some of Georges things inside. He motioned for Hank to come over.

"I just wanted you to see that I wasn't taking anything that didn't belong to George."

"Oh, that's all right." he said.

A loud bell mounted on the back wall rang.

"That's a bell we rigged up to the bar to let us know when

the phone is ringing out there. Gimme a second to answer it and I'll let you out."

Alex hung back as Hank sprinted toward the bar. He sat the box down and ran around to the back of the cooler. Sure enough, he saw a tiny pile of sawdust below a loose board. He pried the board back, reached inside and felt the outline of a pistol through the cloth wrapped around it. He grabbed it, pushed the board back into place and stuffed the gun in the box. He picked the box up and walked to the door just as Hank came back.

"Wrong number," he said. "Get that all the time. Our number is one off from a grocery store on Buena Vista. One of us is gonna hafta change one of these days.

"Well, I see you've got George's box. Tell him I asked about him. Sure do miss him around here. I didn't know how heavy that ice was til he was gone."

Alex walked past the bar. He heard Hank click the lock through its hasp. He resisted an urge to run out the door before someone asked him what was in the box. He breathed easier as he eased out of the parking lot and headed back to Aiken.

"Well here it is Mr. Poole," Alex said, sitting the box with the gun on his desk. He pulled out the towel wrapped weapon, folding back the towel. The light from the desk lamp reflected off the silver initials set into the pearl handle – *E.C.*

"There's certainly no mistaking those initials," Mr. Poole said, "Eric was always proud of that gun. He took every opportunity to flash it around.

"Alex, after you left I took the liberty of calling and old buddy of mine over in Columbia. He works at the state crime lab. I asked him if they had the bullets the coroner dug out of the Leeman children. He said he'd check and get back to me. An hour later he called back and said they were still in the box holding all the evidence from that case. I asked him if I sent over a bullet if he could match it up against those three. He was curious but he said sure, send it over, I'll take a look at it."

"But those bullets were dug out of the Leemans. Won't they look different than one that hasn't been fired?" Alex asked.

"Sure they will, if they haven't been fired. Come with me."

Poole drove Alex far out East Richland, down a dirt lane, to a nondescript building set back in the woods. The stench emanating from the squat brick structure was overwhelming. The sign above the front door read, "Walker Brothers Abattoir."

"What is this place?" Alex asked as they walked up to the front door.

"This is where most of the animals slaughtered for consumption in Aiken meet their fate."

"I never heard of this place before. How long has it been here?"

"Oh, about thirty years I reckon. It's not a place most people want to know about. Slaughtering animals is a nasty, smelly business and the less genteel people know about it the better they feel. However, somebody has to do it if we're going to enjoy steak and ham on our dinner tables."

"Why are we here?"

"The Walker boys and I went to school together. This isn't the first time I've asked them for a favor. On the other hand, I've gotten them out of a few scrapes with the health and agriculture departments. One hand scratching the other you know."

Alvin Walker answered the door. He was taller than Alex and twice as thick. He was the biggest man Alex had ever seen. He had a ten-inch butcher knife in his hand and wiped it on the blood soaked apron straining to control his enormous girth.

"Frammy, what you doing out here in the woods?"

"I need a favor Alvin."

"What is it this time, a twenty-pound haunch of sirloin?"

"No, nothing like that. I need to borrow one of your beef carcasses for a few minutes."

"Borrow! What are you talking about? We don't have a habit of lending out meat carcasses," he said, breaking into a big grin. "Is this like that time you needed to prove that blood found on your client came from a pig and not the man they found lying in his back yard?"

"Not exactly Alvin, but close. I want to shoot one of your cows."

"But Frammy, they're already dead. You can't kill them twice."

"I know, I know, just hear me out."

Mr. Poole pulled the colt revolver from the briefcase he was carrying.

"I need to fire this pistol into a carcass and retrieve the bullet. I want to send it off to see if it matches some slugs that were retrieved in a murder."

"What you up to? They ain't been no killings around here to my knowledge since them Leemans were shot. That was two years ago. I thought that case had done gone away. They won't nobody ever arrested far as I know."

"That's right and I'm not at liberty to discuss this present case with you. Court order, you know," he lied.

Walker took notice of Alex, eyeing him up and down.

"Who's this boy with you?"

"This is Alexander Devereux. He's a newly minted lawyer who's gone to work for me."

Alvin Walker frowned.

"I ain't got no problem with you hiring a colored lawyer, but how's it gonna set with some of the high-toned folks around town. I know there's still some hard feelings about you representing that Leeman girl."

"I understand Alvin, but I had no choice. The judge mandated that I represent her. All the rest that happened was beyond my control."

"Well, Mr. Devereux, welcome to our humble establishment."

"Thank you Mr. Walker."

"You boys follow me and be careful you don't bump into those butcher tables. Gittin' that blood outta your clothes ain't easy."

They followed the giant man toward the back of the building. He opened a heavy door, exposing a long rack of beef carcasses hung by their hamstrings.

"Pick one Frampton," he said.

"How about the first one in line?"

"Fine by me. Where do you want it.?"

"Just push it off by itself."

Mr. Walker isolated the heavy side of beef and stepped back.

"Alvin I'm going to fire this into a muscle where we can extract it afterwards. I don't want it to hit a bone where it will become deformed. Where do you suggest?"

Alvin took his knife and demonstrated the trajectory he recommended. Mr. Poole took the revolver, making sure he aimed away from the two spectators, cocked the hammer and placed the barrel against the beef at the angle suggested by Mr. Walker. He fired. The blast was deafening as it reverberated around the small enclosure.

"Okay, Alvin," he said. "See if you can dig that bullet out for me."

He was careful that Mr. Walker not get a good look at the gun. The less he knew the better.

"There's more to this lawyering business than you knew, huh Alex," Mr. Poole said as they drove back to the office. "Not many lawyers visit slaughterhouses in the pursuit of justice."

"No sir, I guess not."

On Monday, the recovered slug was forwarded to Poole's friend at the crime lab in Columbia. Now all they could do was wait – and hope.

34

The Wait

Days had passed and still there was no break in the case. Wiggin's forays into the Valley had turned up nothing of significance. There was the occasional bar talk about "that nigger that was killed out at Carolina Springs," but none of the participants seemed to have any connection to Eric Caldwell or any of his circles.

Alex took Minnie to the jail regularly. She always carried a basket of fried chicken. Mary came over at least once a week when the club was shuttered. Performances had resumed a week after Jonah's death. Initially, the attendance numbers were down but had recovered as the notoriety died down.

Alex saw Betty only twice following George's arrest. Her talent and the large crowds she drew to the hotel lounge had convinced the Richmond Hill club manager to sign Betty to a six-month contract—with a sizable pay increase. She also charmed him into giving Ben an audition. Milton Rogers was blown away. He asked Mary to prepare Ben for a series of weekend appearances in which he would sing a couple of duets with Betty and a few solos.

Alex had driven Ben over for two of the shows. They were a welcome diversion from the long hours at the office and the steady drumbeat heralding George's approaching trial.

Ben's growing confidence in his singing ability encouraged Alex. He was delighted to see his brother emerge from his dark shell of despair. Ben's newly discovered self-esteem was evident in the way he now carried himself and in how he inter-related with others. It was evident that he no longer saw himself as having to follow a path that relegated him to menial, soul-crushing jobs.

"Betty, Ben's another person now. What you and Mary have done for him and his self-esteem is incredible. Thank you."

"Don't thank me Alex. Thank Mr. Rogers for giving Ben the opportunity, and thank Ben for seizing it. The crowds from Augusta have been unbelievable and the number of folks coming over from Aiken to hear him has gone through the roof. With a little polishing up, the sky's the limit for him."

"What about us Betty? Where do you see us going?" Alex asked.

"Right now I'm very happy that I found this place. I'm happy that I'm having success here. I'm happy that Ben is doing well. And, I'm happy that I found you again. I don't want the bubble to burst. I think we should just go along as we are until this thing with George gets resolved. You don't need to be distracted by anything else. Just know that when it is over, I'll still be here. Then we can talk."

The calendar turned. January arrived. A deluge of gingko leaves inundated Laurens. Icicles hung suspended from the umbrella shielding the two children in the Morgan fountain. The deepening winter layered a gray bleakness onto Alex's already dark mood. He dwelt constantly on the plight of his brother and their inability to help him. Soon it would be two months since George climbed the steps to the jail behind the courthouse to await his fate. Each time Alex reported no progress, the anguish George felt was reflected in his face.

"I'm sorry George but we keep running into dead ends. None of us has been able to find anything to support the theory of another killer in that storeroom. The only good news is that the investigators in Columbia were able to find a partial fingerprint in the blood on the baling hook that killed Jonah. It was the only print besides yours. There were no prints on record that matched it. If it belonged to the man you saw, our only hope is to identify him and get his prints. So far, it's been a blind alley. Wiggins has even had Caldwell followed when he goes home to Warrenville, but he's seen no one with him matching the description you gave. He even had someone watch Caldwell's house with binoculars from a hill across the street. Still no one. It doesn't look good George. Your trial date is only a month away and we've got nothing but Mary's testimony to refute the crime scene.

"We were able to fire the pistol and send the slug over to the crime lab for comparison to the Leeman bullets. We still haven't heard anything back,"

"I know you's trying yo best Alex. It jest seem lak nothin' ain't goin' right for me – 'cept Mary. I don't know what I'd do if she won't believin' in me. You and Ma and Mary is all I got on my side. That sheriff Caldwell, he got all the law with him. I's scared Alex. You think they might hang me."

"No George, I don't think it will come to that. First, it was obviously not a premeditated crime. Secondly, we're going to plead that it was a matter of self-defense. We'll have to paint Jonah as the villain here, that he attacked you and you were just defending yourself. I hope the jury will buy that. If they don't and you're convicted, it will most likely be for second-degree homicide or manslaughter which carry much lighter sentences. The judge makes that decision, and I believe Mr. Poole can convince him to go easy on you. There's nothing in your past to indicate that you are violent, no previous arrests. Finally, I think the judge will take into account your physical problems.

"No George, I don't think you have to worry about the death penalty. I keep hoping we will find something to get you off altogether. Don't give up hope. We're still working on it."

"Alex we have only a few weeks to go before George will come up for trial," Poole said. "We need to go over the arguments we have constructed in his defense. I believe the strongest is self-defense. We'll be able to provide several witnesses that heard Jonah threaten George. If we can make a strong enough case we may convince the jury to acquit. Barring that, we may be able to plant enough seeds of doubt in their minds for a lesser verdict. Do you agree?"

"Yes sir, totally. I just keep hoping something will turn up but it's looking more and more that it won't. I think by now Caldwell is so sure of conviction that he's going to lay low and let nature take its course.

"Have you heard anything from Columbia on that bullet you sent?"

"No. I called just yesterday. My friend said that he was put at the back of the line because of all the work required for those three students killed in Orangeburg. He said it'll probably be another two to three weeks."

"The trial will be underway by then," Alex said. "If that bullet matches the ones found in the Leemans, how could you use that in the trial."

"That's just it Alex. If we can't find anything else tying Caldwell to the shooting in North Augusta, there's no pretext under which to introduce the bullet. We wouldn't be able to show a relationship to George. Besides, without corroborating evidence, we'd just be tipping our hand to Caldwell. No, we have to find something more."

35

The Trial

The Court of General Sessions for Aiken County, Judge Charles Manning presiding, convened on Monday, February 17, 1928. Anyone charged with a felony crime in the past six months would be scheduled before this court. The case of the State of South Carolina versus George Devereux was set for Wednesday, February 19.

Mary came over for the trial. She was to be both a witness and a very interested spectator. Minnie asked Phoebe to let her stay with her. Having Mary and Cleo together at the Devereux house would prove awkward. Family tensions were frayed enough already.

During the week before the trial Alex and Mr. Poole coached George and Mary within an inch of their life – Mary in their offices and George in a jail holding room. It was of paramount importance that they come across as confident and believable. Alex and Mr. Poole pounded them mercilessly with mock questions they could expect from the prosecution and about how they should respond. Tell the truth under oath but be forceful and assured.

Miss Rhodes answered the phone on Tuesday, February 18. She tapped on Mr. Poole's office door. He and Alex were going over last minute strategies for trial the next day.

"Sir, it's a call from Columbia."

"Thank you Miss Rhodes."

He lifted the phone from its cradle.

"Hello. Oh, hey Howard, how are you? Great, great. Yeah the family's fine. You don't say. That's terrific news Howard. Thank you. Can you send those results over to me when you return the slug. Wonderful, I really appreciate this. You take care and say hello to Myrtle for me. We'll have to get together for dinner the next time Gladys and I are in Columbia—my treat. You bet. Good bye."

"Good news Alex. That was Howard Murphy from the crime lab. Just as we thought, the slugs matched. We now know that Eric Caldwell was personally involved in the killing of the Leemans. All we have to do now is figure out how to use that information. If nothing breaks our way during the trial and then everyone lets their guard down, then someone might slip up. I'll keep Wiggins on the case.

"All rise, The Court of General Sessions for the Second District of South Carolina is now in session, the Honorable Charles Manning presiding," intoned the bailiff.

Judge Manning was new to the Second District, having been recently elected by the General Assembly for a judicial term of six years. Previously, he was one of the foremost criminal lawyers practicing before both the South Carolina and United States Supreme Courts. His reputation for a fair but strict interpretation of the law was well known. He ran a disciplined court.

"Be seated," he said. "Will the clerk call the next docket case please?"

"Your honor the State of South Carolina versus Mr. George Devereux, State solicitor Mr. Abner Peabody prosecuting, Esquire Frampton Poole defending."

"Are you gentlemen prepared with your opening

arguments?"

"We are your honor," both answered in unison.

"Well let's get right to it then. Bailiff, bring in the jury."

The twelve jurors and two alternates ranged in age from 25 to 80. Two wore overalls, six wore khaki work pants and starched, white, high-collar shirts, six wore suits. They represented a varied cross section of George Devereuxs' peers, as specified in the U.S. constitution – except none had black skin. The *Plessey vs. Ferguson* decision by the United States Supreme Court in 1896 had enshrined the unofficial *Jim Crow* laws across the South. Separate but equal became the rallying cry for those intent on maintaining segregation as a way of life, especially in the South.

The jury's educational level ranged from grade school to college. Professor Darrell Gooding, a Quaker graduate of the Haverford College in Pennsylvania, and a math teacher at the Schofield school, was chosen foreman.

"Mr. Peabody you may proceed with your opening argument," Judge Manning said.

"Thank you your honor. The state intends to prove that George Devereux did, on Saturday, November 12 of last year, attack and murder one Jonah Page. This will prove to be a simple and straightforward prosecution. George Devereux was found covered with the blood of Jonah Page, and the murder weapon, a common baling hook belonging to the defendant, was found impaled in the head of the victim. Furthermore, the defense's contention that there was some mysterious assailant who sneaked in and murdered Mr. Page while the defendant lay on the floor in an epileptic state, and then sneaked away, is ludicrous on its face."

"Thank you Mr. Peabody. Mr. Poole may we have your opening statement please."

"Certainly, your honor.

Though my learned opponent dismisses the veracity of

our findings, we certainly feel they are with merit. However, since we have been unable to substantiate their stories with hard evidence, George is changing his plea from "not guilty" to "self-defense." If, at some future date evidence is brought forward to corroborate the testimony of George Devereux and Mary Waters, we will petition to re-open the case and seek a new trial.

"We seek to show that the victim had displayed animus toward my client and had, on more than one occasion threatened him with bodily harm. Therefore, if my client did indeed kill Jonah Page, it was in a highly agitated and threatened state and he did so in self-defense before his seizure. As is common with epileptic seizures, the patient often does not remember events that occurred immediately prior to the attack.

"We ask the jury to weigh all the evidence presented and to dismiss any charge of murder, both of the first and the second degree and to dismiss any charge of manslaughter. If my client did cause the death of Jonah Page he was totally justified in protecting himself against an assailant bent on causing him bodily harm and therefore he should be held blameless. .

"Thank you your honor. That concludes my opening statement."

"Very well then. Mr. Peabody are you prepared to begin your prosecution?"

"I am," your honor.

"I call Mr. Kenneth Melton to the stand."

The bailiff swore the witness in.

"Now, Mr. Melton, will you give your full name and your occupation?"

"My name is Kenneth Eugene Melton. I am a police sergeant with the North Augusta Police Department."

"And, will you relate to the jury what transpired on the afternoon of November 12, 1927."

"I received a call from a hysterical woman saying that there had been a killing at the Carolina Springs club. My partner Roy Branch and I responded. When we arrived on the scene, we discovered the victim lying behind a pile of boxes with this hook in his head. I checked to see if he was alive and I couldn't find a pulse. It was pretty obvious that he died almost instantly."

"Is that weapon here today?"

"Yes sir, that's it lying there on the evidence table."

"Has it been tampered with?"

"No sir, it's still in the bag it was put in when the coroner brought it to the sheriff's office. It still has the victim's blood on it."

"And what did the crime lab find when they examined it?"

"They found the blood of the victim, the fingerprints of the defendant, and one other partial, latent print."

"Were you able to identify the person belonging to that print?"

"No sir, there was no match in the files. We checked the prints of everyone that had access to that room and we didn't find a match."

"What else?"

"Well, the woman who called us, Mary Waters, was kneeling beside the defendant. He was on the other side of the room, closer to the back door."

"Did she say that she saw what had happened?"

"No sir, she said she was out front on the stage when she heard a loud noise and shouting coming from the storage room. She said she ran to the room and when she got there, she saw a man running out the back door. Then she said she heard a car drive away. She said she didn't follow the man because she was worried about the defendant."

"I see and what did she say she heard from out front."

"She said she heard a man's voice yell, "Where the hell is it, George? I know you have it." That's the same thing the defendant said."

"And what is the relationship of the woman with the defendant?"

"They both work at the club and they live together."

"So, she's his girlfriend."

"I reckon so."

"And did you conclude that she was repeating his story to protect him?"

"Objection, your honor. That calls for speculation on the part of the witness," Poole said.

"Sustained. Continue Mr. Peabody."

"Was there anyone else at the scene when you arrived?"

"Yes sir, the defendant's brother, Alexander Devereux, had arrived and was helping him. They were giving him water and she was holding a cloth to his head."

"Anything else Mr. Melton?"

"No sir. At that point, we called the Aiken County sheriff's department since the crime scene was in their jurisdiction. We also alerted the coroner to come over."

"Then what?"

"I asked my partner Roy Branch to take them outside and wait for the sheriff. I stayed at the scene."

"Anything else, Mr. Melton?"

"No sir."

"Do you wish to cross-examine the witness Mr. Poole?" Judge Manning asked.

"Not at this time, your honor."

"You may be dismissed Mr. Melton but remember that you are still under oath and you are not to discuss your testimony with anyone else."

"Yes your honor."

"Mr. Peabody?"

"I'd like to call Mr. Ezra Shackleford to the stand."

"State your name and occupation," Mr. Peabody asked after the witness was sworn in.

"Ernest Everett Shackleford. I am a deputy sheriff with the Aiken County sheriff's department."

"What can you tell us about this case?"

"Well sir, when we got the call from Sergeant Melton, Con Massey and I hightailed it over to North Augusta, When we got there we examined the crime scene with Mr. Melton and drew the same conclusions that he did. It appeared that there had been a fight between the defendant and the victim and that the defendant had hit him with that baling hook there," he said pointing at the table.

"Objection your honor," Mr. Poole said. "Mr. Shackleford is stating an assumption, not a fact. It was not in his purview to draw that conclusion until a complete investigation was completed."

"Objection sustained. Mr. Shackleford I will remind you that your testimony must adhere to the facts as you know them."

"Let me get at this in another way." Peabody said. "Mr. Shackleford, in your own words, what did you see?"

"The victim was lying in a pool of blood with that hook through his head. The defendant had been removed from the scene and was sitting with the Waters woman and his brother out by the bar. My partner Con Massey and I agreed with the conclusion Mr. Melton had come to, that it appeared the defendant had killed the victim. As soon as the coroner arrived we took the suspect, his brother and Miss Waters back to Aiken to the sheriff's department where they were all questioned and gave signed statements. At that point, Chief Deputy Eric Caldwell reviewed the statements and interviewed the three of them. When he finished, he told us to lock the defendant up and that he was going to recommend his indictment for murder."

"Anything else Mr. Shackleford?"

"No sir, that's about it."

"Thank you sir, you may step down," the judge said, "I don't need to remind you that you're still under oath."

"Any other witnesses Mr. Peabody?"

"No your honor, I believe the facts of this case are so abundantly clear that any further testimony by the prosecution witnesses would be redundant. I look forward to hearing my colleague try to refute the irrefutable."

"Very well then. It's now approaching noon. We will adjourn and resume with the defense's presentation at one-thirty," Judge Manning said with a bang of his gavel. "This court is now in recess."

Mr. Poole, Alex and Mary went back to the offices where Miss Rhodes had sandwiches and iced tea waiting for them.

"Mr. Poole, what do you make of the prosecutions presentation?" Alex asked. "It seems awfully short when you consider what is at stake."

"I believe Abner thinks that any additional testimony would just cloud the issue and maybe confuse the jury. He's going to wait until I put you and Mary and George on the stand. He's convinced that you and Mary are prejudiced witnesses and he'll tear into you on cross-examination. He'll get into all the history of George and Jonah so he can plant in the jury's mind that this all erupted from a family quarrel over money.

"It's our job to show that Jonah was the aggressor here and that George was just defending himself. That's the only way I see to mitigate the damaging evidence against George."

"Is there no way to show that someone else was in that room and that he killed Jonah?" Mary asked.

"At this point Mary," Mr.Poole said, "if we're going to go with self-defense as the motive, then bringing up the third man theory would weaken our case. Right now I just want to be sure the jury is sympathetic to George and will convict him on a self-defense or manslaughter charge. If we do that, I believe George will be a free man in less than five years."

Mary began to cry. Alex looked downcast.

"I realize this is the best defense for now," Alex said, "but if we can later produce evidence showing there was another man in that room, then we'll be able to petition for a new trial. Barring that I believe we have a case to appeal under the sixth amendment. Those twelve white men sitting in that jury box are not George's peers."

"You and I both know that Alex, but the sixth amendment only states that the jury must be impartial, it doesn't say anything about peers. Until *Plessey vs. Ferguson* is overturned by the Supreme Court, you'll have a hard time getting a South Carolina judge to grant an appeal on that account."

"That's just not fair!" Alex growled. "One more cause I have to add to the long list of discriminations suffered by Negroes."

"You're right Alex, but right now we have to focus on doing what's best for George. We'll go over our strategy one more time while we have our sandwiches."

Both the defense and the prosecution were back at their tables as Judge Manning emerged from his chambers to gavel the afternoon session to order.

"All rise. The Honorable Judge Manning."

"Mr. Poole I trust you had a nice lunch and you are ready to present your case for the defendant."

"I am, your honor."

"Please proceed."

"I call Mary Waters to the stand."

"You swear to tell the truth, the whole truth and nothing but the truth, so help you God." asked the bailiff.

"I do."

"State your name and occupation," Poole asked.

"My name is Mary Elizabeth Waters. I am a singer at the Carolina Springs club."

"How do you know the defendant?"

"George befriended me when I came here from Savannah. I left there under trying circumstances and his friendship helped me to get my life back in order."

"Is George Devereaux more than a friend?"

Mary cast her eyes downward and answered softly, "Yes sir, I live with George."

"Did you know the victim?"

"Yes sir, he was George's brother-in-law, married to his sister Cleo."

"What was the relationship between George and Mr. Page?"

"George told me that he and Jonah had argued over the way he treated Cleo. They had almost come to blows over it. When things didn't get any better George decided to leave home. That's when he came over here to the Springs to work."

"And when was that?"

"George said it was almost two years ago."

"Had you ever seen Mr. Page at Carolina Springs before." "No sir, never."

"And why do you think he was there on the day he was killed?"

"George told me that Jonah believed that the Devereux family had come into a large sum of money and that some of it should be given to Cleo. George said he didn't know anything about any money and told Jonah to leave him alone."

"And did he?"

"No sir."

"How so?"

"Jonah threatened George when we attended his father's funeral. Then, on the Saturday before he came to the Springs someone broke into our apartment. At the time we thought it was just some neighbor kids but thinking back we believe it was Jonah looking for the money he thought George had."

"Objection your honor. That calls for speculation on the part of the witness."

"Sustained."

"Tell me what you observed on the afternoon of November 12. 1927?" Poole asked.

"I was on stage out front when I heard a loud noise coming from the store room and then a man shouting, "Where the hell is it George? I know you have it."

"Then what did you do?"

"I ran around the bar and back to the store room."

" And what did you find?"

"George was lying on the floor near the back door. His eyes were rolled back in his head like they did when he had a seizure. I saw blood all over the floor. It led to a pile of boxes in the right front corner of the room. I went over there and found Jonah lying in a big pool of blood. He had this hook thing stuck in his head. I checked his pulse and there was none. I ran back over to George and tried to wake him up. I threw some water on his face and washed it with a bar towel. He started to respond and that's when Alex came in."

"Who is Alex?"

"Oh, Alex is George's brother. He had come over on other business. He said he saw Jonah's car and reckoned something was wrong. He ran back to where we were and helped me with George."

"Then what?"

"Alex asked me to go out front and call the police, which I did."

"Was there anyone else in that room? "I thought I saw someone running out the back door but in the confusion, I must have been mistaken. We never found anyone else."

"Then what happened?"

"After the police came and the sheriff's people came we were taken back to Aiken where George was arrested for Jonah's murder."

"Do you have anything else to add Miss Waters?"
"Just that George is a gentle and kind man and he would never have killed Jonah if he wasn't threatened. I just know it."

"Objection your honor," Abner Peabody said. "These are

personal observations that have no place in her testimony."

"Sustained. Miss Waters please stick to the facts as you know them and do not offer personal opinions."

"Any further questions Mr. Poole?"

"Not at this time your honor."

"Mr. Peabody?"

"No your honor but I reserve the right to recall this witness later."

"You may step down young lady. Remember that you are still under oath and must not discuss this testimony with anyone other than your legal counsel."

"Yes your honor."

Mary descended from the witness box and was escorted from the chamber. She was weeping and went immediately to the ladies room. Upon exiting the ladies room she stepped around the corner and sat on a bench to compose herself.

36

The Conversation

Two men emerged from the Men's room around the corner. Mary was shielded from their view by two large potted palms. She pulled back a frond and recognized one of the men as Chief Deputy Sheriff Caldwell. The other man looked familiar, but she couldn't place him.

"I think old Abner's got this thing all sewed up," Caldwell said. "That nigger might get off with manslaughter, but they ain't no way that jury is gonna let him go with no self-defense plea. I know some of them boys and they ain't got much sympathy for niggers even if he killed one of their own."

"I hope you're right. The sooner he's behind bars up in Edgefield the sooner we ain't gotta worry no more," the younger man said before they moved out of earshot.

"Mary wanted to scream. That voice. It was the same one she heard yelling at George. She waited until they were out of sight and ran back to the courtroom. The officer at the door stopped her.

"Miss you are a witness. You ain't allowed back in there."

"Please, I must talk to Mr. Poole."

"Can't let you do that while court's in session."

""How about the young black lawyer sitting with him. Could you call him to come out here. It's very important."

The elderly guard looked at Mary's desperate face.

"I reckon the judge won't be too upset if I ask him to come out here for a minute. Now you stay right here and don't come in."

Seconds later Alex emerged through the double doors with the guard.

"Mary what is it? You're as pale as a ghost."

"Let's go someplace where no one can overhear us."

There was a bench at the far end of the main corridor. It was vacant and there was no one around.

"Alex, I know who the man in the storeroom is."

"How?"

"I overheard a conversation between Sheriff Caldwell and this younger man. He was dressed nicer and he didn't have a beard. But I would know that voice anywhere. It's him Alex. I know it's him."

"Whoa. Slow down. Are you absolutely sure."

"Yes, I recognized him even without his beard. And that high pitched voice, I'd know it anywhere."

"Mary, you stay right here. I'll be back in a jiffy."

Alex eased back into his chair as Mr. Poole was beginning to ask George questions. He whispered to him. Poole looked dazed.

"Your honor, if I may have a moment to confer with my associate."

"Make it brief Mr. Poole. At the pace we're going I suspect we may be able to give this case to the jury today."

Alex again repeated what Mary had told him and recommended they ask for a continuance until her story could be verified.

"Your honor may I ask to see you in chambers together with Mr. Peabody. Some new information has arisen which may bear significantly on this case."

"Any objections, solicitor?"

"It is highly unusual your honor, but if you have no objections I will go along."

Judge Manning stepped down from the bench and led the two lawyers into his chambers.

"Mr. Poole I warn you this had better be good. If you have some frivolous excuse for halting these proceedings it will not sit well with me."

"I fully understand your honor. I believe what I am going to divulge will change the course of this trial."

"Go ahead."

"Your honor, when the original testimony of Miss Waters and Mr. Devereux was taken they both swore that there was another man in that store room and that he was the one who killed Mr. Page. Obviously, I was dubious at first but slowly I came around to believe their story. There were several inconsistencies at the crime scene. The victim was all the way across the room from my client. The only blood on my client was transferred by Miss Waters when she went to check on Mr. Page. Mr. Devereux is subject to epileptic seizures, especially when he is under great stress, which obviously he was when he was confronted in that storeroom. We believe that Mr. Page was already dead when my client went into the room. Our problem was that we found no way to corroborate their story. We had reason to suspect certain people but we could come up with no evidence to tie them to the crime. Therefore, we felt the best case for our client was to plead self-defense thinking that if we ever were able to produce that third man we could appeal. Well now we think we have that evidence."

"Your honor," a flustered Abner Peabody said, "This cockamamie story is just a ruse by Mr. Poole to muddy the water and confuse the jury."

"It may be Mr. Peabody but I will hear him out."

"Go ahead Mr. Poole>"

"This will take a while judge so bear with me. It all goes back to the killing of the three Leeman children two years ago. I'm sure you remember that case,"

"Indeed, everybody in South Carolina with even the slightest connection to law enforcement remembers that case. It left a very dark stain on the reputation of our state."

"Your honor, a young black man in our community went to the site of those killings the morning after and stumbled across a piece of evidence that was potentially explosive. He found an object buried in the mud. It had been trampled by the crowd of vigilantes milling around. He took it back to his house and cleaned it up. What he discovered frightened him to death."

"What was it Mr. Poole?"

"It was a pearl handled revolver with three empty chambers. The most chilling part of the story lies in the description of that pistol. Embedded in the pearl on each side of the butt are the initials *E.C.* "

"Abner Peabody turned pale and reached for the glass of water in front of him. He downed a big gulp while composing himself.

"Those initials obviously mean something to you Mr. Peabody."

"Yes your honor, that revolver belongs to Chief Deputy Sheriff Eric Caldwell."

"Go on Mr. Poole. How does this gun tie into the present case?"

"Your honor when we couldn't find evidence to support the testimony of my client and Miss Waters, we fell back on self-defense as the most logical defense for Mr. Devereux.

"You see my client had come into possession of that gun through a series of events that I will describe later. He wanted a gun for protection. He was actually worried about the threats from Mr. Page. Somehow, Sheriff Caldwell found out that the gun he thought had been lost was actually in the hands of George Devereaux. We still don't know how he found out, because there were only three people who knew about it, except for the boy that found it and he's dead.

"As Miss Waters said, when she ran into the storeroom she thought she saw a man running out the back door. George Devereux also swore there was someone else there, rummaging through his belongings when he entered the room. He said the man was wearing overalls, a plaid shirt and an old, oily felt hat. The man ran at George yelling, 'Where the hell is it George. I know you have it.' That's when George had a seizure. That's exactly how Miss Waters described the man."

"Oh for goodness sakes Frampton! This is the most ridiculous fairy tale I have ever heard. I don't know what your ploy is here but it ain't gonna work. Judge Manning, this is patently a scheme to throw doubt on the obvious facts of the case and introduce supposed new evidence to sway the jury. He knows if he can get just one of those men to vote for acquittal he's won."

"I'll admit that this is a stretch Mr. Peabody, but in the interest of full and complete fairness I'll allow Mr. Poole to continue his story."

"Thank you, your honor. Everyone assumed the shout they heard referred to the money Mr. Page thought George had. In fact, we believe it referred to the gun, which George had hidden in the room.

"We suspected all along that Mr. Caldwell was involved in the abduction of those children from the jail, and in their execution, but we couldn't prove it. No one who was there that night would ever admit to it. Eric Caldwell couldn't possibly be found searching through Mr. Devereux's effects, so he hired someone to do it for him.

"After her testimony today, Miss Waters went to the ladies room. When she came out, she sat down on that bench behind the two palm trees around the corner. She heard two men talking as they came out of the men's room. She could see them through the palms but they had their backs to her. One of the men was Deputy Caldwell. She said she thought she had seen the other man but couldn't recall where.

"She said Mr. Caldwell told the other man that he thought Mr. Peabody had the case pretty well wrapped up and even if George only went to prison for five years, he would be out of their hair, and that strange things had a way of happening in prisons. That's when the younger man turned so that she could see him in profile, and even though he had shaved his beard and mustache, she recognized him as the man fleeing the storeroom. She was even more certain when he spoke. Mary had said all along that the man had a high pitched, nasal voice. George said the same thing. She's certain he's the man she saw fleeing the Carolina Springs store room that afternoon."

"I've heard it all now," Abner Peabody said. "Poole, you expect the judge to believe this hearsay evidence by a young girl who has a vested interest in seeing George Devereux go free. And, on the flimsiest of evidence, "*she recognized his voice.*" Give me a break."

"I must agree Mr. Peabody that this is pretty flimsy evidence to throw into the trial at this point. Mr. Poole is there anything more that you can demonstrate that will corroborate this woman's tale."

"There is your honor. Two things.

"First, I took that pistol out to a local slaughterhouse and fired it into a beef carcass. I sent the bullet we dug out to the crime lab in Columbia. It was a perfect match to the three slugs recovered from the site where the gun was found, and where the three Leemans were killed. In my mind that proves a link between Eric Caldwell and the murder of those three children.

"Second, there was a partial print in the blood on that baling hook that didn't belong to George Devereux. The police assumed that someone had touched the weapon after Mr. Page was dead. Everyone connected with the case was fingerprinted and there were no matches to the bloody print. I would like the state crime lab to take a look at that man's prints to see if they match the one on the murder weapon."

The judge leaned back in his big leather desk chair, took a deep breath, and stared at the slowly revolving ceiling fan.

"This seems like quite a stretch Mr. Poole. What you're asking me to do is to command evidence from a man we don't even know in the belief that it will exonerate your client, and on the flimsiest of pretexts. You're also opening up the even bigger matter of the Leeman killings. If you're wrong, and I believe you are, you will have done nothing for your client and you will have impugned the reputation of an innocent man. You will also tear the scab off a wound that most people thought was healed over. I don't know if you really want that hanging over you. Therefore I deny your request."

"I understand your reluctance to go down this path your honor, but I owe it to my client to pursue all avenues that may aide in his defense. It's getting late in the afternoon. I beg the court's indulgence. I would like your honor to grant a continuance until Monday morning. If we are not able to substantiate Miss Water's story by then, I will raise no more objections and plead for a speedy conclusion of this case."

"Mr. Peabody, will you agree to such a request?"

"Reluctantly your honor, but Mr. Poole and I have been friends and adversaries for many years and he is a man of the utmost integrity and while he may resort to questionable courtroom tactics occasionally, I respect his diligence in representing his clients to the fullest extent possible. I will consent, but I will hold you to your promise Frampton. If you have nothing more on Monday morning, I expect the jury to have this case by the afternoon."

"Thank you, Abner, I appreciate your compliment, and your sense of fair play."

"Very well then," Judge Manning said, "I will announce a recess until Monday morning. Considering the delicateness of these proceedings, I will say it is due to a personal conflict. That may be a bit obscure, but still true. It's just not my personal conflict," he said winking. "Mr. Poole, whatever investigation you have in mind, I must remind you to be circumspect and mindful of due process."

"Yes your honor, thank you."

37

The Recess

"All right, Alex," Poole said to those gathered around the office conference table. "We've got two days and the weekend to obtain the evidence we need."

He turned to face John Wiggins who was seated at the foot of the table.

"John, find out who that was Mary saw with Caldwell and get a set of his fingerprints. I don't care how. He just can't know. My license may be on the line here if we mess this up. I'll alert my friend in Columbia that we may need his expedited services this weekend. I hope he can produce for us.

"Meanwhile Alex, you and I have to decide how we're going to proceed with this on Monday assuming we get a match. Okay John get out of here and get your boys into action"

"You bet, Mr. Poole. It'll be a pleasure to nail Caldwell's hide to the wall. He's been running roughshod in this county ever since Sheriff Howard was killed. He's been acting like he's the sheriff and no one has taken him down. Well we're about to do it."

Wiggins talked to Mary to get her story and her description of the man with Caldwell. He next went over to the courthouse. He stopped along the way for doughnuts and coffee. The annex near the courtroom was the hangout for all the courthouse guards and the jailers.

"Afternoon Tom," he said to the bailiff. "What do you make of this delay in the trial of that nigger boy who shot his brother-in-law?"

Most of the courthouse crowd were unreconstructed segregationists. Wiggins always adopted their vernacular when he was looking for information.

"Sure surprised me," he said. "I reckon the judge got called back to Columbia on some personal matter. The boys don't mind gittin' a couple of days off, that's for sure," Tom Morehouse said as he brushed powdered sugar from his vest. "Margaret still makes the best doughnuts in town, don't she?"

"Best I ever had," John replied.

"Say, was that Eric Caldwell I saw sitting in the back of the courtroom this morning? I thought he'd be testifying since he talked to all those folks after the murder."

"Old Abner said he had so much '*incontrosumpin* evidence– some big 'ol word I don't know–that he wouldn't need Eric."

"It sure looked that way to me, too. I bet old Abner was mad as a wet hen that he couldn't close out the case today."

"I saw him when he walked out. He didn't seem too out of sorts. All in a day's work for a lawyer I reckon."

"I reckon so. Say that boy I saw sittin' with Eric, I ain't seen him around the court before. He a new man over to the sheriff's office."

"Naw, that's his sister Bertha's son. They live over in Bath, not too far from Eric's place in Warrenville. He works in that paper plant over there."

"I reckon that's why I ain't seen him around these parts so much. Lots of them Valley folks kinda keeps to theirselves."

"What's Jim Bob gonna do with his time off. They ain't gonna need him until Monday."

"Me'n him gonna go shoot some turkeys up near Edgefield."

"That sounds like a good weekend to me. Wish I could go

with you but my old woman's got me puttin' some new shingles on the house. You git more'n you can eat you know where I live." he said, downing the last of the coffee. "I guess I better git on over to the lumber yard and pick up them shingles. See you on Monday, Tom. You and Jim Bob be careful out there in them woods. Don't you go shootin' each other."

"Don't you worry. I ain't lettin' Jim Bob have none of my brew. He shoots better when he ain't drunk."

Amos Hudgins backed his car out of the rutted driveway of one of the cookie-cutter mill houses lining Posey Street. He drove the two blocks to the Augusta-Aiken Highway and turned east. He took no notice of the rusted, beat up Plymouth coupe with one headlamp that swung in behind him.

Hudgins skirted the two-mile long Langley pond on his left and a mile later, pulled his pickup truck into a bar at the intersection with the Howlandville Road in Warrenville. A westbound trolley rumbled past across the street, headed for Augusta.

John Wiggins parked his Plymouth at the far end of the lot. He sat behind the wheel and had a cigarette. He looked at his watch. He'd give Hudgins five minutes before he went in.

The bar was dimly lit. Smoke swirled around the low-wattage light bulbs hanging over the bar. Several mill workers, just off their shift, sat at the five tables against the back wall. Two billiard tables occupied the far end of the room. Two men were playing a halfhearted match of nine-ball. Amos Hudgins was perched on a high stool watching.

"Caleb you ain't never been able to make a two-cushion shot in yo life. What makes you think you gone make that'un"

"Shut up Amos. Wait'll I take care of Rufus here and you can have a go at me."

"You're on boy. I cain't wait to take some of yore money. I got me a date with Sally Gentry tomorrow night and I can sho use a little extra change," Amos said as he leaned back against the wall and drained his bottle of Schlitz.

"Hey Troy, gimme another beer," he yelled at the squat, bald bartender.

"You'll hafta come up here and git it. We ain't got no table service tonight. Bessie done got sick with the fever," Troy said as he popped the cap on the bottle and sat it on the counter.

"I'll take it back to him," Wiggins said. "I might want to git in on some of that nine-ball action myself."

He walked back toward the pool tables and handed the beer to Hudgins.

"Thanks stranger," Amos said, eyeing John warily. "I don't recollect seein' you round here before," he said.

"Oh, I'm just here for a few days. They got me workin' on one of them new looms up to the Graniteville Mill. They's a mite tricky to operate so they sent me over to help out. I usually spends mosta my time over at the Augusta mill.

John exchanged the full bottle with the empty. He was careful to hold it by the top and sat it on the stool beside him.

"Amos, you so smart, why don't you come over here and show me how to line up this shot," Caleb Porter yelled.

"You betcha, boy. I got that shot down pat. Step aside and I'll show you."

Wiggins pulled the paper bag from his bulky winter coat's pocket and slipped the empty beer bottle into it, quickly stuffing it back into the pocket.

Click, click, click. plunk. The eight ball dropped into the corner pocket.

"Yeah man, that's the way you do it. You ready to take me on?"

"Sho nuff," Caleb said. "Grab yoself a cue stick and let's go."

"How bout you stranger," Caleb asked. "You want to join in with us?"

"I don't think so after seeing that last shot. I'm good but I ain't that good. I think I'll just sit here and drink my beer and watch you boys go at it."

"Suit yoself. Maybe ya'll will learn a thing or two."

"Could be, Caleb, could be."

Wiggins sat through two games and three beers before excusing himself.

"It's been fun watching you two beat up on each other but I gotta be up for the early shift tomorrow. You boys take care. See you around."

Wiggins walked slowly to the door, clutching the bottle in his pocket. He didn't want any slipups on the way out."

"Well, here it is Mr. Poole," John Wiggins said, handing the bag with the bottle to his employer.

"Did you have any trouble getting it."

"No sir, piece of cake. I'll have to add the three beers to my bill though."

"If that's all it'll be worth it," Poole said, grinning ear-to-ear.

"John I want you to take my car and get this over to Howard Murphy at the state crime lab in Columbia. Ask him to run the prints right away against the one found on the murder weapon that was sent over in November and not to tell anyone else in the lab. I don't want it leaking back to Caldwell. If this pans out, I want to surprise him."

Alex was in the office on Friday, but his mind was not on his work. Wiggins did not make it back on Thursday. He called to say that comparing the prints was proving difficult but that Murphy had s new procedure the FBI had just released. The FBI had improved its methodology significantly since Congress authorized them to establish a Fingerprint Bureau in 1924. The new FBI facility in Leavenworth, Kansas had developed the new process.

The mid-winter sun was waning; the shadows creeped up the side of the hardware store across the street. Alex went to the front window and looked down on Laurens Street. Still no Murphy.

"Alex, we might as well go home. John will call me when he knows something. Keep your spirits up. I have a feeling this is going to turn out in our favor."

"I certainly hope so. Everyone around my house is totally stressed out. Ma is a basket case. Cleo is torn between Jonah and George. I haven't told them anything about what's been going on with the fingerprints or bullets. I saw no need to get their hopes up if nothing comes of it."

"Probably a good idea. Go home. I'll be in first thing tomorrow. I hope John comes back with good news."

The rusted Plymouth was parked in front of the office when Alex walked up on Saturday morning.

'Thank God,' Alex muttered to himself.

He vaulted up the stairs, breathlessly bursting into the conference room. The smile on Mr. Poole's face told Alex all he needed to know.

"It's his?"

38

The Proof

"Yes Alex, the print on the handle of the baling hook that killed Jonah belongs to Amos Hudgins. We have an affidavit from the lab to that effect. We will prepare a presentation of evidence for the gun, the slugs, and the fingerprint for Monday morning. I've already given this information to the prosecution as required by discovery law. Needless to say, Abner was stunned. He never thought we'd be able to tie Caldwell to the murder of Jonah Page. I also notified Judge Manning of our findings and he said he would allow the defense to make an opening statement on Monday. He has ordered Eric Caldwell to be available as a witness. He directed the state police to pick up Amos Hudgins and to hold him incommunicado and in their protective custody until Monday. He's ordered the sheriff's department to keep their distance from the courthouse until this is all sorted out. I'm sure all hell is breaking loose in Horse Creek Valley. Monday morning should prove to be very entertaining."

Alex eased himself into a chair. The whole world had just been lifted off his shoulders. George will be exonerated. Eric Caldwell will be brought to justice. Amos Hudgins will be arrested for the murder of Jonah and life will eventually return to normal. Thank God.

"I don't know what to say. This is a dream come true. At least one black man is going to receive justice in this town. With a little luck, three others will soon have their day in court. If justice is served, Eric Caldwell will be brought to trial for the killing of the Leemans. I just wish they could be around to witness it."

"The colored community will see it." Mr. Poole said. "And that's what really matters. It'll be one small step toward equality in South Carolina. However, you and I both know it's a long way from one black man winning justice and an entire race. It will come Alex. Maybe not in my lifetime, but hopefully in yours."

Poole closed his eyes in deep thought as if he was having an epiphany. He opened them, stood up and looked at Alex.

"I'm going to ask the judge to allow you to question Eric Caldwell. I don't know if he will, but if he does it will go a long way toward establishing the place of black attorneys in white courts. It will represent a level of fairness and recognition that has not been present in our courts.

Alex couldn't believe what he was hearing. His heart began to race. He didn't know if he was up to the task. He took a deep breath and reminded himself of why he had spent seven long years at Howard and why he was back here in Aiken. He remembered the long ago conversation with Miss Eustis when she first told him about his scholarship.

"Alex, the black people in Aiken need a voice in the community. It has to start with fair and equal representation in the courts. I want you to be part of that crusade. I want you to help make the promise of our constitution come true. All men are created equal."

Alex couldn't sleep Saturday night. He wanted to tell Mary

and his family what was going on but the judge's order precluded that. The family had gathered in the kitchen for breakfast prior to Sunday morning church services.

"I want all of you to be in court first thing Monday morning," Alex announced. "I am not at liberty to tell you why, but it's very important."

Minnie looked at her son with fear in her eyes. "They gone be a verdict on George? He gone go to jail?"

"I don't think so Ma. There have been some new developments in the case that may help George."

"Does it have to do with what you and Mr. Poole were trying to find out," Mary asked excitedly.

Alex looked at Mary and winked. "I can't tell you," he said.

"Ma, will Cleo be at church today?"

"She say she be comin' when she go home yesterday."

"Good, I want her to be there, and Phoebe too."

Mr. Poole had scheduled a rare Sunday afternoon in the office. He and Alex sat around the table going over the particulars of the next morning's proceedings.

"You understand the importance of getting Caldwell to admit that the revolver we will present is his and that he does it under oath."

"Yes sir."

"Then you will ask him about Crosland Park?"

"Yes sir. Do you think he'll answer the questions?"

"No, I think he'll plead the fifth amendment, and then we'll have to bring Amos Hudgins in and question him about Carolina Springs."

The two went back and forth for three hours until Alex had virtually memorized his role.

"Alex I don't think there's anything we've left uncovered. You just relax when you get him on the stand. Remember, I'll be sitting there right beside you if you need to clarify anything. Now go on home and try to get some sleep tonight. It might be a long day tomorrow."

Telling Alex to sleep was as good as telling him to fly. He went to bed early after supper. He slept briefly, waking up before eleven. No matter how much he tossed and turned, he couldn't get back to sleep. Finally, he gave up and dressed. The night was clear and crisp with a bright full moon overhead.

Alex slipped out the front door and headed toward South Boundary. He crossed Banks Mill. He heard the neighing of horses as he approached Mr. Dunbar Bostwick's training track. He had accompanied Tommy Hitchcock to this track many times to see Pete Bostwick race trotters. A lone beagle, wakened by the horses, began to bugle beyond the stables.

Alex went over and over in his mind the upcoming court session. He didn't see how anything could go wrong. While there was no proven direct connection between Eric Caldwell and the murder of Jonah Page, he was certain that before the day was over the testimony of Amos Hudgins would establish one. There was nothing more to be done. He reversed his course and returned home. This time he slept until dawn.

The courtroom was empty when George's defense team arrived. A single guard lolled on the bench outside the entry doors.

"Mornin' Mr. Poole," the guard said. "Guess we gonna git back to the trial this morning".

"Yes Jake. It should be a good day."

The guard looked perplexed. He thought it sure looked like the defendant was going to be convicted when everybody went home on Wednesday. Maybe ol' man Poole'll just be happy to get a self-defense verdict. We'll see.

Around 8:30 others started to filter into court. The bailiff arrived and saw to water for both lawyers and the judge. He checked the jury box for anything left behind from Wednesday. Satisfied, he wandered back to the waiting room for coffee and a doughnut.

The fourth estate was represented by a beat reporter from *The Standard.* A cub came over from *The Chronicle* in Augusta just to get in a little practice at trial reporting. The guard strained to see the press badge of a stranger entering with his camera. Best he could make out it said *The State.* Jake was familiar with the largest newspaper in Columbia. Its reporters besieged Aiken after the Leeman killings in 1925 and again in 1926 when they were brought back for trial—and wound up dead in Crosland Park. He sensed that something unusual was in the air. It was almost impossible to keep leaks from seeping out of the state crime lab.

Abner Peabody strolled in about a quarter to nine among a group of spectators from the Horse Creek communities. Word had spread over the weekend about Hudgin's arrest.

The bailiff walked to the front of the courtroom to announce that court was now back in session.

"All rise."

Judge Manning climbed to the bench. He surveyed the room before taking his seat. He saw that the pews in this temple of justice were filled—as many wearing overalls as Kuppenheimer suits. He attributed the increase in interest to the swirling rumors and not to any willful disobedience of his orders.

"This court is ready to reconvene the trial of the state versus George Devereux. I am told that there have been new developments in my absence. Mr. Poole, I believe you were in the process of presenting your defense when we adjourned on Wednesday. Do you wish to continue?"

"Yes your honor. You are correct that there have been new

developments in the past few days. Evidence has come to light that, I believe, changes the entire perspective of this trial."

"Have those discoveries been made available to the prosecution?"

"Yes your honor."

"Mr. Peabody have you reviewed the new evidence?"

"I have your honor."

"And are you in accord with its presentation by the defense."

"I am your honor."

"Then you may proceed Mr. Poole."

39

The Trap

"If I may, your honor, I have a rather unusual request. In light of the evidence that is about to be disclosed and its predicted effect on the family of my associate, I would like to have Esquire Alexander Devereux present the new findings."

The whispers and rustling in the court attested to the apparent reckless nature of Poole's request. No Negro man had addressed this court since Walter White, a lawyer for the NAACP from Spartanburg, appeared at the retrial of Demon Leeman. Due to his near white complexion, White was able to infiltrate the racially fanatical elements of the community and amass a list of lynch-mob names. When his identity as a Negro ("My skin is white, my eyes are blue, my hair is blond, but I am a Negro") was revealed in court, it was necessary for local blacks to escort him out of town to avoid the same fate as his clients, due to violent threats from the KKK. That episode was etched in Aiken's collective memory—and not lost on this crowd.

"Do you have any objections Mr. Peabody?"

Abner Peabody looked nonplussed. He appeared to be at a loss for words. After a few ahems and uhhs, he realized how it would look to the press if he objected.

"No your honor," he reluctantly answered.

"Very well. Mr. Devereux you may begin."

Alex rose, leaning on the table to steady himself. His legs trembled. Every eye in the chamber was riveted on him. He picked up his briefing papers.

"Your honor I would like to call Mr. Eric Caldwell to the stand."

"Bailiff, please produce Mr. Caldwell."

Tom Morehouse went to the antechamber witness room.

"Mr. Caldwell, you are called to testify."

Eric Caldwell moved warily down the aisle. He didn't know exactly what was about to occur, but he certainly didn't like what he saw. There was that uppity nigger of Poole's that had been at the murder scene, the brother of the defendant, the one I talked to and got a statement from. What's he doing standing there.

"State your name and occupation sir," the bailiff said.

"Eric Roger Caldwell, Chief Deputy Sheriff of Aiken County."

"Place your left hand on the bible. Do you solemnly swear that the testimony you are about to give is the truth, the whole truth, and nothing but the truth, so help you God."

"I do."

"Be seated."

Alex cleared his throat and approached the witness stand.

"Mr. Caldwell, do you recognize the gun I am holding in my hand?"

Caldwell blanched. He had no idea the defense had gotten hold of the gun. Since Amos hadn't found it he thought maybe George Devereux had thrown it in the river.

"I do," he answered sullenly.

"Would you describe it to the court?"

Caldwell looked around the room, sweat popping out on his forehead. The jury members leaned forward in rapt attention.

"It's a six-shot, Colt revolver."

"And have you ever seen it before?"

Caldwell hesitated.

"I have."

"Where have you seen it?"

"That's my gun. It was stolen from my house."

"How can you be certain that it's your gun?"

"It has pearl handles with my initials set in silver."

"I see. And you say it was stolen. When was that?"

"Oh, musta been two, three years ago."

"Would you be surprised to know that this gun was found in Crosland Park the morning after the Leemans were killed."

The sweat rolled off his brow. Dark semi-circles bloomed under his armpits.

"I don't know nothin' bout that. I told you it was stolen before them young'uns was killed."

Ignoring the answer, Alex continued to bore in.

"Would you be further surprised to find out that the young man who found the gun saw you in Crosland Park that same morning after the killings. He said you were walking around kicking at the dirt as if you were looking for something."

"I was just out there looking for any evidence we could use to catch whoever killed 'em. It was pitch black that night and we couldn't do a complete search."

"I see. And did you know that gun had been found and was in the possession of the defendant George Devereux at the Carolina Springs ice house when Jonah Page was murdered?"

"I don't know nothin' bout that."

"Furthermore," Alex continued, ignoring Caldwells protests. "were you aware that a slug from a bullet fired from that gun just last week is a perfect match to the slugs removed from the Leemans.?"

"I ain't seen that pistol since it was stolen. Whoever stole it musta had it out at Crosland Park that night. It won't me."

"Oh, I think it was you Mr. Caldwell, and my next witness will prove it.

"Mr. Caldwell I am going to ask that you be excused temporarily while we bring the other witness to the stand."

"You may step down Mr. Caldwell," the judge said. "Bailiff please take Mr. Caldwell to the witness room."

"Yes your honor."

When Caldwell was out of sight and the bailiff had returned Alex called his next witness to the stand.

"The defense calls Mr. Amos Hudgins."

Murmurs ran excitedly around the room. Hudgins was well known in the Valley. It was obvious that many in the gallery knew him and were stunned by the unfolding of events.

"State your name and occupation," Westmore said.

"My name is Amos Gerald Hudgins. I'm a baler at the Bath Paper Mill."

"Do you know Mr. Eric Caldwell?"

"Yeah, I do."

"And how do you know him?"

Amos hesitated. He knew that he and his uncle were in big trouble.

"Eric Caldwell is my uncle."

"He's your mother Bertha Hudgin's brother?"

"Yeah."

"Did you know your uncle owned a pearl handled, colt revolver with silver initials."

"Yeah."

"When's the last time you saw him with that gun?"

"Oh, musta been two, maybe three year ago, fore it got stole."

"Is that what he told you, 'it got stole'.

"That's right."

"Isn't it true that he told you he lost it out at Crosland Park the night you and he were out there and the Leeman kids were killed?"

"Naw, I ain't never been out there."

"When did your uncle tell you that his gun had turned up and was at Carolina Springs?"

"He ain't never told me that."

"Then why were you there on the afternoon of November 12?"

"I won't never there."

"Then how do you explain your bloody finger print on the handle of that baling hook that killed Jonah Page."

Amos Hudgins looked set to faint.

He coughed, composed himself and answered.

"That cain't be my finger print cause I won't there."

"I have an affidavit from the state crime lab that says you were. Your Uncle couldn't very well go rummaging around that storeroom himself so he told you to do it. When Jonah Page came in the back door and caught you going through George Devereux's belongings, you panicked and grabbed that baling hook. Then you swung it at his head, impaling it in his brain. You'd had a lot of experience with baling hooks before, working on the loading dock at the Bath mill—dragging all those bales around.

"Your honor I have another other witness I want to call. Following her testimony I would like to recall the first two witnesses."

"Very well, bailiff stash Mr. Hudgins in a different room than Mr. Caldwell for the time being."

"The bailiff took Hudgins to another holding room.

"Proceed Mr. Devereux."

"I would like to call Miss Mary Waters."

"Miss Waters, would you repeat your earlier testimony

where you said there was a third person in that storeroom when you entered?"

"I saw a man running out the back door. He was wearing Bib overalls, a plaid shirt and a felt hat. He had a short beard and a mustache."

"What else do you recall about him?"

"When I started back toward the storeroom, I heard a high-pitched, nasal sounding voice yell out, 'Where the hell is it George? I know you have it.' "

"And you swear that was not the voice of Jonah Page."

"I swear. Jonah's voice wasn't anything like what I heard."

"Thank you Miss White. Please remain seated. Judge would you ask the bailiff to bring Mr. Hudgins back in."

"Bailiff, bring him in."

Amos Hudgins reentered the court, only now he was wearing Bib overalls, a plaid shirt, a felt hat and he was sporting a beard and mustache. Unexpectedly, there were three other men with him. They were dressed exactly as Amos Hudgins and looked for all the world like three of John Wiggin's employees.

"What is this Mr. Devereux?"

"Your honor, if a fingerprint on the murder weapon isn't sufficient to prove the guilt of the witness this should. If I may your honor?"

"Highly unusual, but go ahead."

One by one, Alex had the four men repeat what Mary said she heard in the storeroom.

"Now, Miss Waters do you recognize any of these men as the one in that room with George?"

"Yes, the second man from the left. I will never forget that voice."

"Let it be noted that Miss Waters has pointed to Amos Hudgins. You may remove the facial hair now Mr. Hudgins.

"No further questions of this witness your honor."

"You may be excused Miss Waters."

"I recall Amos Hudgins to the stand."

Amos Hudgins was a deer in the headlights. His shoulders slumped and spittle formed at the corners of his mouth.

"All right, Mr. Hudgins we now have your fingerprint on the murder weapon and we have an eyewitness who identifies you as being in that room when she came in. Do you still want to stick to your story?

"We have the three slugs that killed the Leemans. We have a slug fired from this gun here," Alex said picking up the evidence bag, "so we know this is the gun you or your uncle used to kill those Leeman children. We have your bloody fingerprint on the weapon that killed Jonah Page. We know that you were just a pawn for your uncle. Are you going to sit there and take the fall for him. Let him go scot free?"

Amos' head fell into his hands. He began to shake all over. His earlier bravado melted into sobs.

40

The Confession

"It was him what done it! I won't nowhere near that gun that night. He tol' me he lost it after the shootin.' One of his neighbor boys what works as a orderly at the hospital tol' him that some nigger boy at the hospital was carryin' on 'bout some gun he done found out to Crosland Park after them shootin's. He said the boy was dyin' and he was yellin' 'bout the sheriff and the gun. They was enough sense in what he was sayin' to know what gun it was. They won't no mistakin' them silver initials. Uncle Eric asked around and found out it was some nigger boy named Quincy Patterson. He was able to git that boy to tell him what he done with it before the boy died. That's when he told me I had to git it back cause it would tie him to them killings at Crosland Park. I won't aimin' to hurt nobody, but when that skinny nigger came running at me with that hook, I jest grabbed it outta his hand and swung it at him. It hit him right in the head. Blood come spurtin' out all over the place. He fell over behind some boxes. I knowed he was dead. His eyes was open. That's when I heard somebody else come in the door. It was this other nigger what was limping and talking funny. I knowed it had to be George Devereux. That's when I grabbed him and asked him where the gun was, cause I knowed he had it. I done already broke into his house and it won't there.

"George started foaming at the mouth and fallin' down. He was jerkin' and moanin'. Then I heard somebody else coming from the front and I skedaddled outta there.

"I didn't have nothin' to do with killin' them Leeman niggers. I didn't mean to kill that other nigger either. I was jest lookin' for that gun like Uncle Eric told me. He said if I found it, he'd give me twenty dollars. But, when that nigger come at me with that hook I had to protect myself."

"Judge Manning, I believe the evidence we've presented here today, along with the sworn testimony, proves that George Devereux is guilty of no crime. I ask the court to dismiss the charges against him and to set him free to rejoin his family."

"Bailiff, produce the defendant."

"Mr. George Devereux It is my judgment that you are not guilty of the crimes for which you are charged and the case against you is hereby dismissed. You are free to go."

George broke down and cried. Mary and Alex helped him to a seat.

"Bailiff, bring in Mr. Caldwell."

"Yes your honor."

"Mr. Hudgins continue standing in the well."

Eric Caldwell was a beaten man. He shuffled into the courtroom with the knowledge that he would never breathe free air again.

"Eric Caldwell, you are hereby remanded to the custody of the South Carolina State Police. You will be brought before this court tomorrow morning and arraigned for the murders of the three Leeman children, for conspiracy to commit burglary, and for aiding and abetting the murder of Mr. Jonah Page.

"Mr. Hudgins, you will also be remanded to the custody of the state police. Tomorrow morning you will be arraigned before this court for the murder of Mr. Jonah Page.

"I will allow no bail for either of you.

"Mr. Poole, Mr. Devereux, I commend you for your

perseverance in the pursuit of justice for your client. I also applaud you for shining a bright spotlight on the corruptness of the Aiken County sheriff's office. No longer will they be allowed to sweep their crimes under the jail. I earnestly pray that their trials will help to expunge at least a part of the dark blot on our state that resulted from the Leeman lynchings.

"This court stands adjourned until nine tomorrow morning."

41

Redemption

"Mr. Poole, I can't ever repay you for what you did to save George," Alex said.

"Give credit where credit is due," Poole responded. "Without your idea for the lineup and without John Wiggin's detective work, this never could have happened."

"Lawsy, Mr. Poole," Minnie said, wiping her eyes as she burst through the gate to the well, "You done got me my boy back. Now Cleo, she gone come on back home knowin' it won't George what kilt Jonah. They gone be a whole lotta celebratin' round my house tonight."

"You're welcome Minnie. There's an old saying—all's well that ends well—and I can't think of a better ending than this.

"I know that it was Miss Eustis' hope that Alex would come back to Aiken and represent his people. I don't think she could possibly have had exactly this in mind, but it's a great start in a long crusade, and a great career. As I said before, Alex has a great future in law, and I look forward to sharing it with him."

Mary, Cleo and Phoebe were all gathered around George, hugging him and crying, as another young woman passed through the well gate. She tapped Alex on the shoulder. His broad smile welcomed her. He placed one arm around Minnie and one around the new arrival.

"Mama, I want to introduce you to Miss Betty Carlton."

The End